T3-AKD-852

MUGGSBOTTOM AND ME

A Study in Anglo-Arkansas Relations

Muggsbottom and Me

A Study in Anglo-Arkansas Relations

By

Patrick Adcock

BASKERVILLE
PUBLISHERS, INC.
DALLAS • NEW YORK • DUBLIN

BASKERVILLE Publishers, Inc.
7616 LBJ Freeway, Suite 220, Dallas, TX 75251-1008

Library of Congress Catalog Card Number: 93-70993
ISBN: 1-880909-10-3

Manufactured in the United States of America
First Printing

For Margaret

1. Prologue

A rcady is a community of ten thousand souls, of whom, I am happy to report, a very significant number are "saved," according to the Southern Baptist interpretation of that crucial term. Our town is located in southwestern Arkansas, a healthy distance down the interstate from that Sodom on the river, Little Rock, but, alas, within easy sinning distance of the resort city of Hot Springs. Arcady is the county seat of Dean County, and in Dean County the public sale of alcoholic beverages is prohibited by law. Tourists seem to view this practice as quaint or worse, but we have chosen to keep the demon rum at bay, let the rest of the world do as it will. Arcady is home to two small colleges, and rumor has it that some of the students are still able occasionally to lay their hands on spirits. I suspect that this is true, although I cannot personally attest to the fact. I try to avoid the more sordid goings-on which one will find even in the most upright of communities.

Our town would therefore seem an unlikely refuge for four middle-aged, bibulous expatriate Englishmen, but such was the case. I, who have traveled little and have always found strangers somewhat menacing, would seem an unlikely prospect as resident expert on our British cousins but, again, such was the case. My eventual intimacy with these local curiosities grew out of a series of coincidences so improbable that one would certainly never put them into a novel.

Charles Pierpont Muggsbottom was the first of the Englishmen to arrive in our town. He stepped down off the bus from Little Rock on the sixteenth day of April in either 1979 or 1980. Bud Howard, who runs the bus station, has always favored 1979, while I have insisted upon 1980. We are agreed, however, that Muggsbottom came on the sixteenth of April, because Bud remembered that he had just beaten the deadline with his jiggered-up tax return the night before (he was audited later and is truly fortunate to be walking the streets today a free man). We all grew accustomed to Muggsbottom and his three cronies during the months that followed, but he must have seemed quite a spectacle that day to Bud and the bench jockies down at the bus station. The bench in front of the station is filled to capacity every day with smokers (especially cigar smokers), tobacco chewers, and snuff dippers. The nonsmokers are up in arms here, as they are everywhere, and the pool hall and the bus station are like reservations, the last for those still enslaved by the filthy habit. These isolation units have smelled so sour for so long that the detritus of tobacco can scarcely do them any harm. But back to Muggsbottom.

He arrived in a tweed jacket and flannels, attire far too heavy for an Arkansas springtime. On his head, he wore a short-billed woolen cap in a brown and black plaid—he would later characterize it as "my single working-class affectation." He was accompanied by a battered steamer trunk—at which the bus station regulars looked askance, despite the stranger's offer to "pay the lad well who will help me carry it to my lodgings"—and a Gladstone bag of a very advanced age. When Muggsbottom sought directions to the Caddo Hotel, his accent so addled the nicotine-stained wretches on the bench that a long pause ensued before someone finally blurted out, "Six blocks due east."

Bud, whose brother-in-law, Eddie Nunn, provides the only public transportation in town, said, "I can have a taxi for you in five minutes."

Eddie is usually at the station to meet the bus, but old Mrs. Davidson was late with her grocery shopping that morning, and Eddie was, at the moment, entering her kitchen, a sack in each arm, and vainly attempting to shake Fideau, the widow's sex-starved toy poodle, off his right leg. As it turned out, Eddie's presence at the bus station would have brought him only disappointment.

"I'll walk, my dear fellow, stretch my legs a bit," Muggsbottom replied—"just the ticket after a morning spent in the cramped confines of an omnibus."

When the Englishman found no takers for his steamer trunk proposition, he was neither offended nor deterred. He marched across the street to the Exxon station and engaged in conversation a black youth who was airing the tires of his bicycle. After Muggsbottom had produced what appeared to be a money clip and gesticulated toward the trunk, the boy nodded an affirmative, slipped a lock through the rear wheel of his bicycle, and accompanied the Englishman back across the street. Within moments, the two of them were headed downtown with the steamer trunk between them. With his other hand, Muggsbottom swung the Gladstone bag jauntily at his side. He was continuing to talk expansively, despite the brierwood pipe clenched between his teeth. The boy responded only with a curious, but not unfriendly, look. For weeks thereafter, every detail of this exotic émigré's arrival was told and retold by the boys on the bench.

I met Muggsbottom a few days later in, of all places, the county tax assessor's office. I needed to renew the tags on my venerable Rocinante, and the assessment of personal property was an unavoidable prerequisite. I knew instantly that the florid, corpulent gentleman sitting at the other end

3

of the long table was the Englishman everyone in Arcady was talking about. Muggsbottom had removed his cap, thereby revealing a horseshoe of graying, rather unkempt hair surrounding his bald pate. He was sucking ruminatively on his brierwood pipe while listening to the assessor's rather disjointed explanation of tax liability. Our tax assessor is an incumbent whose years in the courthouse have rendered him complete master of the routine of his office. However, Muggsbottom was not routine, and the assessor was clearly rattled. Further, Muggsbottom's tobacco had filled the room with cumulonimbus layers of blue smoke, while its aroma reminded one of a grease fire. The clerk who was waiting upon me had ostentatiously plopped a bottle of Airwick onto the table, but the Englishman took no note of it.

"I want to get off on the right foot here, don't you know?" said Muggsbottom.

"I understand," said the assessor, a desperate look in his eye, "but even if you *had* tax liability as a resident alien, I don't believe it would come into play."

I could tell that the young woman who was assisting me could hardly keep her thoughts focused on my mundane tax liabilities because of the conversation that was going on just down the table from us.

"You see," the assessor continued, "you rent, and you don't own a car, a boat, a TV set, furniture. You don't have anything that we can tax."

"Quite right, my dear fellow. Quite right. The Inland Revenue took it all, every last farthing. Damned disgrace, the British system of taxation. Robbery under law, that's what it is. It's driven some of the very best people right out of the country."

I could discern neither pomposity nor self-mockery in Muggsbottom's manner. It was not possible to tell if he had consciously referred to himself.

"So, Mr. Muggsbottom," said the assessor, rising to signal the end of the conversation, "it's admirable of you to come forward like this but, unless the situation changes, I think you needn't concern yourself about county taxes."

"And it well may. Change, that is. This is the Land of Opportunity, after all. I may make my fortune here."

Muggsbottom chuckled to himself over this pleasant prospect, pumped the assessor's hand vigorously, and sallied out of the office, contentedly puffing away at his awful tobacco. I finished my business almost simultaneously and followed him into the hallway.

"Pardon me, sir," I called.

It is very much out of character for me to impose myself upon a stranger as I did that morning. I am a shy and retiring man by nature. Since I teach at the state college, the townspeople hold me somewhat suspect. Nor am I completely accepted by my colleagues, owing to my having voted for Richard Nixon . . . twice. Once might have been excused. I keep pretty well to myself, though I do not wish to exaggerate my lack of sociability. At any rate, I introduced myself to the Englishman.

"Muggsbottom, my dear fellow—Charles Pierpont," he replied, and pumped my hand as heartily as he had the tax assessor's.

"I teach in the English Department at the local state college, Mr. Muggsbottom, and I'm a shameless Anglophile. So you can see that a real-life Englishman visiting our town is an extremely exciting occurrence to me."

"Flattering, my boy, very flattering. I fear, however, that 'exciting' is not an adjective which has often been applied to me. I shall do my best, naturally . . . You mentioned a state college—I thought the local citadel of learning was an Anabaptist institution."

"We have two colleges in town. One state supported, the other Baptist."

"Ah, I see. The sacred and the profane. This unexpected diversity comes as a bit of serendipity to me. And I must correct one thing you said, old man. I've not come for a visit. I'm settling here, as my discussion with that exceedingly pleasant exciseman would indicate."

I hoped that Muggsbottom would tell me more, and he did.

Laying his finger beside his nose, he whispered conspiratorially, "Actually, I'm only the advance party. Reconnoitering the area, as it were. Three of my chums will arrive within the week. Doing a bit of recolonization, what?"

Muggsbottom laughed and clapped me good-naturedly on the shoulder. I was seeing him at his most expansive. His good humor on that occasion was genuine, but I would discover later that his personality was mercurial. He could suddenly plunge into the gloomiest of funks.

"That is exciting," I said, unimaginatively repeating the adjective to which he had earlier taken polite exception. "Please call on me if I can be of any help. I'm in the phone book, or you can reach me at my office on campus during the day."

"Deucedly kind of you. May well take you up on that offer. My digs at the hotel are quite satisfactory for a few days' stay, but when the other chaps arrive we shall be requiring a house. If you should hear of anything at all suitable . . . ?"

"I'll ask around and let you know what I've found out."

"Capital, my boy, capital. We shall keep in touch."

We shook hands again and parted. I now knew that four Englishmen would soon be residents of our small, homogeneous community. But the question burning in my brain was, *why*? I would have an opportunity to pursue the answer, though. I would have entree to the group through Muggsbottom. Suddenly my solitary, sedentary, rather predictable life had taken on a slight air of romance.

Before another week had passed, just as Muggsbottom

had told me, his three cronies arrived. The boys at the bus station, in whom Muggsbottom's arrival had also stirred a feeling of excitement mixed with awe, viewed the arrival of three more Englishmen with unambiguous disapproval. A disturbing trend was apparent in Arcady.

We had nothing to fear from our new neighbors, of course, but they were as different from us as could be imagined. Indeed, as I achieved some familiarity with the other Englishmen, I found them so eccentric as to render Muggsbottom rather colorless by comparison.

The eldest of the group was Sir Montague Capulet, a baronet—real or spurious, I never really knew. Sir Monty, as he was familiarly addressed by his chums, was a man of seventy or more years of age. He had a full head of iron-gray hair, a beetling brow, eyebrows like tangled horsehair brushes, small watery blue eyes, and a bulbous nose over-wrought with broken purple veins. He affected the physical decripitude of a very aged man, although he could be spry enough on those rare occasions when something caught his fancy. His appearance suggested that any wealth which might have once accompanied his title had long since been dissipated. He wore clacking, ill-fitting dentures. "Damned boobies in the National Health Service," he explained. As Sir Monty snored and snorted through his noisy naps, the false teeth seemed to come to life and travel around his mouth at will. He enjoyed giving an impression of advanced senility because, I believe, it allowed him to behave exactly as he pleased. And his companions paid due deference to his title and age when doing so did not truly inconvenience them, which was most of the time.

"Biffy" Smythe-Gardner was a small man of middle age, whose thin reddish hair was going gray and who sported a neat ginger moustache. Smythe-Gardner claimed to have held a captaincy in Her Majesty's Navy "until the balls-up." He was never more specific than this in the charac-terization of his retirement, and I never pressed him. He certainly had a martial bearing and manner about him . . . when sober. I quickly noted, however, that he was a tippler whose consumption of spirits stood out even among his bibulous companions. He drank one gin and lime after another from morning till night. He liked to joke that he could consume with impunity any number of these libations, his rationale being that during his years at sea he had sucked so many limes he had inoculated himself against their toxic effects. Alas, the limes usually struck around dinner time, and Smythe-Gardner would spend the rest of the evening decidedly boiled. I could guess that "the balls-up" had in some way featured limes. His cronies called him "Biffy" because, so the story went, he had relentlessly harangued his men about "biffing" the enemy. But so erratic was Smythe-Gardner's seamanship that he was usually "biffing" Portsmouth or Dover. "Fortunately," Muggsbottom once whispered to me, "Biffy insisted upon training the gun crews personally. Thus it was that none of his ill-conceived volleys ever fell within a mile of the target."

The fourth, and youngest, member of the little colony was Reggie Dipswizzle. Apart from Muggsbottom, Reggie was my favorite. He was the most financially secure of the Englishmen, for he was a remittance man. That is, Dipswizzles pere and mere paid him a healthy annual stipend to keep himself well away from Hertfordshire. As with Smythe-Gardner's cryptic "balls-up," I never learned precisely what series of offenses had rendered Reggie *persona non grata* in Hertfordshire, but he did recount for me many adventures from the checkered career which had followed his leaving home. During his peregrinations, he had for a time even acted in television commercials in London. The performance of which he was most proud was the stoic sufferer from constipation he had once played in a "tastefully done" laxative commercial. Reggie was tall, slender, and fair to the point of wanness. Although he was in his early forties, he had a deceptively youthful face. His dreamy blue eyes seemed forever fixed upon some ideal vision not vouchsafed the rest of us, and seemingly forever beyond his grasp as well. In short, Reggie was a romantic.

As luck would have it, I was able to aid the Britishers in their house hunting almost immediately. One morning, a colleague in the English Department mentioned that his next-door neighbor, a lady of extremely advanced age, had just died. She had been found in her garden, where she had expired amid her tomato plants, her venerable right hand encircling her favorite hoe in a literal death grip. "Just as she would have chosen," my colleague allowed lugubriously. A few delicately phrased questions on my part elicited these facts: her house was a white frame, turn-of-the-century structure with three large bedrooms and a study among its six rooms. A wide gallery ran across two-thirds of the facade and was embellished with gingerbread latticework. Protruding beyond the porch was a large bay window, featuring three high, oldfashioned window frames stretching up toward a gabled roof. The old lady's sole survivor, a daughter, had her own home elsewhere in town. She had no use for her mother's home but was reluctant to put it on the market, its having been in her family for over eighty years. My colleague assumed, therefore, that the daughter might be willing to rent it in its present, rather shabby but furnished, condition. Just the thing for my Englishmen, I thought.

I immediately called the Caddo Hotel and there being no telephones in the hotel save the one at the desk, was obliged to leave a message containing the pertinent data with Miss Amanda. Miss Amanda was a curious (in multiple senses of the word) hostess. She seemed actively to resent the guests who chose to stay in her little downtown hotel (few, in fact, did) and delighted in telling anyone who would listen how greatly her clientele discommoded her morning and night. She would barely acknowledge the most civil request a guest might make concerning the most basic of hotel accommodations. On the other hand, she was ravenously eager to learn any detail of a person's private life that he might be least expected to share with a total stranger. Consequently, any guest who sought a few quiet moments alone in the lobby was interrogated mercilessly until he fled to the street or back to the sanctuary of his room. The lobby of the Caddo Hotel was seldom occupied.

"I'll be glad to give Mr. Muggsbottom this message," said Miss Amanda, managing, despite her words, to convey the clear impression that I had discommoded her, "if he ever comes down. He and his pals follow a different daily schedule, don't you know?" Here, Miss Amanda mimicked an Oxbridge accent, especially in pronouncing the first syllable of "schedule" as "shed." The posh accent overlaid only slightly her native twang and was very amusing. "They eat four meals a day, you know, and none of them at the same time as anybody else."

I left my number, and within half an hour Muggsbottom returned my call. His first inclination, as always, was to walk to the house. I offered my car, however, pointing out that, although I had already spoken to the daughter on the phone, he would need to go by her home first to pick up the key. I also suggested that he speak to her alone. Then, if she did not wish to accompany him on an inspection tour of the house, we could swing back by the hotel and pick up the others.

"Ah, I see. Don't descend on her like a pack of old queens, eh? Sort of ease her into the notion of *four* foreigners possibly living in her dear old mother's house. Good thinking, lad. Don't worry, I'll charm the lady right out of her knickers. I used to be quite a hand with the ladies, although to look at me now I shouldn't wonder that you're a bit sceptical."

The house is located on one of the oldest and quietest streets in Arcady. The narrow street extends for three blocks from the campus of the Baptist college to the river.

Its entire length is shaded by walnut, magnolia, and sweet gum trees of great age. I dare not provide further descriptive details, for the family currently in residence complains that passers-by already pause on the sidewalk or at the curb in front of the house to gawk, point, and even to take photographs of the house "where those crazy Englishmen used to live."

To make a long and potentially tedious story short, the house suited the expatriates "down to the ground." (Alas, I find that increasingly I tell stories more in the Muggsbottom manner, two steps backward for each step forward, so that my chances of surviving long enough to reach the dénouement seem ever less likely.) There were bedrooms for Sir Monty, Captain Smythe-Gardner, and Reggie. Muggsbottom, being the only member of the group with literary interests, chose the study. Against one wall was an old-fashioned daybed, upon which the late mistress of the house had probably taken her afternoon nap. "This shall be my bed," declared Muggsbottom. "I've slept on far worse many a night." He also announced that he had sufficient books in storage to fill the built-in shelves around the other three walls of the room.

The landlady, as Muggsbottom (and I) had feared, was considerably less keen on renting to Muggsbottom when she discovered he would be sharing the house with three other strangers—yea, even foreigners. I rather foolhardily vouched for the Englishmen. The landlady would have viewed my testimony on their behalf more favorably had I not been "with the college." Those of us who had come to Arcady to be "with the college," no matter how long we remained in residence, could never truly be considered as townspeople. But Muggsbottom called forth the considerable charm of which he had boasted, and eventually an agreement was concluded.

Well, now the Englishmen were more or less permanently situated in the community, and for the next year or two I would have the closest relationship with them of anyone in town. The first purpose to which I wished to put my special relationship was the discovery of what unlikely circumstances had bound these men together in the first place and what even more unlikely circumstances had led them to Arcady, Arkansas. In as subtle and as politic a manner as I could, I set out to get this information.

2. Exposition

Gradually, from a chance remark here and a casual reminiscence there, I pieced together the background of the Englishmen. Most of my information came from Muggsbottom, and it was ironic that, although I was always closer to him than to his friends, I knew far less about his past than about the others'. He was circumspect almost to the point of secretiveness about his life in the mother country.

I shall now claim the privilege of the New Journalism and convert my friend's remarks, made over a period of many months and within many contexts, into a coherent narrative. Thus the reader may more easily acquire that information for which he is, I hope, by now hungering. Let us listen as Muggsbottom, whom we may imagine to be slightly in his cups, mulls over the circumstances which brought him and his cronies together and, later, to Arkansas.

Politics was the glue that cemented Sir Montague Capulet and me together. Or rather, our common abhorrence of politics as practiced in the twentieth century. Sir Monty is a Tory of the eighteenth-century stripe, who would have been very much at home among the Queen Anne wits provided, of course, that he did not have to be witty himself. He still longs for a leader who will make the trains run on time, even though he no longer has anyplace to go. I, on the other hand, rather see myself as a modern day Edmund Burke. Over the years, unperceptive individuals have occasionally called me a reactionary. I deny this appellation and feel that those who employ it ought to be shot.

Sir Monty and I met one Sunday afternoon at Hyde Park corner, where we were listening to an Australian socialist loudly advocating vicious policies in a vile accent. After hooting him down together, we fell into conversation and have been, more or less, boon companions ever since. Sir Monty was considerably more alert in those days, less apt to trump his partner's aces and that sort of thing. Still, in his lucid moments a spark of the old aristocratic fire will glow forth, reminding us of noblesse oblige and the duties imposed by our sacred heritage.

We later came across Smythe-Gardner at a meeting of the Cassandra Club. The club's membership agrees without exception that western civilization is at the point of total collapse. On discussion evenings, they debate the imminence of this collapse and what specific occurrences might precipitate *le déluge*. On this particular evening, Smythe-Gardner was ventilating the argument that the present difficulties of western man are caused largely by the Irish. I was moved to observe that this seemed as absurd as to claim that our present difficulties are caused by the . . . Canadians. "Aha," quoth Smythe-Gardner, "I have long suspected the Canadians of being in league with the bloody Irish." Well, I learnt one doesn't attempt to argue with Smythe-Gardner, who takes a bit more drink than is quite good for him. He becomes most belligerent at about nine-fifteen post meridiem but, if one can just hold on, he usually loses consciousness by nine-thirty.

At that point, Sir Monty voiced his curious notion that tea bags constitute the appropriate metaphor for the ills of the world. "Beginning of the end," he said lachrymosely.

"Next thing you know, they'll be chilling beer." We have been so far successful in keeping from Sir Monty the knowledge that this barbarous practice has indeed spread even unto that sceptered isle.

After the discussion period petered out in its usual inconclusive fashion, Sir Monty and I invited Smythe-Gardner to have a drink with us. As it turned out, we had several drinks together, not concluding the evening until the early hours of the next day. By that time, we were as thick as thieves. I was then sharing digs with a cousin of mine, of whom the less said the better. He was a Fleet Street hack— my mother's family, I fear, cultivated mediocrity all too assiduously. He paid his half of the rent most of the time and, having made that observation, I have enumerated his virtues in full. Sir Monty was living in a small bed-and-breakfast establishment run by a pimply little man named Colin. Colin read the *Manchester Guardian* all day long and railed against the royal family. As you might guess, Sir Monty was not happy there and was even fearful that he might lose his head one day and give Colin a good thrashing with his stick. So both Sir Monty and I were receptive when Smythe-Gardner highly recommended to us his own lodgings.

Smythe-Gardner resided at the Flotsam and Jetsam Hotel at Number Two, Bloomsbury Place. The Flotsam and Jetsam catered to, though not exclusively so, bachelors and widowers with military or naval backgrounds. "Grand bunch of chaps," Smythe-Gardner assured us. "Not a poof in the lot." The hotel faced onto Bloomsbury Square, a nice little patch of greenery where a fellow could enjoy a stroll, provided he was prepared to run the gantlet of winos and panhandlers who had taken up residence there. The British Museum and several cozy pubs were within easy walking distance. Sir Monty and I paid a visit, liked what we saw, and promptly moved in. Sir Monty, Smythe-Gardner, and I have been under the same roof ever since.

Early the next year, we met Reggie Dipswizzle. More precisely, I met Reggie and later introduced him to my friends. I wound up standing next to Reggie at the Flotsam and Jetsam's intimate little bar shortly after he had moved in. He was recounting to the barman details of his acting career, which I gathered from his remarks to then be in an extended hiatus. The aged barman, a former sergeant major in India, had spent twenty years listening to the doleful tales of thwarted subalterns. He was a sympathetic but not an enthusiastic auditor, whose contributions to the conversation were, "Ah yes, sir," "Quite true, sir," and the like. When I interjected myself—subtly and skillfully, of course—into their colloquy, he instantly melted away to the other end of the bar. I do not generally join into barroom conversations unbidden—or bidden, for that matter. But Reggie's personality attracted me. He is such a delightful mixture of good humor and melancholy. One of his favorite expressions, you know, is, "I've never met a chap I didn't like but, of course, I've not yet met Harold Wilson."

That particular evening, Reggie was lamenting his limited appeal as a performer in television commercials. "Directors seem always to see me as the fellow who needs an antacid for his heartburn, a laxative for his irregularity, or a suppository for his hemorrhoids. Once I got a commercial for an anti-itching salve, because the director said I looked exactly like a fellow who was frantic to scratch his bum. Naturally, one would like one's first impression to be otherwise. As of late, however, I'm not even getting *those* parts. Had quite a dry spell, actually."

Reggie went on to tell me that, fortunately, his lengthy period "at liberty" had produced an artistic crisis only in his life. He was financially secure, due to a generous annuity from a loving but impatient father in the south of England. Of course, Reggie should not have revealed these intimate details to a complete stranger, as I then was to him. Such is, however, his nature. I have often heard him say to people, "Please, do not share your secrets with me, because I tell everything I know to everyone I meet." Reggie's total openness—which by no means conforms to the national character—is a considerable part of his charm, but it also makes him vulnerable. I must constantly keep my eye on Reggie, for there are those about who would take advantage of him.

Well, Reggie was soon taken up by the others as well, since he was deferential to Sir Monty's whims and indulgent of Smythe-Gardner's sea stories. Our threesome became a foursome.

Now, as to our emigration: Sir Monty and I, the most politically astute members of our little band, had finally concluded with deep regret that the welfare state was too firmly established in Britain to ever be dismantled. The Labourites were a patent abomination, but Sir Monty and I had lost faith in the Tories as well. For, while crying they would ne'er consent, they had consented to virtually every egalitarian lunacy put forward by the socialists. We had desperately examined one course of action after another and been ultimately forced to accept the idea that emigration was the only choice available to the Briton who would live as a free man. The idea appealed to Smythe-Gardner, I believe, less for political reasons than for the opportunity it would afford him to leave the unpleasant circumstances associated with his retirement far behind. Reggie had been pretty much apolitical when we met, but he is an impressionable lad. I suppose it was our nightly diatribes against Labour that eventually persuaded him of the leftward leanings of those television directors who had declined to hire him. I do not apologize for leading the boy into the light of truth.

We could not simply leave England. We had to leave England *for* somewhere else. We spent many weeks debating what our ultimate destination should be. Sir Monty suggested South Africa, having while at university spent a pleasant holiday there as guest of an undergraduate friend. Smythe-Gardner objected strenuously. While serving with South African naval officers during the war, he had developed a virulent prejudice against them. "Impossible blokes. Especially the ones of Dutch descent. Every bit as hard-headed as the bloody jerries." Reggie then placed Canada's name in nomination—he knew a fellow at the Canadian Broadcasting Corporation. "Too damned cold for these old bones in Canada," thundered Sir Monty. "For God's sake, let's not seek out a *worse* climate than Britain's." As a matter of form, I put Australia and New Zealand forward. But we all agreed that socialism had progressed just as far down under as at home, and the radicals seemed to be firmly in the saddle there. "Besides," said Sir Monty, "could you bear listening to that accent for the rest of your life?" (In case you are wondering, my dear fellow, at that time Sir Monty had not yet heard an Arkansan speak.) We flirted briefly with the notion of removing to the West Indies. But a good long look at ourselves gave proof that none of us were the beachcomber type. Ireland, of course, was out of the question from the very beginning. So we had pretty well narrowed our choices in the English speaking world down to the United States.

Now, why Arkansas?

I do hope that what I am about to say doesn't give offense, since none is intended. Our research indicated that Arkansas, perhaps for reasons as much geographical as sociological, is the most culturally remote state in the union. Precisely the environment we sought! Amidst the decline and fall of practically everything and everybody, we wished to withdraw to some private place. There we would seek what solace is afforded by the grape and the grain, while we awaited the collapse of western civilization. Our consolation would be that said collapse would reach Arkansas last, as everything else seems to.

And why Arcady?

Why not? The climate is pleasant. The townspeople are courteous, if a bit suspicious. And their standoffishness is not unwelcome—it suits our English temperament. Admittedly, we were a bit taken aback by the "dry" status of the county, a political condition to which we were completely unaccustomed. Even so, we were only slightly discommoded. During my first evening at the Caddo Hotel, Maynard, the dimwitted but obliging porter, offered to "make a run" to Hot Springs in his motor car in order to secure what liquor I might require. For a very nominal gratuity, he has been performing this service on a weekly basis ever since, and not even Smythe- Gardner has found himself in want. Oh, we have been quite comfortable in Arcady.

Yes, I thought, quite comfortable on poor innocent Reggie's annuity. This was one of the few occasions upon which Muggsbottom made me a little angry. Although my loyalty to my home state does not blind me to her blemishes, I found Muggsbottom's bland references to our backwardness offensive. I kept my anger to myself, however. I dared not risk estrangement from the Englishmen, thereby denying myself this rare cross-cultural experience.

3. The Phlegm Club

Muggsbottom telephoned me at my office one midsummer afternoon. He was calling from his neighbor's house, and his voice betrayed more excitement than I had heard in it up to that time.

"My dear fellow, I fear I must impose upon you again. Might I have the use of your motor car for an hour's time . . . and of you as driver, of course?"

Muggsbottom and Sir Monty openly admitted—indeed, almost with pride—that they could not drive an automobile. Smythe-Gardner claimed to have had some experience with "the wretched things," and Reggie even alleged that he could "operate a motor frightfully well." I was unpersuaded. Besides, none of the Englishmen possessed a valid driver's license from Arkansas or any other state. I found it less stressful to chauffeur them about than to lend them my car.

"Certainly. I'm through with classes for the day. I'll be there in about twenty minutes, all right?"

"Good lad. We shall be ready."

I found myself getting excited. Muggsbottom's enthusiasms were always worthy of interest, and usually a bit piquant.

When I blew the "hooter," as Muggsbottom had once referred to it, the door flew open and the Englishmen came bustling down the steps. Even Sir Monty had speeded up his customary shuffle. The others were obviously as excited as Muggsbottom had seemed on the phone. I was captivated by their enthusiasm. Where were we going? What place— within an hour's drive—could, at this time of the afternoon, stir Sir Monty from his torpor, lure Smythe-Gardner from his gin and lime, and snap Reggie out of his reverie?

Muggsbottom joined me in the front seat. His cronies wedged themselves into the back, reminding me, for no very rational reason, of the Marx brothers. Muggsbottom drew a slip of paper from the handkerchief pocket of his jacket and studied it at arm's length.

"Do you happen to know, dear boy, the AMVETS Club? My informant tells me it is on Highway 67 as one goes toward Malvern."

"I've often driven past it, and I know it by reputation. It has . . . it *had* a reputation for serving a pretty rough clientele. Supposedly it was a private club, but that was a local joke. I understand that the state alcohol control board closed it down several months ago."

"Exactly the intelligence I have received. Please take us there forthwith."

The AMVETS Club was a small, boxy, concrete-block building nestled in a bend of the highway, seven miles north of Arcady. It stood well off the shoulder of the road and appeared to be trying to hide itself in a little stand of pine trees. Without the neon Pabst Blue Ribbon sign flickering in the window, without the semicircle of pickup trucks and rattletrap cars-—like mine, I thought wryly—in front, it looked abandoned and disconsolate. To me, it was architecturally and aesthetically depressing, like an old whore pushed out of the car onto the side of the road. But its effect upon the Englishmen was strangely salutary.

"Let us take a look through the windows," said Muggsbottom. "I have not yet secured the key."

We could see that the AMVETS Club was little more than one bare room. Doors led to the men's and women's restrooms and to an office in the rear—all must have been very tiny. The floor was a slab of concrete, heavily spotted and stained. A narrow bar stood on one side of the room, looking empty and neglected. Three booths squatted against the opposite wall. The backrests of one had been repaired with strips of tape that did not match the color of the vinyl. The stuffing was leaking, unimpeded, from various lesions in the other two. Several sets of cheap tables and chairs were jumbled together in the middle of the floor.

"Perfect, wouldn't you say, Reggie?" Muggsbottom inquired with a tilt of his head.

"The *size* is certainly perfect," Reggie responded.

"We should be able to lease it for a song," Smythe-Gardner observed.

Sir Monty, having been on his feet for two minutes, was obviously tiring, and he mumbled something unintelligible.

"Quite so," said Muggsbottom. "Let us return to town, and I shall commence negotiations with the estate agent."

As I drove back to Arcady, I was pretty sure I knew what the Englishmen were up to. But, by way of verification, I asked, "What in the world do you want that dump for?"

"Why, for a club, dear boy." In Muggsbottom's voice was a hint of disappointment at my obtuseness.

"But you have that big house just for the four of you?"

"If you were English, old fellow, you would understand. A man's home is merely his home, but a man's club is his refuge."

And so was born the Phlegm Club. In short order, Muggsbottom had leased the building and commissioned sufficient redecoration to make the place at least presentable—using Reggie's money, I assumed. Maynard, porter at the Caddo Hotel, was already in the Englishmen's employ as an importer of spirits from the adjoining "wet" county. Muggsbottom raised Maynard's salary and expanded his position to part-time barman, waiter, and fry cook. Muggsbottom worked out an arrangement with Eddie Nunn whereby, for a special rate, Eddie would drive the

Englishmen out to the club each evening at six, then bring them back to town at ten.

Reggie was credited with giving a name to the club. He thought he remembered encountering a Phlegm Club in the works of P. G. Wodehouse and was very taken with the appellation. Reggie, by the way, read these works with no hint of humor, apparently taking them as literal representations of English life as he remembered it from his boyhood.

Few guests would be admitted to the club—and those few only under very special circumstances—since privacy was, of course, the Phlegm Club's *raison d'étre*. (I wondered how much more privacy the Englishmen could desire, for no one other than I ever visited them at their residence.) Muggsbottom gave me to understand that, due to the many services I had rendered him and his friends, I was the exception to the rule. I might come to the Phlegm Club as often as I liked.

And I eventually began to come several times a week. There, while Muggsbottom sank deep into his cups, I would sit at his elbow and listen to his misanthropic views on a wide range of subjects. I found him, on the whole, a delightful old curmudgeon. I have written down as many of his observations as I could recall, under the title *Praejudicia Muggsbottom*. I will share these with the reader in the next chapter.

At first, I visited the Phlegm Club very sparingly. As the months passed, as I grew more comfortable with the Englishmen and they with me, I drove out to the club more frequently. But I resisted the temptation to drop by every night, or even every other night. Although Muggsbottom's invitation to me had been open-ended, I knew that he and his mates expected me to practice restraint while keeping an eye open for those signs which would encourage greater intimacy.

Each Englishman staked out his territory almost immediately. Sir Monty found that, until suitable furniture was acquired, he could sleep quite comfortably with his back against the wall (protected from the concrete blocks by two plump pillows) and his legs stretched out along the seat of one of the booths. Smythe-Gardner gravitated to a bar stool, from which he could hector poor Maynard while the latter prepared one gin and lime after the other. Muggsbottom and Reggie claimed tables of their own. Muggsbottom would read the *Arcady Harbinger*, carrying on an indignant commentary throughout, for none of the news—international, national, state, or local—particularly pleased him. He was relatively quiet only while working the crossword puzzle. His companions appeared to pay no attention to him whatever. Reggie also read, after a fashion. He enjoyed leafing through slick magazines devoted to the beautiful people, magazines containing photographs that were numerous and large.

Eventually each of the Englishmen acquired for himself a large overstuffed, leather bound chair. These pieces of furniture did little to improve the ambiance. They seemed merely to be at odds with, rather than to enhance, the tawdry decor of the former AMVETS Club. But, to me, the Englishmen were clearly—to use the Arcadian vernacular—as contented as a dead pig in the sunshine.

Seldom did the outside world intrude upon the Phlegm Club. Seldom was the placid routine of its members disturbed. I was fortunate enough to be present on two such occasions. I say "fortunate" because the Englishmen were always the most entertaining after having been disturbed in some way.

After the Phlegm Club had been in existence for about a month, it attracted the attention of the local authorities. And at dusk one evening, Sheriff Briscoe "Red" Birdsong presented himself at the door of the Phlegm Club, in the company of Deputy Sheriff Ero "Slim" Appleseed. It had been bruited about Dean County for some time that the high sheriff made no calls, no matter how routine, unaccompanied by another lawman. This practice supposedly resulted from an indignity he had suffered in 1978. One afternoon, while searching perfunctorily for a band of wild pigs that had been rooting up rural gardens, Sheriff Birdsong was cruising, alone, deep down a country lane. He happened upon the family farm of two brazen young marijuana growers, brothers, who were harvesting their crop literally within sight of the roadway. When he attempted to arrest the young men, they overpowered him (here, he was decidedly vague about the details), took away his weapon, dismantled his patrol car, and left him bound hand and foot in tall grass that was severely infested with ticks and chiggers. Many hours had passed before the sheriff was found and freed, by which time he had been gnawed upon by scores of vermin and had peed all over himself. The miscreants were eventually captured and brought to what passes for justice in such cases, but Sheriff Birdsong had never truly recovered from the experience. Hence, the presence of Deputy Appleseed during the interview which follows. I realize that the entire anecdote about Sheriff Birdsong has been a digression, but this is the way we small town folk tell our stories.

"Howdy, boys," began the lawman, uncovering his russet head. "I'm Sheriff Red Birdsong, and this here's Slim Appleseed, my chief deputy. How are y'all getting along this evening?"

Birdsong signaled with his hat for Appleseed to remove his own. The sheriff's affability was greatly exaggerated, for he was by nature a melancholy, even a dour man. But it was obvious that he was not quite sure of what he was up against in the Englishmen. So if he should err, it was going to be on the side of forced good humor and excessive courtesy.

Muggsbottom, acting as spokesman, introduced himself and his companions. I did not know Deputy Appleseed, but the sheriff and I were very slightly acquainted. I am pleased to report that I had never dealt with him in his official capacity. He knew, of course, that I was "from the college," so he probably considered me nearly as much of a resident alien as the Englishmen.

"What can we do for you gentlemen?" Muggsbottom inquired.

"Well . . . " Birdsong was trying to maintain an avuncular tone but was clearly pleased by the directness of Muggsbottom's question. Small talk was not his long suite.

"Well, Eddie Nunn tells me y'all have reopened a club out here. Is that right?"

"Oh, my goodness," said Muggsbottom. "Why, I never thought that Eddie might . . . But then I forget that Arcady's class structure is virtually nonexistent, except for three or four rich old relics whom everybody sucks up to. Not to put too fine a point upon it, we have established, not 'reopened,' a club—the Phlegm Club."

I saw at once that the key term had not been properly defined and that, unless this were immediately accomplished, the discussion was bound to produce a gross misunderstanding.

"I don't suppose your club is open to the public?"

"Well, of course not, my dear fellow. What sort of club is open to the public? Besides, if that were the case, poor Eddie would have had no reason to feel excluded, now would he?"

"Mr. Muggsbottom, do you have a license to operate a club?"

Muggsbottom's expression indicated how curious he considered Sheriff Birdsong's question to be.

"Why, my dear old minions of the law," said Muggsbottom, with an expansive gesture clearly intended to include the taciturn Appleseed in their colloquy, "this is a *private* club."

"Got to have a license to operate a private club. Maybe that ain't the way it is overseas. That's the way it is in Arkansas."

Muggsbottom and Me

I felt it was time for me to offer some lexical assistance.

"Muggsbottom, just as your public schools are not 'public' in our sense of the word, our private clubs are not 'private' in your sense of the word."

Sheriff Birdsong did not speak to me aloud, but he gave me a look that said, "What business is this of yours, you barracks room lawyer?"

He eyed the bar, behind which were a dozen or so bottles and Maynard in a dirty apron.

"Bet you ain't got a liquor license neither. Got to have a liquor license to sell liquor. I reckon you do *sell* that booze over there behind the bar?"

"We each sign a tab, of course," Muggsbottom replied. "A gentleman is naturally obliged to pay his share."

What Muggsbottom said was technically correct, but it worked to the detriment of the argument I knew he should be making. True, the Englishmen signed their tabs punctiliously but had no intention of ever paying them. A portion of Reggie's periodic remittance check had and always would represent the entire financial support of the Phlegm Club.

"Dean County's dry as an old maid schoolteacher's twat, boys," said the sheriff. "Can't sell liquor in Dean County 'less you have a liquor license. Can't get a liquor license 'less you run a private club. Can't run a private club 'less you have a private club license. Sorry, boys—but them's the rules, and that's the law."

"Sheriff," I said, "I believe I can clear up this little . . ."

"I'll biff the first of you blighters to lay a hand on me," Smythe-Gardner said, springing from his bar stool and landing very unsteadily on his feet.

"Have these men come about the roof?" Sir Monty said, barely lifting his chin from his chest.

"We haven't offered the gentlemen any refreshment," said Reggie, smiling his beatific smile.

Muggsbottom raised his hand imperiously and silenced

us all.

"Please, lads. I shall attend to this matter. I have been, in my time, plagued by agents of the Inland Revenue and vexed by awful female canvassers for the Labour Party. The Dean County legal system does not terrify me." He presented his wrists. "Shackle me, gentlemen, and take me away. Let us learn if in Dean County the weary, careworn immigrant can find justice."

"Ain't no need to arrest nobody, Mr. Muggsbottom. I'll just cite you for this violation, and you'll be notified when to appear before the District Judge. Might be a week, might be a month . . . But now, if y'all are out here again tomorrow night, we'll have to come back and cite you again . . . and, I reckon, confiscate that liquor."

As the lawmen left, Deputy Appleseed was heard to speak his first words.

"The way they talk—it's a lot like English, ain't it?"

We small town Southerners do not resolve misunderstandings quickly. Whereas the big city types seem to advocate confrontation until there is resolution, we favor pouting, snubbing, and a period of estrangement sufficiently long for both parties to tell their side of the story to everyone they know. So this matter was resolved rather quickly by Arcadian standards. When Sheriff Birdsong presented his charges to Darnell Witherspoon, our prosecuting attorney, the latter consulted his memory of the British fiction he had been required to read at the University of Arkansas and declined to prosecute.

According to the story I heard, Darnell told the sheriff, "Red, it's not like the AMVETS. It's more like the Mickey Mouse Club . . . with booze."

I mentioned two specific intrusions to which I bore witness. The second involved the telephone, and I was partly responsible for what occurred.

In the little room at the rear of the building, which had served the previous lessee as an office, was a telephone. It sat disconsolately on the floor but was still plugged into its jack. I saw that service could be easily and immediately reinstated, and I forcefully—for me—argued that course of action. Each evening at the Phlegm Club was spent seven miles up the highway from Arcady, and the Englishmen had no automobile. True, Eddie Nunn had been engaged to deposit them at six and pick them up at ten. But they might need to reach Eddie, or me or an ambulance or the police, in the interim. What if one of them should fall ill or suffer an accident? What if criminals should break in and molest them? These were not likely occurrences, but why risk them when the charge for telephone service was so nominal? I had as an ally in pressing my case Maynard, the majordomo. He had a car, but it was a beat-up old rattletrap—affectionately called "the Dent"—which belched black smoke and had an engine that sounded like a faulty washing machine. He insisted, quite convincingly, that the Dent could not be relied upon in a pinch. However, a stray word here and there convinced me that Maynard's argument was not entirely disinterested. A telephone at the Phlegm Club would give Maynard's several white trash girlfriends the means to reach him during the evening hours.

Maynard and I lobbied Muggsbottom hard, for we knew that he was the man who had to be convinced. He had a natural aversion to the telephone. "The damned contraption was made for liars," he thundered. "I can spot a liar instantly when I look into his eyes, but on the telephone . . . " Still we kept at him, virtually promising that we, ourselves, would never call, virtually promising that the Phlegm Club telephone would be a one-way only instrument of communication, like a factory whistle or a warning siren. "Who else would call you?" I asked—naively, as things turned out.

We finally won him over or, rather, he decided to stop playing. I believe the more we inveigled him, the more he enjoyed resisting. But Muggsbottom's threshold for boredom was very low and, when he tired of the game, he suddenly acquiesced. The members duly met to discuss the proposal but, since Muggsbottom had already made the decision, the Phlegm Club voted unanimously to have a telephone. I conducted the negotiations with Ma Bell. An unlisted number seemed a pointless extravagance, and I recommended against listing the number under "The Phlegm Club" for fear of stirring up Red Birdsong all over again. "Then I suppose it *will* have to be in my name," said Muggsbottom, adopting the tone of a martyr. However, Reggie was the only Phlegmatic with a bank account, and when the young lady representing the communications giant learned that all checks would bear his name, she courteously but firmly insisted that the number should be listed in his name as well. The formalities were quickly concluded and, the next afternoon, a lineman scrambled up a pole near the little concrete-block building. His nimble gloved fingers worked their magic among the tangle of lines and wires, and the Phlegm Club had phone service.

For over a week, the telephone never rang once. So far as anyone knew, not even Maynard's girlfriends had called. He and I appeared to be prophets. And then I happened to be visiting the Phlegm Club on the evening when the first call was received.

Maynard emerged from the back and said, "Phone for you, Mr. Dipswizzle."

Reggie's melancholy countenance instantly brightened.

"What?" said Muggsbottom, as he gave me an irritated look. "Who is it?"

"Don't know. It's a man wants to speak to Mr. Reginald Dipswizzle. Sounds like a yankee to me."

"Ask him what he wants," said Muggsbottom.

"It's *my* phone call, Muggsbottom," said Reggie, show-ing more spunk than I had seen heretofore. "I may have won one of my contests."

Reggie entered every contest for which he could find an entry blank in a magazine, but he was so lax in his attention to detail that we assumed he could not be technically eligible for any of the prizes.

After Reggie had left the room, Muggsbottom sat brooding for several minutes in silence. Then he turned to me and said, "Who can that be? Reggie doesn't know anybody in America."

I got the decided impression that Reggie's telephone call was my fault.

"I can't believe they've worked this fast," I said hesitantly.

"Who do you mean by 'they'?" Muggsbottom asked, with an even sharper edge to his voice.

"Well, in this country we have a huge industry called telemarketing. Surely you have the same sort of thing in Britain. Entrepreneurs—and, I'm afraid, sometimes outright crooks—set up phone banks, some of them huge, and call people all day and into the night, trying to sell them things they don't need or want."

The expression on Muggsbottom's face was turning from concern to dismay.

"These people buy lists of names and telephone numbers from every source they can find. I wasn't really concerned about them though. How would they find Reggie? He isn't even listed in the Arcady directory yet . . . But perhaps I underestimated them."

Muggsbottom rose and said, "Good God! Poor Reggie is no match for such persons as that."

But before Muggsbottom could go in pursuit of his friend and meal ticket, Reggie reentered the room, looking very smug.

"Ah, Muggsbottom," he said. "You scoff, but that *was* one of my contests. It seems that I have won a piece of property, potentially quite valuable, in Baja California. Some chaps are developing what they call 'condominiums' there for what will soon be an absolutely boffo retirement community. I get the impression my property is quite near the beach." He turned to me and said, "There are beaches in this Baja California, are there not? A very personable fellow named Lennie gave me all the details, but I can't recite them off the top of my head."

"And what has this . . . Lennie . . . asked you to do?" said Muggsbottom.

"Oh, the Baja government, or the Mexican government, or whatever it is, does require the payment of some rather modest property taxes. These developer chaps are just preparing to put down the sewer lines and gas mains, that sort of thing. Once that is accomplished, I shall have one of these condominium things within a matter of months. Then I shall be able to lease it to hordes of retiring Americans for thousands and thousands of dollars. My name was drawn, you see, and I am able to get in on the ground floor, as Lennie puts it, because this is what's called a 'promotion.' I'm prepared to ignore the dismissive attitude you lads have shown towards my contests, and we will, naturally, share equally in the income."

"But what has Lennie asked you to *do*, Reggie?"

"What? Oh, yes. I'm to send a certified check for five hundred dollars—those property taxes I mentioned—to an address in . . ." He fumbled through his jacket pockets and eventually drew out a slip of paper. "Yes, here it is. In San Diego, California."

I stood and said, "I think it's time I was getting home."

"Reggie," said Muggsbottom. "I believe that Baja California is inhabited almost exclusively by snakes and scorpions, creatures generally avoided by superannuated Americans."

I slipped as unobtrusively as possible out the door.

The next evening, the Phlegm Club reconsidered the issue of telephone service. During the brief discussion, Muggsbottom managed simultaneously to recant his earlier favorable recommendation of the idea and to insist that he had been right all along. He moved to nullify the original proposal, and Smythe-Gardner seconded. When the question was called, three Phlegmatics voted for reversal, and one petulantly abstained.

Shortly thereafter, the telephone in the back room went dead once more.

4. Praejudicia Muggsbottom

Again, I will resort to a practice as old as Herodotus and Thucydides and reorder history slightly, not to misrepresent it but to make it more readable. Muggsbottom was a man of many antipathies. Some I found quite reasonable, since I shared them with him, while others I considered rather singular. Our discussions ranged very widely, for Muggsbottom's association of ideas was often as curious as his views. Nor was he always the lecturer and I a mere audience of one. As I grew less intimidated by him, I began to have my say as well.

But it is Muggsbottom's opinions in which we are chiefly interested here. Therefore, in an effort to systematize our very unsystematic discussions, I have arbitrarily chosen seven of Muggsbottom's most deeply held prejudices and treated each in the form of a daily lecture. Seven is one of the mystical, talismanic numbers. It is also the number of days in a week, providing us with a handy organizing principle for the study of my friend's eclectic ratiocinations. Let us listen as Muggsbottom holds forth on each day's particular aversion.

Sunday: You need not infer that I make these remarks in confidence, dear boy. Feel free to share them with others. I believe that my observations may be an extremely valuable contribution to my American cousins, for the correction or elimination of those things which most irritate me will, in turn, have a salutary effect upon the community as a whole. I shall begin with the rather—alas, I can use no other word—perverse practice of Christianity here in Arcady.

While Biffy Smythe-Gardner is a complete materialist and poor Reggie draws his spiritual insights from astrology columns in the popular press, Sir Monty and I are staunch Church of England men—and High-Church men at that. We learnt of the existence of a local Episcopal parish, no mean feat since most of Arcady's inhabitants appear to be Anabaptists who have no knowledge of it. We procured the services of the loquacious Mr. Nunn and set off to attend Sunday matins. "I know that little church," said he. "Ain't they a lot like the Catholics?" I had little enthusiasm for an ecclesiastical discussion with Eddie Nunn, so I simply responded, "One might say so."

The "little church" was St. Augustine's of the Wood. It was nestled in an arbor of oaks and pines and was safe from discovery by anyone who was not fervently searching for it. The parishioners were few in number, all seemingly related in some degree to one another, and obviously fascinated by the appearance of any new communicant. The Eucharist was administered in a satisfactorily traditional manner, but the sermon was a bit hard to swallow. The padre, a pudgy, bland-faced little fellow, suddenly began to carry on about bringing racial justice to South Africa, saving the whales, eliminating acid rain, and doing something or other to the ozone. Whales and acid rain indeed! And we don't even have ozone in Arkansas, do we? At any rate, these remarks so stirred Sir Monty that he was unable to go to sleep during the sermon, as is his practice. After services, Sir Monty engaged the padre in conversation. Actually, *interrogation* might be a better choice of words. Sir Monty put to the fellow the key ecclesiastical questions upon which our approval or disapproval depended, and the answers were as unsatisfactory as we had feared. When asked his position on women in the priesthood, he not only voiced enthusiastic support for the practice but also—quite gratuitously, I thought—launched into an anecdote about a lesbian priest he liked so much that he always tried to have dinner with her during diocesan meetings. Sir Monty, growing quite apoplectic of mien, commenced to sputter and quickly lapsed into total incoherency. I recognized these danger signals, and Mr. Nunn and I rushed Sir Monty away before physical harm could come to either him or the padre.

Need I say that St. Augustine's of the Wood has been *terra non grata* to us since that day?

Sir Monty is so High Church as to be almost "turned." Only his long-held dubiety of the doctrine of transubstantiation has stood between him and Rome. He announced his intention to attend the local R.C. church with an eye toward finally receiving instruction. I thought this action imprudent, too analogous to a man's making a bad marriage immediately after having been jilted. But he was determined to attend mass the next Sunday morning, whether I accompanied him or not. And so he did. Fortunately, my friend was saved from any extreme and precipitous action by two specific disappointments that he suffered during the mass. Actually, the first occurred *before* the mass. The parishioners of the Church of Our Lady of Wise Counsel had either failed to seek or failed to heed that wise counsel. The result was an extremely tacky grotto of painted concrete which they had constructed on ground some yards behind the sanctuary. The mere presence of a concrete grotto in Arcady was . . . exotic, but the fact that this one was seen against the background of the barbecue drive-in restaurant on the lot immediately behind the church property made it seem even more mislocated. The odor of burning hickory chips and sizzling ribs filled the shrine with what Sir Monty considered a most inappropriate incense. My friend's second disappointment was the vernacular mass. "Taking those prayers out of the Latin," Sir Monty said to me later, "was a catastrophic mistake. God must grow very weary indeed of listening to such jejune and insipid recitations. One wouldn't half blame Him for nodding off."

Sir Monty's first visit to Our Lady of Wise Counsel was also his last.

The Episcopal Church had been ecclesiastically unsound. The Roman Catholic Church had proved aesthetically unsatisfying. Clearly, we had to search elsewhere for that spiritual guidance which even an Englishman requires.

One afternoon, I was chatting with that colleague of yours who lives next door. I told him how the local Anglicans had let us down and how Sir Monty had subsequently failed to receive sustenance from the R.C.s. He grew very excited.

"Why," said he, "you and Sir Monty must visit with our Unitarian group. Our services are extremely stimulating. None of this psalm singing and sermonizing. We play tapes of Bach and have rousing discussions on crucial issues of the day. Twice we've given sanctuary to illegal aliens fleeing persecution in Central America. The last time, I was questioned by people from the Immigration Service, but I wouldn't tell them a damned thing. We don't have any creed, you know—just the brotherhood of man under the fatherhood of God. In fact, belief in the brotherhood of man may be all that's actually *essential*."

He was awfully keen, but why he thought Sir Monty and I would find all that self-conscious benevolence appealing I can't imagine. In the long run, his sort do much more harm than the villains of the world. I am amazed that he is permitted to teach impressionable young men and women.

At the other extreme is our Anabaptist landlady. Perhaps I should withdraw the term "extreme," since I am informed that some of the other chapel congregations in Arcady are more stridently Nonconformist in their practices than even the Anabaptists. Well, setting degrees of apostasy aside, I shall continue with my anecdote.

The good lady, ascertaining that Sir Monty and I were two of the very few European Christians she imagined to exist, never ceased inveigling us to accompany her to chapel. The flesh is weak, and the Sunday morning eventually came when we acquiesced. Our arrival inspired great joy among the lady's coreligionists, who seemed to be laboring under the misapprehension that she had brought us there as converts. We seated ourselves at the rear of the room, which gave more the appearance of a union hall in Sheffield than a sanctuary. No recorded Bach cantatas greeted us there. A large, leather-lunged choir sang every verse of several melodically pleasing but lachrymose hymns. Their performance was apparently intended to set a suitably somber mood for the sermon, which the preacher then rose to deliver.

He was an enthusiast, in the eighteenth century sense, and was not without a certain Bunyanesque eloquence. He was a small man whose riot of blond hair had been subdued into an immense pompadour. He wore a shiny suit fashioned from some indestructible-looking synthetic material which reminded me, for some reason, of television pictures of astronauts exploring the moon. His brightly colored tie was embroidered with a huge gold cross. He preached with a Bible in his hand and constantly lifted it skyward, as if inviting the Lord to reread the pertinent passages. He made frequent references to "the lost," and it was my clear impression that in each instance these were directed particularly at Sir Monty and me. Our landlady was much affected and cast doleful glances in our direction throughout the entire peroration. At one point, she was even moved to pat me empathetically on the back. The sermon seemed about three hours long but Sir Monty, who awoke near the end of it and consulted his timepiece, tells me that I exaggerate. During the altar call, all eyes were once again upon us. But despite repeated pleas of "Won't you come?" we—and, presumably, the other sinners in attendance—sat tight. The preacher was visibly disappointed. The only person to make her way tearfully to the altar was a young woman who, our landlady later informed us, "rededicates her life about every other Sunday—it's sort of her hobby."

The service ended with a call for "witnessing." Here, our landlady had hoped to distinguish herself by witnessing to her role in our conversion. Alas, her disappointment was written large upon her face. She had earlier passed our names forward on a visitors' card, and about what happened next Sir Monty and I remain in disagreement. Sir Monty views the preacher's behavior as outright retaliation for our obduracy, while I take the more charitable view that it merely represented a curious Anabaptist practice.

Reading from the visitors' card, the pompadoured Jeremiah said, "Now, would Brother Montague Capulet lead us in the benediction?"

For a moment, I thought Sir Monty was not going to respond at all but, with great dignity, he lifted his hoary head and replied, "In my church, the Anglican Church, we engage professionals to do our praying for us. We call these men 'priests.'"

As Sir Monty was scuttling down the front steps at what was for him a brisk pace, he harrumphed, *"Brother* Montague Capulet, indeed!"

Our landlady did not invite us to church again. In fact, she was noticeably cool towards us thereafter. Sir Monty opined that she was embarrassed by the gauche behavior of her minister and knew not what to say to us. I always suspected there was more to it than that.

Not long after our visit with the Anabaptists, a delivery van drove up with a television set in the back.

Reggie announced, rather sheepishly, "Well, you two are forever going on about your spiritual needs and how you can't find a church that suits you. The salesman tells me that on Sunday mornings there's a religious service on every channel. Surely you can find one that isn't too objectionable."

Now, Reggie is generous to a fault, and I have no doubt that what he said was true so far as it went. But Sir Monty and I agree that the television set also gave our friend the opportunity to imaginatively reexperience his past triumphs. I was strengthened in this belief by noting that tears often came into Reggie's eyes during laxative commercials.

We found that indeed the salesman had not misrepresented the plethora of televised Sunday morning services. But, to our dismay, we discovered also that the most dreadful horde of television evangelists were on the air at all hours of the night and day. However, my dear fellow, this is the lamentable subject for another conversation.

Monday: Today, I continue my commentary on the most hateful aspects of the modern world. I have adumbrated the corruption of Anglican theology in the New World and the evils of the Nonconformist worship service. This afternoon, I turn to a producer of malaise that, if not more serious than those mentioned, is, at least, more omnipresent. I speak of recorded music. I am not hostile to recorded music per se—well, not completely. I once owned a phonograph and would have continued, no doubt, to listen to it had I not lost the crank. The tragic mistake we made, of course, was in allowing recorded music to be played over the wireless, thereby insuring the eventual pollution of even the most remote hamlet—such as Arcady. Up from the primordial ooze has come something called "rock and roll." It features aboriginal rhythms and such lyrics as, "Hey, baby/Let's get naked and nasty."

Nor is it America alone which has fallen prey to this degeneracy. I understand that even in my homeland a group called the Centipedes, or something very like, achieved a passing notoriety. I am told, however, that these young musicians came from Liverpool. Thus, I do not consider them in any way representative of British life.

This issue was brought jarringly to my attention in recent days, when a rather primitive young man called at the Phlegm Club. He represented, said he, a firm specializing in automated music—"juke boxes" was the puzzling term he actually used. He appeared before the Membership Committee, composed of Smythe-Gardner, Sir Monty Capulet, and myself—Reggie is far too impressionable to serve on this crucial committee. This was the first time that an outsider, other than yourself, had visited the club since the local Episcopal priest had come in hopes of luring us back to services. I wonder, do you know the vicar here? Under ordinary circumstances, we would have considered him for membership, but he's so patently proletarian, don't you think? We're pretty sure he wouldn't fit in. Sir Monty suspects that he may even have voted Labour, or whatever the American equivalent of that is. But I digress.

The salesman sang the praises of his juke box, showering it with hyperbole, and urging us to rent it for the Phlegm Club. Then he made his fatal mistake—he played a couple of "country music" records for us by way of demonstration. The first was a lugubrious little ballad entitled "It's My Rabbit, My Dog Caught It." We had scarcely recovered from the effects of this experience, when he played the bucolic lament: "Send Me to Glory in a Glad Bag." Naturally, we tossed the young man out on his ear without a further word.

During our entire intercourse with the commercial traveler, Maynard, our dipsomaniacal barman, was smiling broadly. Could he have conceivably put that wretched boy up to calling on us? I wonder.

Tuesday: My prejudice for the day is election campaigns—*all* election campaigns, local, state, and federal. We also have election campaigns in Britain, of course, and they are ghastly exercises as well. But they are so much shorter and less numerous than those in the New World. Here, it seems that there is never a time when some gaggle of patently undeserving petitioners, usually unsuccessful barristers, aren't seeking one sinecure or another from the taxpayers. We witness a marathon round of caucuses, conventions, primaries, and general elections. Invariably, this round ends just in time for another to begin. The process is enervating in the extreme, both for the politicians and the public. The problem is *not* that we learn too little about the office seekers; it is that we learn too much. Having taken note of the degree of their obtuseness, shallowness, and mendacity, how could we conceivably vote for any of them? (Here I speak figuratively, of course, since, as a British subject, I may not vote even for so efficacious a measure as the installation of public houses on Pine Street.)

We nightly witness on the television the spectacle of the presidential candidates zooming from one speaking engagement to another in jet aeroplanes. During his speech, each man will clearly reveal his unfitness to govern anybody. Then the mob will clamorously cheer some puerile sentiment, and reveal its fitness to be governed by *just* anybody.

See, for example, what the vagaries of democracy have wrought in Arkansas—Mr. Clinton, a governor not long removed from puberty, who must occasionally postpone public appearances until his face clears up. But, enough. I am not, as you well know, one to deal in personalities.

Wednesday: My dear boy, please allow me to continue pointing out to you those things in life which I find most bile-making. Today I shall document and defend my antipathy for modern poetry. Actually, my prejudice against contemporary verse is decidedly of the second rank, nowhere nearly approaching the animosity inspired by television evangelists, civil servants of every stripe, joggers, reformed smokers, and commercials for products of feminine hygiene. However, having just read what is often called a "slim volume" of verses—this one was not slim enough—I find the subject presently in my thoughts.

The source of these muddled and elliptical obliquities is a fellow I knew slightly at university. His name is Twinksly Murk, and he is now taken rather seriously as a bard. We were not at the same college. Murk, who is somewhat younger than I, matriculated at Ponce College, where the atmosphere was permeated with all of the Wildean qualities, save wit. I recall that young Twinksly's customary drink in those days was a creme de menthe frappé, served to him in an unchilled glass. This he referred to as "taking it neat." After four or five of these vile libations, he would pull off his trousers, run up the length of the High Street, and throw himself into the fountain there. From thence, he would accost the passersby, shouting: "Oh, save me, old darlings, for I feel the Nereids nibbling at my toes." Suffice it to say that any Nereid consorting with Twinksly Murk would have found the encounter to be singularly unrewarding. Well, I took small note of the fellow in those long ago days—except that I *may* have once set fire to his trousers. I have a vague recollection of doing something very like that.

Then, the other day at the Phlegm Club as I was taking a glass of port for the stomach's sake, Smythe-Gardner made his unsteady way over to my chair. He handed me this little book and asked my opinion. He had come across it somewhere and, mistaking it for one of the little books which come to him regularly through the mail wrapped in brown paper, he had settled down to read it. But, finding it unintelligible, he had brought it to me. After a cursory examination, I assured Smythe-Gardner that, although tasteless in the extreme, it was not lubricious in the straightforward, unambiguous way preferred by the English. Without a word he returned to his gin and lime and to his self-imposed task of checking from time to time whether Sir Montague Capulet were napping or dead.

Thus it was that I came to read Twinksly Murk's book, *Water Skiing in Erebus*. The poems did not rhyme, nor could one scan or gloss them. The ideas were largely inchoate. In those few instances in which they were comprehensible, I found them trivial. A note in the front of the book informs one that Murk's *oeuvre* consists of two other tomes: *Diddling at the Dorchester* and *Simpering at the Savoy*. Nothing short of the Chinese water torture could induce me to read them. At any rate, British poetry was interred with the bones of Pope, and American poetry was destined to be stillborn from the moment that George Washington and his renegades rejected the culture of the mother country. This is all that need be said regarding modern poetry.

Thursday: British television, my boy, is a scandal. I do not pretend otherwise. But the very purpose of American television appears to be obliteration of the demarcation line between sanity and madness. I am pessimistic, but it is devoutly to be wished that something salubrious shall eventually come from this powerful medium. Something other than the salacious, the scatological, the double-entendres employed each evening by one degenerate cast after another. In short, something other than the tasteless material which numbs one's mind and lays waste to one's soul at any time one is viewing the television machine.

Let us take as an example last night's television schedule. At six o'clock, we watched the Arkansas news from Little Rock. Four "reporters" sat behind a desk cut into the shape of the station's channel number—and very awkwardly arranged they were, too. On either side of the point at the top of the number sat a middle-aged man and a young woman called, for some reason that no one seems to understand, "anchors." The male anchor, who was coiffed much like an Anabaptist preacher, wore a vacuous look throughout. He obviously understood little of what he was reading. At one point where he had used the word "magnolia," thereby rendering his sentence very cryptic indeed, he was obliged to go back and change the term to "Mongolia." The female anchor was extremely attractive but, alas, the expression in her eyes was no more penetrating than that of her male counterpart. Her profusion of golden hair was—purposely, I assume—all a-tangle, giving her the appearance of someone who has just stuck her finger in a light socket. Her smile was radiant but often inappropriate, as if beauty contests, watermelon festivals, and fatal highway crashes were all one to her. To her left sat the "weather-girl," a slender brunette, who would later stand before a huge map of the United States and point wildly from one to another of a bewildering accumulation of graphic symbols. She seemed delighted that the meteorological tedium of recent days was to be shattered by the imminent arrival of a killer tornado. To the male anchor's right sat the sports reporter. To communicate the degree of his excitement over the several games you Americans are so keen on, he shouted at us for nearly ten minutes, as though to reach into our home without the aid of his microphone. By the end of the half-hour, their manic presentation had quite exhausted me.

At six-thirty, we watched dumbfounded a show in which a group of the dimmest young newlyweds ever gathered together in one spot played some sort of game. I asked Sir Monty if he could discern the object of the game. His reply was, "I believe they are attempting to outdo each other in relating intimacies. The couple which most embarrasses themselves, the studio audience, and the viewing public wins a Caribbean cruise or something of the sort." An oily master of ceremonies fed these jejune troglodytes and troglodettes a list of questions designed to elicit lewd responses. The producers had made an obvious effort to represent several racial and ethnic groups, and their egalitarian experiment had proved totally successful: all the couples were equally smarmy and puerile. The studio audience, who should have been either sitting in silent mortification or noisily explaining what they were doing there, roared with apparent pleasure. I was appalled, and Smythe-Gardner said, "These creatures shouldn't be allowed to breed, you know." But Reggie smiled his gentle smile and observed, "Oh, they're just high-spirited, I should say. Kids are like that." Reggie practices Christian charity to a fault.

From seven to eight, Smythe-Gardner tuned in a crime show. He rather enjoys these because of all the biffing that goes on in them. I find the dramas of this sort interchangeable. I can never tell which American city is being featured. Its streets are populated exclusively by black and Latin hoodlums, all speaking an impenetrable argot. They work for the "big boss," who is the scion of a venerable Anglo-Saxon family. This villain ordinarily holds a position such as mayor of the city, president of a leading bank, or chairman of the Carnegie Foundation. The nihilistic, monosyllabic hero spends half the show in his motor car, careening about the city streets at excessive speeds. He pots gangsters like grouse with his Magnum, holstering this immense phallic symbol only long enough to use the genuine article on a host of beautiful young women who keep throwing themselves beneath him. The mayhem lifts Smythe-Gardner's spirits noticeably, but he seldom is conscious for the dénouement. Lime poisoning sets in around seven-thirty, and by eight o'clock his snoring is competing on equal terms with the rattle of gunfire from the television set.

Last night, the crime show was succeeded by what

Reggie tells me is a "nighttime soap." These are melodramas set in various cities of the modern West. All of the characters are rich (but greedy for more), amoral, and libidinous. I am told that over time all the characters have illicit affairs with the spouses of all the other characters, so that eventually a kind of incestuous extended family develops which includes everybody. Reggie said, "It's just romance. You can't take it seriously." Indeed I could not, and at that point I retired to my study. I am, therefore, unable to relate the television schedule beyond nine o'clock. My stultification had proceeded quite far enough by that hour.

What's that, old fellow? Do I ever watch public television? I have tried on occasion. But men in dinner jackets and women in evening gowns are perpetually begging for money, not unlike those holy rollers on the other channels. And I haven't taken to the programs, as a matter of fact. I mean, those interminable contemporary ballets where, to the accompaniment of atonal music, the prima ballerina dances for hours with forklifts and other symbols of technology. And all the programs about wildebeest, schizophrenia, and the rings of Saturn. I know one should find these shows riveting, dear boy, and I wish one did.

Friday: This evening, let's chat for a bit about American education, shall we? The subject is much on my mind because of an experience I had a week ago today. A few days earlier, a Miss Grendel from the Arcady High School had sent me a note asking if I would come to talk with her senior English class about British mores, folkways, that sort of thing. Broaden their understanding of the subject, don't you know? Well, I imprudently responded in the affirmative and committed myself to an appearance on Friday last. And on that day, at what was for me an exceedingly early hour, I engaged the good Mr. Nunn to convey me to that citadel of learning at the edge of town. *I* was soon to learn why the high school had been erected so far from all other human habitation.

Miss Grendel was a veteran of many campaigns. Her grey eyes were wary, her thin lips drawn tight. From the salt-and-pepper bun at the back of her neck to her orthopedic shoes, she was a schoolmistress. But a weary schoolmistress. She welcomed me as General Gordon might have welcomed reinforcements at Khartoum. The opportunity to put her charges into the hands of another, even for an hour's time, she obviously viewed as a great blessing. By way of orientation, she told me that the class had been reading *Macbeth*, then gestured that the floor was mine.

"Before we get started, Miss Grendel," said a ruddy behemoth sitting at the back of the room, "is this Macbeth a dude or a chick?"

"A dude, Bill Ed," Miss Grendel responded with resignation. "*Lady* Macbeth is the chick."

"Oh, yeah?" Bill Ed's knitted brow indicated some effort at thought. "I guess I ain't got to her yet."

Despite this unpromising beginning and my general state of disarray, I launched into a discussion of the England of the Tudors. I have already alluded to the earliness of the hour, but I confess that I was more than usually untidy as a result of oversleeping. I had thus been forced to rush directly from the shower into my clothes. In fact, my hair—what remains of it—was still wet when I reached the high school. I pulled myself together and spoke with the aplomb which, I believe I can say without boasting, is characteristic of my public lectures. I was obliged, in regard to *Macbeth*, to explain to these adolescents that the Scots and the English are *not* the same people and, alas, in the minds of all too many Englishmen, are by no means created equal. Also I found that smiling faces and heads nodding up and down do not necessarily mean, "I understand." At one point, I began to fill my pipe. Miss

Grendel's grey eyes narrowed, her taut mouth mouth grew still more taut, and her salt-and-pepper head wagged just perceptibly from side to side. It was the classic schoolmistress signal—"Forbidden." Second thoughts began to race through my head.

Eventually, I realized that I had reached a point of diminishing returns, for most of my young auditors were either asleep, doodling, or surreptitiously passing notes. I closed and called for questions. A black lad wearing a genuinely curious expression raised his hand.

"Say, do all Englishmen be dressed like you?"

I requested amplification.

"I mean, you be wearing your tie too long."

You may wonder that the query stumped me so completely, but that was certainly the case. The necktie in question was my school tie. I assumed—correctly, as it turned out—that a school tie is not customary at the Arcady High School. But I digress. The lad's remark was tantalizingly ambiguous. Had he used the term "too long" in the spatial or the chronological sense? I decided to leave the matter unresolved.

A nubile brunette, attired in the costume of what I believe you call a "cheerleader," spoke next.

"Mr. Muggsbottom, you're the most entertaining guest speaker we've ever had."

Before I could articulate a suitable reply to this compliment, she added, "It's been so much fun watching your hair dry."

At this point, Miss Grendel mercifully called the question and-answer period to a halt, thanked me, gave my hand a masculine squeeze, and sent me on my way.

Further requests for lectures have not been forthcoming.

Saturday: You know, old man, we culture lovers are sorely beset on every hand. And amidst the widespread moral chaos of our time, it is no easy task to single out a prejudice for us to discuss each evening. One is almost driven to shout one's jeremiads to the skies. But one soon grows weary of playing Cassandra in the wilderness. In Arkansas, one is positively beaten down by the unwillingness of the natives to discuss anything other than the prospects of their rugby team, the Razorblades. One eventually retires to one's club to enjoy whatever amenities one finds there, while one awaits the apocalypse.

It seems to me that this enthusiasm for games—poor Maynard babbles about almost nothing else—is the cultural focal point for much of what we have previously discussed. For example, let us consider the young Neanderthal who was in doubt as to Macbeth's gender and his classmate who found my tie more fascinating than the history of the English-speaking peoples. No doubt each could name all sixty or seventy members of the Razorblade aggregation and cite their athletic achievements down to the most recondite statistic. And what of the wench in the cheerleader costume? Doubtless her greatest motivation for completing her high school studies is the thought of matriculating at the University, where her vocal support will help the Razorblades achieve victory over Texas.

The coach shamelessly encourages the natives in their pseudo-religious attitude toward the team. I have seen him on the television. He says things like, "In life, even when it's fourth and long [whatever that means], we should never punt. We only have to ask that Great Quarterback in the Sky to diagram the right play for us on His Heavenly Blackboard. His play selection never fails, because He's got the best won-lost record of all time." Life as a football match ignores a number of the theological complexities, wouldn't you say?

This mania for sports can sometimes produce the most unhappy results for those who do not share in it. On a recent evening, Sir Monty was reading one of the Little Rock newspapers. He voiced some disapproval—quite sensibly, I thought—of the excessive number of Razorblade stories, even in the news section of the paper. Maynard, who by the look and smell of him had been into our Scotch again, took offense. He pouted ostentatiously for the next hour. When Smythe-Gardner and I called for our nightcaps, Sir Monty was napping in his chair, as is his custom. As Maynard was making his unsteady way toward us with the tray of drinks, he stumbled over Sir Monty's ottoman and deposited the drinks in the old gentleman's ample lap. Sir Monty, quite understandably, awoke. A flurry of noisy recriminations and howls of innocence ensued.

I could not prove that Maynard's faux pas was purposeful, but I am convinced that it was. The rascal is well aware that, Arcady's market for servants being what it is, we can scarcely discharge him for any offense short of a capital crime.

"Muggsbottom," I was finally moved to say, "you left England because you found life intolerable there. But, if you had your way, you would make Arkansas over into the England you have abandoned."

He smiled and replied, "My friend, you point up a penchant of the Englishman which many others have noted. But I believe some well-known American writer once said that consistency is one of the very minor virtues, or something to that effect. And of course Oscar Wilde, an authority on virtue, whatever else might be said of him, called consistency "the last resort of an impoverished imagination.""

5. The Ol' Perfesser and Homer Joe Tennyson

Another American phenomenon Muggsbottom purported not to understand was junk mail.

"My dear fellow," he said, "we get things through the post addressed to 'Occupant' and 'Resident.' How effective can that be for your merchants? It seems rather like stuffing a note in a bottle and tossing it into the ocean."

"If the cost exceeded their sales, I suppose they would stop doing it," I sagely opined.

"Yes, but surely one can form only the most tenuous relationship with a tradesman who addresses one as 'Occupant.'"

"Well, as I said, it must work," I replied. "My mailboxes at home and at school are stuffed full with that crap nearly every day."

Muggsbottom ruminated for a few moments, then said, "I must admit that poor Reggie *is* susceptible. Last month, 'Occupant' received two complimentary boxes of dry cereal. They were tiny and grotesquely labeled. Flakes of cereal with arms and legs and little faces, cavorting about in garish colors—that sort of thing. Their names were so strikingly awful that I remember them vividly . . . Cinnamon Asteroids and Blueberry Mega-Missiles. They instantly attracted Reggie's attention and, with his childlike enthusiasm, he sampled them the very next morning. As I recall, both turned the milk in his bowl a disgusting color.

They were sugar-coated, and sugar has always acted as a stimulant for Reggie. He absolutely loved his wretched breakfast and has insisted upon having dry cereal every morning since. Now when we go to the market, Reggie's off like a shot in search of Cinnamon Asteroids and Blueberry Mega-Missiles . . . But then Reggie is the atypical consumer, I should think. He's certainly the exception to every rule I've ever learnt."

"What about Smythe-Gardner?" I said.

"I beg your pardon, dear boy?"

"Didn't Smythe-Gardner tell me he got the first copy of that girlie magazine he holes up with every month with a coupon that just came in the mail one day?"

"Perhaps . . . Yes, I believe he may well have done."

I was pleased with myself, because I always loved to catch Muggsbottom up in one of his many blatant inconsistencies.

He sniffed, began to refill his pipe, and said, in a tone clearly meant to close the subject, "Still, in *principle* the practice strikes *me* as unsound."

Had I wished to embarrass Muggsbottom or make him angry (the latter would have been more likely than the former), I could have mentioned another instance in which American marketing practices had succeeded with my Englishmen.

It was the practice of the *Arcady Harbinger* to throw newcomers a complimentary copy of the paper every afternoon for a week. Ours is a typical small-town newspaper. It seldom has momentous events to report. It is fleshed out with stories on local sporting events, goings-on at the colleges, activities of the area churches, and special promotions by the local merchants. The photographs are mostly of the high school and college teams in action, and of home-town girls just married or engaged to be. There is also a liberal sprinkling of dead deer in the beds of pickup trucks, and men holding long strings of fish or snake carcasses. I had not believed that the Phlegmatics would find this fare very appetizing but, to my amazement, they all read every complimentary issue from front to back. Judging by the behavior of my Englishmen, a quasi spiritual involvement with the newspaper must be a national trait. By the second week in their new home, Muggsbottom and his friends were regular subscribers to the *Arcady Harbinger*.

Muggsbottom had no desire to involve himself in local affairs, beyond the hit-and-run criticisms he offered in our wide-ranging conversations. I am certain he never dreamed he would be drawn into a literary controversy in Arcady, Arkansas, but such was the case. His adversaries were to be two Arcadians as atypical as he: the Ol' Perfesser, a thrice-weekly columnist with the *Arcady Harbinger*, and Homer Joe Tennyson, poet laureate of Dean County.

Homer Joe I knew only through his work, but the Ol' Perfesser had once been a reasonably close acquaintance. He and I had come to teach at the little state college in the same year. He was, I believe, a good historian, but the provincial atmosphere of our little slice of academe caused him quickly to grow restive. After a faculty meeting in which he had referred to the Board of Trustees as "that bunch of cretins," his relationship with the Administration steadily deteriorated. At the end of his third year of employment, his teaching contract was not renewed. He maintained that he had resigned, while the Vice President for Academic Affairs insisted that he had been discharged. As is so often the case in these situations, the exact nature of the breach remained pretty much in the eye of the beholder. So bitter was the parting, however, that the historian came to view those of us who remained on the faculty as morally obtuse—we became his former friends.

As my one-time colleague had no immediate prospects, he began nosing about for some temporary work he could do until an academic vacancy materialized somewhere. He had done a little newspaper work during his teens and early twenties, and it happened that the *Arcady Harbinger* was just then in need of a general assignments reporter. He took the job with the *Harbinger* expecting, I am sure, to be there only a few months. But, like so many of us who had come to Arcady planning to stay only until our ship came in, a decade later he was still in town, still with the paper. Before long, his skillful use of language and mordant wit had garnered him a 700-word column three times weekly. Because of his academic background and the animosity he continued to display toward the college community, he adopted for his column the persona of a cracker-barrel, anti-intellectual philosopher called the Ol' Perfesser. His real name is not important, for it is the role he played under his journalistic cognomen that is of interest in the drama I am about to relate.

It is ironic that he and Homer Joe Tennyson were to become allies in their aesthetic battle with Muggsbottom, since the two men could hardly have been more different. Where the Ol' Perfesser was sly and subtle, Homer Joe was straightforward and appallingly sincere. Prior to the controversy, their relationship was only tenuous and accidental in nature—both wrote a column for the *Harbinger*.

Homer Joe Tennyson's "Verses from the Vale" appeared in the *Harbinger* each Thursday afternoon. The essence of Homer Joe's poetic works might best be described as the pastoral tradition gone to seed. Some representative titles: "The Ballad of the Bayou," "Soybean Serenade," "The Plowman's Plaint at Eventide," and "Ruminations While Skinning a Doe." He was variously known as the Bard of Dean County, the Minstrel of the Marshes, and the Antoine Songbird (so named for the hamlet which had produced him). His poems were like the lyrics to country songs, except with pretensions. But I must admit that he had developed a following, just as any artist will who, no matter how awful, believes in himself totally.

Perhaps the best thing I can do at this point is to quote

the entire text of the poem which was the *casus belli*. It was entitled "The Lonely Lover's Lament" and went as follows:

'Tis Spring when beauteous flowers blossom,
When love stirs e'en the humble 'possum.
All creatures mate in Nature's way,
While thou and I do nought but pray
That we may be together soon,
Beneath yon circling golden moon.
Our day of sweet consort is nigh,
And 'cause of this our hearts is high.

I happened to be visiting the Phlegm Club on the evening Muggsbottom came across "The Lonely Lover's Lament" in that afternoon's *Harbinger*. I recall that he read the poem aloud, chuckled, and scratched a note on a pad he always kept close at hand. Muggsbottom was constantly committing to paper the curious notions that swarmed through his brain. These notes, he said, were the basis for a philosophical treatise he planned someday to write. I never took them seriously, since I considered my friend to be just another author manqué, gathering material year after year for a book that would never be written. So I was not really curious about what Muggsbottom had jotted down and thought no more of it until a few days later, when one of the letters in the *Harbinger*'s "To the Editor" column caught my eye. It read:

Re Homer Joe Tennyson's 'The Lonely Lover's Lament'
To paraphrase someone or other:
  For there be poets fair as he,
  Whose nouns and verbs do more agree.
      C.P. Muggsbottom

It was up to that time very much out of character for

Muggsbottom to send even so brief a letter to the editor. Normally, he enjoyed playing the role of detached observer, imagining himself far above the drolleries of the hoi polloi. But when Homer Joe's awful little poem had caused the phrase from Bret Harte, I believe it was, suddenly to come into his head, he must have decided the comment was far too good not to share with the general public. Consequently, his letter to the editor.

The thin-skinned Homer Joe was quick to respond. The lead poem in the next Thursday's "Verses from the Vale" was entitled "To the Men without a Country." It was as close as Homer Joe could come to a Shakespearean sonnet and went as follows:

We blessèd boys and girls of Arkansas
Were reared to love our fathers and our land.
We sought no foreign clime. Each pa and ma
Taught us upon our heritage to stand.
We long ago dispelled the tyrant's pow'r;
The satin breeches of the king, we kicked.
Yet, even at this late arrivèd hour,
Some Englishmen forget how they were licked.
These Englishmen come to our state as guests,
Although transported from their native soil.
We welcome them, but not their tasteless jests,
Belittling a home-grown poet's toil.
So if they find us Arkies too outré,
Remember—ships still sail the other way.

I couldn't help thinking that this was one of Homer Joe's better efforts.

"How does he know that I'm an Englishman?" Muggsbottom asked me that night. "I've never met the bugger."

Muggsbottom had never understood that he and his fellow members of the Phlegm Club were celebrities merely by virtue of their origin. There was scarcely a resident of Arcady who did not know them.

"Well, you and Homer Joe are even now," I suggested, although I could see that the look in Muggsbottom's eye said otherwise.

"We would be if the blighter had attacked only me in his wretched bit of doggerel. But did you notice that he used the plural throughout? He aimed a broadside at my friends as well, who had nothing whatever to do with my innocent little remark, and he impugned by implication all my countrymen. He should never have got my patriotic juices flowing."

"What are you going to do?"

"I believe another letter to the editor is warranted, don't you? And this time, my analysis of Homer Joe's art will be somewhat more definitive."

I felt that my friend was making a mistake. In a prolonged public battle between a resident alien and a native son, Arcadians would rally behind the native son. During the Englishmen's first weeks in Arcady, I had seen definite signs of suspicion and resentment in some local circles. But as the four Britons were observed to keep to themselves, moving only occasionally and unobtrusively about the town in Eddie Nunn's taxicab, these negative feelings had waned. I was convinced that Muggsbottom's proposed counterattack would stir up xenophobia all over again. But I also realized how pointless it was to argue against a course of action to which Muggsbottom had already committed himself in his mind.

The counterattack took the form of the following letter:

"I understand that Homer Joe Tennyson, our bard of the bayou, took offense at my passing reference to him in a recent letter to the editor. I further understand that he voiced a veiled suggestion that I and my friends should

return whence we came. Being one of the last gentlemen whose existence I can actually verify, I view the defense of my honor and that of my friends as a solemn duty.

"Further, as long as the Harbinger continues to allow Homer Joe to ventilate his execrable doggerel in its pages, I believe the public have a right to defend themselves. Surely Homer Joe's wretched rhymes and mangled metrics are in violation of several anti-pollution statutes.

"Ah, well. Homer Joe has not been the same, I am told, since the Antoine Lions Club gave him its 'Artist of the Year' award. I fear that unless someone can stop him he will permanently join the ranks of those trinomial poets who live to extremely advanced ages, writing a ghastly new poem every day, decade after decade. In Homer Joe's case, alas, ars brevis, vita longa.

> *Objectively yours,*
> *C.P. Muggsbottom"*

The war of words was on.

Homer Joe interpreted—misinterpreted, Muggsbottom insisted—the letter as a suggestion that assassination might be an appropriate means of terminating his poetic career. He understandably found such a response *too* fundamental, even to the work of a "natural genius." He fired back with another poem, the crucial lines of which read, "I heed no critic who no poet is/And raise a stouter arm and fist than his."

Within days, Muggsbottom's rejoinder was in print: "Homer Joe Tennyson has insinuated . . . no, the term 'insinuated' suggests more subtlety than Homer Joe has ever possessed . . . he charged that since *I* am not a poet I may not remark that *he* is not a poet. *Au contraire*, Homer Joe. *Au contraire.* One need not be a hen to smell a rotten egg. In addition, this backwoods booby clearly made a threat against my person. He had best beware what actionable remarks he commits to print. I understand that America is teeming with barristers who ache to represent an injured party before the bar of justice."

It was at this point that the Ol' Perfesser entered the fray. It was at this point also that I played my small part in the contretemps. Perhaps I suffer from a natural inclination to pad my part, but I do believe I was originally the source of the Ol' Perfesser's hostility towards Muggsbottom. We had never actually been on bad terms personally, but to the Ol' Perfesser I represented the college, and he and the college were still on very bad terms. I had befriended the Englishmen, thus linking them with the college through me. Homer Joe was scattering poetic small arms fire in the direction of Muggsbottom's cannonades. Homer Joe could certainly use some help, and by coming to his aid the Ol' Perfesser could strike back at his old nemesis through Muggsbottom and me. He chose to do so in this way:

"Veteran readers of this newspaper are aware that Homer Joe Tennyson has been writing a poetry column for a decade and more. The publisher has been pleased with it. The editor has been pleased with it. The readers of Dean County have been pleased with it.

"What we have always liked about Homer Joe's 'pottery,' as he sometimes jokingly calls it, is that we can understand it. It ain't like the stuff put out by those guys the state college sometimes invites down here to lecture. Homer Joe is an outdoorsman and, I will admit, he writes a little more about the slaughter of God's creatures than some of us would prefer. But when Homer Joe writes about shooting and skinning a rabbit, we know that's a *rabbit* and not some Freudian symbol.

"So old Homer Joe has been highly honored around these parts, made county poet laureate and all. Now, along comes a fellow named Muggsbottom, new not only to Arkansas but also to these shores, and he claims Homer Joe ain't much of a poet after all. Of course, he is so much more refined than folks around here that we are expected to take his judgments and put them right in the bank.

"Muggsbottom has a friend, and perhaps a poetic advisor, who teaches English out at the state college. He shall remain nameless here, and I am told that in scholarly circles he definitely *is*. We are all aware of how the crowd out there keeps bringing in fags and revolutionaries—sometimes revolutionary fags—to speak at the college auditorium. The idea is that these weirdos are bringing enlightenment to the hinterlands. Now, the folks at the state college have imported Mr. Muggsbottom and some friends of his all the way from England, so that they can chip off our rough edges.

"Well, the Ol' Perfesser has a challenge for Mr. Muggsbottom. If he can write a better poem than any of Homer Joe Tennyson's, we just might pay some attention to his criticisms. But if he cannot, I would suggest that he limit his literary discussions to evenings with his pals out at the old AMVETS Club, and leave the rest of us sitting in darkness."

"Who is this Ol' Perfesser person?" Muggsbottom asked, as he tapped the newspaper meditatively with his spectacles.

"An apostate professor from my college."

"Ah, his apostasy accounting for his misspelled title, his pretentiously ungrammatical prose, and his resentment of you? I assume you *are* the friend and 'poetic advisor' of whom he writes?"

"Yes, although I would never presume to advise you on artistic matters, Muggsbottom," I said with mock solemnity.

Smythe-Gardner, who had been peering over Muggsbottom's shoulder as he read the column, interjected, "Let's call the poet and this blighter out and give them both a good biffing, shall we?"

I did not really fear that Muggsbottom would follow Smythe-Gardner's lead, since no one ever followed poor Smythe-Gardner's lead, but I hastened to say, "Oh, I don't think the Ol' Perfesser is all that serious. He has to fill three columns a week, and we don't have many controversies in Arcady. Your spat with Homer Joe has given him something to write about. The way he damned Homer Joe with faint praise shows that he really knows you're right on the merits."

"Still," Smythe-Gardner muttered, "the fellow has openly challenged you."

"Yes, and proved himself no gentleman by also choosing the weapons. But he has overreached himself. He does not realize that he is dealing with a one-time finalist for the Newdigate prize. I shall compose a poem that will set Homer Joe Tennyson on his tin ear and will make the Ol' Perfesser rue the day the name Muggsbottom passed through his typewriter."

Smythe-Gardner grunted and returned to his armchair, from where he signaled to Maynard for another gin and lime. He was clearly disappointed that Muggsbottom would not pursue a military solution to the conflict. Sir Monty was hardly aware of the conflict, having been in one of his more soporific phases during its entirety. And Reggie, typically, tended to minimize the affront to his friend. Of Homer Joe, he had said, "Poets are like that, you know . . . sensitive blokes."

The next day, Muggsbottom did not stir from the house, not even to join his friends in their nightly sojourn to the Phlegm Club. He closeted himself away with his writing materials in his book lined, smoke filled study and awaited the coming of his muse. She eventually made her appearance, for (I was told by Reggie, whose bedroom is next to the study) Muggsbottom emerged at two a.m., announcing, "By God, I've done it." Later that morning, he sent his handwritten creation to the editorial office of the *Harbinger* by personal messenger—the redoubtable Maynard. And in the afternoon edition of the *Harbinger* (which is, in fact, the *only* edition of the *Harbinger*), the entire "To the Editor" section was devoted to Muggsbottom's "Ode to Arcady":

Oh, Arcady—thou bourne of sober men,
A storm-tossed pilgrim thanks you yet again.
You welcomed him. You shared with him and his
Your churches' quaint Protestant practices.
You offered country ballads by the score,
Truckers' laments, adult'rers' plaints, and more.
You lavished him with lore of Razorblades,
Accounts of games whose mem'ry never fades.
Now what can he, this trav'ler from afar,
Offer those who his benefactors are?
His wisdom, judgment, taste, panache, élan—
These only can he grant his fellow man.
But, culture lovers, there are those who say,
'That Brit presumes too much. Send him away.
This realm's ideal. His musings we'll not stand.'
Thus speak our Platos of the hinterland.
One writes in verse, a wretched verse withal;
The other writes in prose that doth appall.
I urge a flow'ring of high culture here,
While they would see this flow'ring brown and sere.
I nurse, I water every fragile shoot,
While they would tear up Beauty by the root.
I, your obedient servant, dared oppose
These Philistines. I trod upon their toes.
Muggsbottom, truest friend of Arcady,
Was vilified with every calumny.
Vermin critics launch attacks in swarms.
Against a sea of troubles I take arms.
This old grey head is bloody but unbowed,
For of my native land I'm justly proud.
Surely, sirs and dames of Arcady,
You could expect no more nor less from me.

I am a man not prone to lavish praise;
That does not mean I came to change your ways.
You'll not condemn me if from time to time
I make a small suggestion. That's no crime.
And if my feud with locals bothers y'all,
I'll sue for peace with Homer Joe et al.
My friends and I desire your good opinion
While we reside 'neath Arkansas' dominion.

After Muggsbottom had reread his effort and passed it round the Phlegm Club, he remarked, "I struck just the right tone, if I may say so. Firm but not strident. Steadfast but conciliatory. And I believe the regionalism in the penultimate couplet goes down rather well, don't you?"

Perhaps Muggsbottom was right. Perhaps his heroic couplets were so effective that they silenced his critics and enraptured the Arcadian public. Or perhaps the Ol' Perfesser and Homer Joe—or their editor—had grown weary of the feud. For whatever reason or combination of reasons, Muggsbottom's adversaries allowed him the final word—in this controversy. Homer Joe returned to the writing of poems featuring coon hunting conceits and bucolic bathos. The Ol' Perfesser returned to his more generalized diatribes against high culture and the life of the mind. But Muggsbottom had made two implacable enemies, with whom he was destined to cross swords again.

6. Of Politicians and Porkers

In the autumn of 1980, the Englishmen had been residing in Arcady for either six or eighteen months, depending upon whether Bud Howard or I have the most reliable recollection of the year in which they arrived. Even if Bud is correct, the Brits had been in Arkansas for the crucial months of the presidential and gubernatorial campaigns. Smythe-Gardner and Sir Monty took a passing interest in the proceedings, while Reggie took almost none at all. He affected enough curiosity to ask an occasional question because, I believe, he thought doing so would please me. Reggie was basically kind and apolitical, qualities I have found people often possess in tandem. Muggsbottom was, however, fascinated by the way we Americans practiced politics—sometimes amused, sometimes deeply troubled.

I found that even a person as opinionated and intractable as Muggsbottom could be taught certain rudimentary Southern concepts. For example, we—primarily Maynard—finally broke him from the habit of beginning a pronouncement with the words "You Yanks." Each time he did so, Maynard, in his role as unlicensed manager of the Phlegm Club, would fix a bloodshot eye upon him with a sudden hostile expression. To remind the Englishmen that he was not a "Yank," Maynard frequently wore a T-shirt on the front of which a Confederate flag was barely visible beneath the wine stains and accumulated grime. The relationship between the two men was always in a state of delicate equilibrium. Muggsbottom once remarked to me, "You know, Maynard can visit my study for only a few minutes, and his ambiance lingers for several days thereafter."

But whereas Maynard and I were attempting to educate Muggsbottom to the degree that we could, other Arcadians were turning to him for instruction. One evening, about two weeks before election day, he said to me, "Guess who came to visit me this afternoon. The editor of the *Harbinger*. Your fears that my occasional criticisms of certain community practices—mild and well-meaning as they are—will earn me the enmity of my neighbors are completely unfounded. The gentleman from the *Harbinger* came to interview me—actively seeking my opinions, mind you.

"You . . . Americans are just about to conduct your quadrennial presidential election, in case you haven't noticed. The editor informed me that the really prestigious newspapers feature foreign experts, commenting on the significance of the American elections. We four expatriate Britons, the charter and so far only members of the Phlegm Club, seem the editor's sole prospects for such expert commentary. Since Sir Monty has napped throughout the entire campaign, he was not considered the ideal choice. Smythe-Gardner concerns himself a bit more with current events than does Sir Monty, but he suffers from the same . . . weakness, shall we say, as does Maynard, and the editor could not be entirely sure that, come his deadline, Smythe-Gardner's comments would be completely comprehensible. And poor Reggie would not recognize a politician if he should find one with a hand in his pocket. Ergo, the task of analyzing this capricious and irrational process devolved to me. Muggsbottom accepted the challenge with relish."

"For God's sake, Muggsbottom, what did you tell him?"

"I believe I spoke somewhat in this wise: I realize that some of your readers may have wondered why Muggsbottom continued his sojourn here in the land of cotton, where old times are not forgotten, etc., etc. even after the Labour Party fell from power in the mother country. I can only reply that I am always cognizant of the Anglo-Saxon's burden—'by slow prudence to make mild a rugged people.' I shall not desert you, dear friends, until the manifold blessings of the Empire have been reasserted in all their majesty."

"Oh, dear. Why is it that every time your declamations appear in the local press you sound like Rudyard Kipling?"

"Please, dear boy, don't interrupt. I am attempting to reconstruct my remarks . . . Then I turned to the presidential election. I said: It may well be that you will choose as your president a soon-to-be septuagenarian with hair considerably younger than the rest of him. I shall withhold judgment—but, one cautionary note. His candidacy is strongly supported by a group of Puritan clergymen. Perhaps I am revealing merely the biases of a Church of England man, but if Mr. Reagan should begin suddenly to quote Oliver Cromwell, my advice is to double the fire insurance and hide the silverware. On the bright side, Mr. Reagan's election would send the Carter family back to their popcorn farm, or whatever it is—a very agreeable prospect. I shall say no more about the presidential election at this time. I am adopting a wait-and-see attitude regarding Mr. Reagan's relations with the British Empire."

Muggsbottom was certainly prescient in his belief that Reagan would win easily, for in the last weeks of the campaign the public opinion polls were still indicating a close election. Although he did not admire the Republican candidate, Muggsbottom had taken a definite dislike to his opponent. Not long before the day of the conversation I am recounting, Jimmy Carter's campaign had made a swing through our part of the country. The

President had spoken in Texarkana, a city on the border between Texas and Arkansas. By speaking from a podium set in the middle of State Line Avenue, President Carter had one foot in Texas and one foot in Arkansas, thereby moving toward fulfillment of his pledge to campaign in each of the fifty states. Texarkana is only an hour's drive from Arcady and, thinking this might well be the Englishmen's only chance to see a President of the United States in person, I drove them down to hear the speech.

The day was warm for autumn, the crowd was a bit unruly, and the President's address was uninspired. I believe that most people look better in person than they do on television, but such was not the case with the President. Muggsbottom had already developed an aversion to Mr. Carter by watching him on television. Standing about with tired feet and sweaty shoulder blades while being jostled from every side was not conducive to improving Muggsbottom's attitude toward the candidate. As we were walking back to the car, I was trying to explain "yellow dog Democrat" to Smythe-Gardner, he having heard the term employed by a red-faced man at his elbow. Muggsbottom suddenly drowned out all other conversation by exclaiming, "The man is sure to be defeated. And, thank God, with his departure the puerile pronouncements of Billy, little Amy, Miss Lillian and the rest of that remarkably uninteresting family will no longer be heard on the television."

My mind was drawn sharply back to the present, when Muggsbottom said, with an edge in his voice, "You asked me what I told the journalist, old man—are you interested in hearing it?"

"I'm sorry. I was just thinking about . . ." No, better to leave well enough alone regarding the Carter clan. "Never mind. What else did you say?"

"Well, we then turned to the gubernatorial election. You may recall that in the past I have suggested that you

Arkansans are taking the admonition 'and a little child shall lead you' rather *too* seriously."

In 1980, Governor Bill Clinton was completing his first two-year term. He was the youngest governor in America, having been elected when he was barely thirty years of age. In physical appearance, he seemed even younger. In the years since, I believe he has attained a certain degree of national eminence . . . or notoriety—the appropriate term depends upon one's attitude toward the sort of celebrity achieved by politicians. Muggsbottom had nothing in particular against the governor but was much amused by his youth. Mr. Clinton's opponent was a Republican named Frank White, a man who at the beginning of the campaign had been known only to his relatives, friends, and neighbors. Mr. White had a firm grasp on Ronald Reagan's coattails and based his hopes in Arkansas upon a substantial Republican victory nationwide. The inexperienced young governor had also made a number of maladroit political moves, which had bred some resentment around the state. (Much to the surprise of even his most fervent supporters, Frank White *did* upset Bill Clinton by a narrow margin in that election, although in a rematch two years later the Democrat reclaimed the governor's office and began to serve in perpetuity from that time forward.)

"I suggested," Muggsbottom continued, "that if the electorate should choose to sack Mr. Clinton, they could not be certain that their action was a wise one, but they could take comfort in this thought: he would then have ample leisure to complete his education and decide what he really wants to be when he grows up. Further, I for one would compliment the people of Arkansas for their innovative decision to try the next couple of years with no governor at all.

"I concluded with an obliquely applicable quotation from your Benjamin Franklin, I believe it was: Just remember as you are voting, Arcadians, that 'no man's life or property is safe while the legislature is in session.' Sometimes I make up quotations, but I believe he really said that."

When Muggsbottom's interview came out in the *Harbinger*, the editor had toned down his remarks considerably. Or perhaps in retrospect my friend's comments seemed more barbed and incisive than they had been in fact. I was constantly surprised, and pleased, to discover that Muggsbottom's words seldom produced ill feeling. Arcadians regarded him as an amusing curmudgeon, not an offensive one. Only Homer Joe Tennyson and the Ol' Perfesser had been permanently alienated by my friend's observations on their performance.

The election season was also the football season, and I hit upon the idea of taking the Englishmen to one of the University of Arkansas' games in Little Rock. First, I thought their reactions to their first American football game would be extremely entertaining. And second, I thought I could rustle up five tickets—the first time in years that such a feat was possible so late in the season. The Razorbacks had been disappointing that autumn, losing three games that they were expected to win. Further, the upcoming game was against Rice, an institution which had decided years before that it is more blessed to lose with real students than to win with players majoring in Recreation and Personal Hygiene. The Rice game had been sold out for months, but I determined that under the circumstances some patrons might be willing to part with their tickets.

I approached an assistant football coach at my own college who was kindly disposed toward me. During the preceding semester, he had been grateful when I had passed a talented but dim behemoth through Freshman English (after three other professors had declined to do so) by pretending not to notice that the young man's girlfriend had written his essays for him. I make this confession not as an act of penance but to show the reader why the assistant coach owed me a favor. I asked him to canvass his contacts in Little Rock until he found someone from whom I could purchase five tickets to the Rice game. He did, and I did.

The tickets indicated a seven-thirty kickoff, so at midafternoon of that Saturday I dropped by the Englishmen's house to check on their preparations. Sir Monty was asleep in his chair but he, or more likely Muggsbottom on his behalf, had set out on the hatrack beside the front door his mackintosh (a threat of rain had been in the air all day), the huge old woolen scarf which put one in mind of a plaid python wrapped round his neck, and the crumpled brown hat that one more often saw protruding from his coat pocket than sitting on his head. Biffy Smythe-Gardner was filling a huge thermos with gin and lime, for I had told him that alcoholic beverages were not offered for sale at the stadium. "Further," I had informed him, "fans are expressly forbidden to bring spirits into the stands." To which comment he had responded with some warmth, "What barbarous customs you Southerners have!" Then, after having my bit of fun with him, I had assured him that in practice the rule was seldom enforced. Smythe-Gardner indicated that Reggie and Muggsbottom were in the latter's study, and there I found them, each man preparing for the evening's adventure in an eccentric but totally predictable way.

As I entered Muggsbottom's book lined, smoke filled study (something about my friend caused me to think in such Homeric epithets), I found him thumbing through a tattered volume.

"Something to read," he said, "in case the football match should bore me. And they always have done. Don't you think *Martin Chuzzlewit* would be an appropriate choice?"

"Muggsbottom," I said, half seriously, "if you begin to read a book during a Razorback game, you may get arrested."

His only reply was a noncommittal grunt. He clenched the brierwood pipe even more firmly between his teeth and continued his riffling through Dickens well-read piece.

I was startled to find Reggie reading as well. He was hunched over a large volume of some kind and was perusing it with such rapt attention that he had taken no notice of my entrance or of the few words Muggsbottom and I had exchanged. This was the first intellectual effort from Reggie Dipswizzle that I had ever witnessed, and I was impressed. I looked over Reggie's shoulder and discovered that he was reading a volume of the *Encyclopedia Britannica*. The book was open to the page whereon the article "FOOTBALL (AMERICAN)" began. I was even more impressed. I had not credited Reggie with the capacity for such forethought. I had wronged him.

I touched Reggie lightly on the shoulder and said, "Ah, boning up for our first American football game, are we?"

Reggie turned and gave me a look of mingled relief and joy. I was intensely pleased.

"I say, my dear fellow. Didn't realize you were here. Glad you are, though. You're precisely what's wanted."

Now Reggie gave me the puzzled, slightly bewildered look which was pretty much his normal expression. It was not always easy to recognize the source of Reggie's befuddlement, his condition being so generalized. But this time I could truly be of some help.

"Well, I'm by no means an expert on football, but I believe I can outline the basics for you. I can teach you enough so that you won't be cheering at the wrong times. That could be dangerous at a Razorback home game."

"Oh, don't bother, old man. I'm hopeless at that sort of thing. Never could understand *our* football either. You know, beyond the fact that one group of chaps want to take the ball *this* way and the other group of chaps want to take the ball *that* way. What I'm really wondering about is what to wear. There are pictures of the players here and all sorts of graphs and things, but no pictures of the fans."

Reggie the actor. Reggie the male model. Reggie the resident alien eager to fit in and wary of giving offense. I should have known.

"What you're wearing should do nicely. With your top-coat, of course."

Reggie was wearing a tweed jacket over a beige sweater vest embellished with brown scrollwork, chocolate-colored corduroy trousers, and plain-toed brown shoes, shined to a high gloss. Reggie always took great pains with his grooming. I had heard him say, "A chap is rather judged by his personal appearance, you know." This was as close as Reggie had come to articulating a philosophy of life.

"Oh, and you might find something red. The team colors are cardinal and white, so Razorback fans usually wear red."

"I see. When in Rome, eh? Thanks awfully, old fellow. I believe I have a red cravat and a red muffler as well. Perhaps I shall wear them both."

Reggie, having achieved peace of mind, bustled happily out of the room.

"Well," I said, "Reggie, at least, is looking forward to our little excursion."

"Reggie's enthusiasm for any new experience," Muggsbottom replied, "is an appealing characteristic of his childlike nature. His melancholia and penchant for exotic phobias are, alas, the other side of the coin."

"Let's leave Reggie's psychoanalysis for another day, shall we? Please have the boys ready by five-thirty. I'll pick you up then."

Muggsbottom smiled mischievously.

"My friends and I and Dickens will await your return."

Happily, the threat of rain had lifted, but the evening was a brisk one, and when I picked the Englishmen up they were dressed accordingly. Reggie Dipswizzle was wearing a long camel hair coat. It was buttoned to the throat so that I could not see if Reggie was wearing the red cravat, but he had wound the red muffler loosely round his neck. Further, he had located a little short-brimmed Alpine hat with a big red feather on the side. Sir Montague Capulet had changed to his customary heavy overcoat. The coat was of pure wool and was about twice the thickness of any garment ever seen in our parts. I had joked that it looked like government issue from the Russian army, intended especially for the Siberian forces. To me, the night was not cold enough to warrant such a heavy coat, but Sir Monty obviously thought differently. He habitually donned the coat whenever the temperature dipped below sixty degrees. Biffy Smythe-Gardner gave the appearance of a skipper who had momentarily misplaced his ship and crew. His jacket was the one in which he had stood on the bridge while braving many a North Atlantic gale. His captain's cap was on his head. His thermos of gin and lime was in the crook of his arm. Charles Pierpont Muggsbottom, his brierwood pipe between his teeth, was wearing his soft plaid cap and what used to be called a car coat. I could see a bit of the cover of a book protruding from each of the coat's pockets.

"Well," said Muggsbottom, "let us be off, to discover what it is that excites you Arkansawyers so every autumn."

Despite the football traffic, I drove the seventy-five miles from Arcady to the stadium in Little Rock in good time. The trip was marked by little conversation. I suppose the miles of Southern pine forests rolling by on either hand lulled the Britons into somnolence. However, about forty minutes into our journey, Sir Monty, the most somnolent of them all, had roused himself enough to observe, "Arkansas is largely uninhabited, is it not?"

We located our seats, which were rather good ones—on the thirty-five yard line, a third of the way up the stadium. We were barely in them before I was forced to abort a bit of unpleasantness. I noticed that Muggsbottom was staring at a middle-aged man sitting across the aisle from us. More precisely, he seemed mesmerized by the man's feet. Little wonder, for the feet were wearing Razorback shoes.

The shoes were like the bunny slippers that children used to wear, except that the ears were pig's ears. The leather was stained a bright red, save for the white pig eyes, narrowed into a baleful expression. The toe of each piece of this remarkable footwear was fashioned in the shape of a porcine snout.

"Dear God," Muggsbottom finally muttered. "Can it be a delusion?"

"Please, Muggsbottom," I implored, "say nothing to him."

"But, my dear fellow, perhaps no one has had the temerity to point out what an absurd spectacle he has made of himself. Would it not be an act of Christian charity to make that fact known to him?"

"Despite all the praying coaches claim to do, Christian charity is not much in demand at football games. Besides, 'tastefully-dressed football fan' is an oxymoron. Please, just read one of your books."

Muggsbottom shrugged, and I relaxed. The crisis had passed. Muggsbottom did, however, take one more long look at the shoes before inquiring, "What do you suppose he paid for them?"

"Quite a lot, I believe."

"What a remarkable country."

"I suppose those are our chaps in the red pullovers," said Reggie, who was the only one of my companions who was genuinely eager to get into the swing of things. "My, what shoulders and thighs they all have."

"Most of that's padding," I explained. "American footballers wear a great deal of padding."

"Ah, I see," said Reggie who, I could clearly tell, did not see at all.

"Those helmets make them look somewhat like creatures out of H. G. Wells, don't they?" said Muggsbottom.

"It's our passion for technology," I said. "They'll soon

have rocket packs on their backs, and we'll need intensive care units at either end of the field."

It occurred to me that, although my companions' comments had been few and largely innocuous, I was already becoming defensive. The natural tendency, I supposed, of an American Anglophile hosting four Englishmen at a quintessentially American event.

The game was neither especially exciting nor especially dull. Reggie worked hard at maintaining, or dissembling, an interest and would ask me a question from time to time. Sir Monty napped precariously but soundly on the narrow board. Smythe-Gardner, predictably, emptied his thermos during the first half and grew progressively crankier during the second. Muggsbottom did indeed turn eventually to one of his books.

I should have known, I suppose, that the sight of a corpulent man in a plaid cap, his head buried deep within the collar of his heavy overcoat, sedately puffing on a pipe and reading a dogeared volume of Dickens would soon excite interest on the thirty-five yard line. And that interest was of the sort that cats excite in mockingbirds.

"There's a man reading a book down there," said a woman sitting a couple of rows above us. She spoke ostensibly to her male companion but made no attempt to keep her observation a private one.

She was around fifty years of age, with hair that was too long and too black. She wore a Razorback sweat shirt, a red knitted hat that climaxed in a hog snout just above her eyes, and dangling earrings, two little red pigs. She wore yet another little red pig as a beauty mark on her left cheek. She had been drinking steadily from a large plastic cup—decorated with the picture of a charging red Razorback—into which her companion would periodically pour an amber liquid from a bottle concealed inside a paper bag. As the evening had progressed, she had found more and more to say and was pretty much saying it at the top of her lungs.

The Razorbacker's husband, for so I took him to be, leaned forward and studied Muggsbottom for a moment.

"Obviously a Rice fan," he said. "I wonder what he's doing in this section."

Although *I* could hear the couple's remarks plainly, and would not have been surprised to learn that the players on the field could also hear them, Muggsbottom did not stir in his seat.

The woman in red began to sing, her rendition breaking off occasionally in a fit of giggling. "I don't give a damn 'bout the whole state of Texas, the whole state of Texas, the whole state of Texas. I don't give a damn 'bout the whole state of Texas. 'Cause I'm from Ar-kin-sa-a-a-w."

Some of our neighbors attempted to join in, although the song leader's beat was so erratic as to make that difficult. Others noisily responded to the musical interlude in a variety of ways, and the resulting hubbub attracted attention from the twenty to the fifty yard line. Muggsbottom licked his finger and turned the page.

During the first half, I had casually exchanged a few words with the stranger sitting to my immediate left. Now this gentleman leaned toward me and asked, "Is that guy reading a book a friend of yours?"

"Yes," I said, "he is."

"I thought so. I don't believe I've ever seen anyone read a book at a Razorback ball game before . . . or at *any* game, come to think of it."

I realize that I was not obliged to explain or defend anything, especially the actions of another man. Still, the social sanctions are very strong, and Muggsbottom's behavior had deviated so far from the War Memorial Stadium norm for a Saturday night in autumn that I attempted to explain.

"He's from England."

"He is?" replied the gentleman. "Why, I'm from just up

the road at Lonoke."

"No, not England, Arkansas . . . England, the United Kingdom . . . England, the British Isles."

"O-o-o-h . . . Well, I guess that explains it then."

"Does it? . . . Yes, I suppose it does. The English are great readers, you know."

The lady in red, however, was still adamant in her disapproval of Muggsbottom's indifference. "Take that book away from him," she shouted, then giggled and snorted.

"Now, calm down, Eunice," said her husband, who had put the paper sack away.

The fan in the Razorback shoes chose just this moment to investigate the source of so much interest. He leaned across the aisle and inquired, "Where you boys from?"

Smythe-Gardner snapped, "Where a bloke doesn't intrude himself upon chaps to whom he hasn't been introduced."

I have already reported that Smythe-Gardner seriously miscalculated the quantity of gin and lime required to get him through the game. As a result, his usual grumpiness had worsened into a really poisonous mood.

The fellow in the Razorback shoes did not seem put off. I supposed a man who went about with such things on his feet was accustomed to abuse and had learned to handle it. He had heard Smythe-Gardner's accent, and now he looked the old sea dog up and down. He knitted his brow and thought visibly.

"Y'all makin' a movie round here or somethin'?"

Still, Muggsbottom did not look up from his book. He was, I thought, being willfully perverse. So, again, I felt a duty to clarify the situation. I rose from my seat and called over to the man in the Razorback shoes, "These four gentlemen are all from England."

"Well, I'll be damned," he said. "I have a cousin who farms between England and Humnoke. His name is . . . "

"No . . . England, *England*."

"Oh. Well, I'll be damned."

"These bores who latch on to one in a public place need a good biffing," muttered Smythe-Gardner.

Reggie had only now noticed the gentleman's feet and, in his childlike way, was captivated by what he saw there. "I say, do you suppose he had those made to order, or could one find them in the shops?"

An admonition floated down to us from above.

"Make him (giggle, giggle) put down that (giggle, giggle) book (giggle, giggle)."

"And I've had about enough of that cow," quoth Smythe-Gardner.

"I see now," said the man in the Razorback shoes to our disgruntled mariner. "I thought at first you must be puttin' on. But if you're really English, I guess you don't have to put on to talk that way."

Smythe-Gardner started up out of his seat. I put my hand on his shoulder and devoutly wished that I had never attempted to expose my Englishmen to this particular bit of Americana.

At that instant, Muggsbottom closed his book with a bang and interposed himself between Smythe-Gardner and the man in the Razorback shoes. To the latter, he said, "My dear fellow, perhaps you could help me. I'm altogether fascinated by that pig cheer you and your fellow fanatics have been at intervals performing. Is it possible, do you suppose, that a resident alien might master it?"

"Pig ch— ?" Then, the meaning of Muggsbottom's inquiry finally discernible behind its rococo trappings, the fan understood. "You mean the *Hog call.* We're famous all around the country for 'Calling the Hogs,' you know . . . Why, I can teach you to call the Hogs in just about two shakes."

"How fortuitous that we were seated within such proximity. Shall we begin my tuition at once?"

The fan was delighted. He instructed Muggsbottom in

both the words and the cadence of the cheer. He spoke very slowly and in a loud voice, as if addressing a deaf person or a nonspeaker of the language.

Then, he stood and called out, "Hey, folks. These boys is from England. England, *England*—you know. And this one here is gonna lead us in 'Calling the Hogs.' Let's all help him out, okay?"

He waved his arms, exhorting the crowd in our section to stand. And, row by row, they complied.

Now, Muggsbottom rose decorously to his feet. He turned to face the spectators above him, raised his arms, stood poised for a moment like a maestro about to give the downbeat to his orchestra . . . and led the crowd in "Calling the Hogs."

"O-o-o-o-o *pig* sooie. O-o-o-o-o *pig* sooie. O-o-o-o-o *pig* sooie. *Razorbacks*!"

The cheer for the team was followed by a cheer for Muggsbottom. Any suspicion and hostility which we might have incurred was dispelled utterly. The fans loved nothing better than sharing this passion for their team with receptive strangers.

The Hog calling had even been spirited enough to waken Sir Monty.

"What the deuce was all that awful caterwauling?" he grumbled.

"That was great," said the man in the Razorback shoes. "Say, would you boys care for a drink?"

He opened his binocular case and withdrew a fat flask.

He winked and said, "I cain't see nothing through them glasses anyway."

Smythe-Gardner's clouded brow brightened instantaneously.

"Hold on, Smythe-Gardner," I said. "We still haven't been introduced to this man."

"Oh, bugger off," he growled.

A few minutes later, I put my mouth close to

Muggsbottom's ear and said, "You rascal, I'd swear you had been the actor instead of Reggie. You think every situation in life is created just for your amusement. Well, you nearly let that little drama get out of hand."

"Don't be too cross with me, dear boy. One must seek whatever entertainment one can find during these interminable football matches of yours."

There was some drama late in the game, though it was not the sort that suited the Arkansas fans. Rice, trailing by a couple of points, got the ball deep in Arkansas territory. With only enough time remaining for one play, the visitors lined up to attempt a field goal—a field goal that would win the game. The chant of "Block that kick," growing in intensity as the snap of the ball became imminent, distracted Muggsbottom from *Martin Chuzzlewit*, to which he had returned.

"What have we here, dear boy?"

"Rice is attempting to kick a field goal."

"Ah, I've been wondering about that. The lads have been carrying the ball about in their hands all evening. Why don't you call the game handball?"

At that moment, the foot of the Rice kicker met the ball. His kick was not a thing of beauty, but it fluttered down just beyond the crossbar like a quail filled with buckshot. The bated breath of fifty thousand spectators gave way to a huge moan, which was followed in turn by a pall of silence. Arkansas had lost to Rice for the first time in eight seasons.

"We already have one by that name," I said.

"I beg your pardon?"

"We already have a game called handball."

"Ah."

"I say," said Reggie, "did we lose the match?"

"We did."

Reggie adopted an appropriately somber expression, but it was clear that my friends did not grasp the enormity of the catastrophe. As we made our way down the crowded aisle, we found ourselves behind the party of our friend in the Razorback shoes. He was of the opinion—loudly expressed, so that all might hear—that the coach should be fired on the spot.

As we were driving back to Arcady, Muggsbottom asked, "What subjects are those lads reading at university?"

"Football mostly," I replied.

"I see. And is that considered an adequate preparation for their later lives?"

"We don't care about their later lives."

"My dear fellow, and you call me a cynic."

Sir Monty, who had not spoken for hours, blurted out, "Why do they call the damned business football?" The same vagrant thought to which Muggsbottom had earlier given utterance had finally flitted through Sir Monty's brain.

"Our American friend has explained it all to me, Sir Monty," said Muggsbottom. "The lads carry the ball about and toss it back and forth throughout the match, but at the end they kick it to determine the winner. It's such a very American way of doing things, don't you think?"

"Well, I've learnt one thing," added Smythe-Gardner grumpily. "If we ever attend another of these shows, I shall damned well require a second thermos."

7. The White Man's Burden

One evening, Muggsbottom stirred himself from deep thought, turned to me, and said, "Your coloreds are not African, are they?"

I was startled, as I often was when Muggsbottom experienced an epiphany and blurted it out.

"No, they're Southerners, like me," I said. "Well, sort of like me. At any rate, they wouldn't like being called 'coloreds.'"

"Ah, I see. A bit sensitive, are they?"

"Their ancestors were brought here on slave ships, and I think some of them are holding a grudge."

Muggsbottom ruminated for a moment more before saying, "Quite understandable. But this is not a recent occurrence then?"

"Of course, it's not a recent occurrence. Don't try that game with me, Muggsbottom."

My friend enjoyed feigning an almost total ignorance of American history. With just a word, with even the twitch of an eyebrow, he could suggest that ours was a history so brief, so devoid of significance, that one might be excused for having missed it altogether. On the other hand, there were genuine gaping holes in his knowledge of his adopted country, so that I often could not be sure whether he was teasing me or not.

"Quite understandable," he repeated. "My dear old

grandfather, Rob Roy Muggsbottom, professed a lifelong aversion to the English, despite his being removed from Scotland in infancy and residing for eighty-two years in Derbyshire. Oh yes, my roots are Gaelic, dear boy. The family name is geographical, you see. My clan long dwelt in the lowlands along the River Mugg, whose waters gently wend their way from the bonny village of Kilbannock to the quaint market town of Drumgoole. The Mugg is not navigable, but she is in every other respect all that one could ask a river to be. However, I must say that the Muggsbottoms, over time, eventually became somewhat Anglicized."

"I've noticed," I said.

"What *do* you call them?"

"I beg your pardon."

"The coloreds. What *do* you call them?"

"I think calling them by name is the safest course to follow. Opinion on the appropriate generic term is sort of mixed right now. I would strongly recommend against following Maynard's example, however."

"My dear fellow, your admonition is entirely unnecessary. I have become rather attached to Maynard, but I am not blind to the fact that he represents a subhuman species. I should never dream of following his example under any circumstances . . . What do they call you?"

"What? . . . Oh, they use a variety of epithets, but one of them is *not* bwana. Why this sudden interest in our black brethren, Muggsbottom?"

"Are you acquainted with a dusky young clergyman by the name of Abednego Aftermath?"

"Everyone in Arcady is acquainted with the Reverend Aftermath. Although, I'm surprised to learn that you are."

"Reggie and I met him yesterday afternoon at the courthouse. Reggie was called in to the assessor's office—a slight matter of taxes on the Phlegm Club property—and I accompanied him. Poor Reggie hasn't the slightest head for figures. At any rate, there was the Right Reverend Aftermath, patrolling the sidewalk in front of the building, pressing his card upon each passerby, and inveigling that person to support his candidacy. Under the circumstances, I concluded that he could not possibly be an African."

"Aftermath is running for office *again*?"

"A special election for city director, he tells me."

"That's right. Old Mr. Drabny, the druggist, had a heart attack out at the country club. Fell dead on the seventh green—dogleg to the right."

The Arcady Board of Directors was composed of six members. This arrangement encouraged and, therefore, produced frequent three-to-three votes, so that our municipal government was in a perpetual state of gridlock. I found it implausible that Abednego Aftermath could succeed old Drabny to the board, but if he could, one likely result would be a change of most of those three-to-three votes into five to one.

Abednego Aftermath had turned up in Arcady in 1977, having been called as pastor to the Fifteenth Street Communion of the Holy Ghost, a splinter group from the Four Square Church of the Apostolic Fellowship. The rupture had resulted from some doctrinal dispute, probably—as the name of the new congregation suggested—over the nature of the third person in the Trinity. Aftermath was a man in his early thirties, with animated features, a milk chocolate complexion, and lithe, athletic movements. He made his presence felt immediately. He decided that Arcadian race relations were not up to snuff and instantly set about making himself unpopular with the white community. He badgered the school board, the city board of directors, the police chief, the county sheriff—insisting that all were demonstrably biased in their treatment of the twenty-two per cent of Arcady's population that was black. My barber had once remarked, "That Aftermath is a Chicago n---x you know," and then had nodded sagely to indicate that he had explained all.

The Reverend Aftermath affected expensive suits with pegged trouser legs and colored shirts that were darker than his ties. Maynard's characterization was, "Looks like a damned pimp to me." Aftermath had already run once for the city board, and for the school board as well. But his support was limited almost exclusively to the aforementioned twenty-two per cent, and he had not been successful. He was a speaker of great energy and some ability. His oratorical style prominently featured slogans, epigrams (usually rhyming or alliterative), and puns. It was rather impressive to the neutral observer and extremely irritating to his enemies.

"I believe that I have his card here," said Muggsbottom, rummaging through his pockets.

He handed me a small card of bilious green. The lettering itself was ordinary enough, but each line began with a huge gothic character. The card read:

Who is the man the peoples cheer?
Who is the man the racists fear?
Who'll make the bosses tell what they know?
The voters' friend, Abednego.

Vote Abednego Aftermath for City Director, Pos. No. 3.

Aftermath had been too flamboyant for my tastes from the beginning. It was significant, no doubt, that I was a diffident white Southerner and he was so stridently none of those things. But the fact that Aftermath was so loud did not mean that he was not clever. I thought about his campaign card. The first line was addressed to his core constituency, the second to any whites prepared to admit guilt at the drop of an epithet. The third line was designed to appeal to all of us who, despite varying ideologies, suspect that our elected officials are flimflamming us most of the time.

"So the coloreds may stand for office then?"

"*Yes*, Muggsbottom." My voice must have betrayed my irritation, because my friend turned and studied my face carefully for a moment. I felt that I was being asked to review a hundred and twenty years of history for a willfully uninformed pupil. "They may do anything that anyone else may do . . . theoretically."

"Ah," said Muggsbottom knowingly. "I believe the same situation obtains in Britain . . . The candidate invited us to his upcoming rally, on Wednesday next. Do you think it would be amusing to attend?"

"Where is the rally to be held?"

"At his church, I believe."

"Well, that would certainly be an interesting experience for you. But I should warn you that Aftermath's invitation was strictly *pro forma*. You and Reggie would be absolutely the only white people there."

"Ah, yes . . . As it happens, I wasn't planning to take Reggie, who is, as you know, apolitical in the extreme. I thought you might be the better choice."

Seeing that an objection was forming on my lips, he hurried on.

"Wait, wait. First, there is your avowed interest in local government." I could remember making no such avowal. "Second, if this Fifteenth Street Church of the . . . Congregation of the . . . ?"

"Communion of the Holy Ghost."

"Yes. If it's very far, we might take your motor car and save the taxi fare. What do you think?"

"I think, as you would say, I'm not keen on being one of the only two white men in a throng of black enthusiasts."

"Pish. Pish and piffle, dear boy. Why, in my African days, I was often alone among ten thousand natives—the only white man within a radius of three hundred miles. One need only maintain one's attitude of quiet authority.

Be gentle and kindly, but firm."

"What African days, Muggsbottom?"

"Have I not mentioned them before? Some evening when the wind whistles about the eaves and the fire burns low in the grate, I shall recount in detail that most fascinating period of my life. But back to the matter at hand. Shall we go? The Reverend Aftermath seems an entertaining fellow, and I should also enjoy observing the local tribal customs at first hand."

It was no good talking reason to Muggsbottom when he was in one of his Kiplingesque moods and the old Empire was burning brightly in his imagination. He had an uncanny ability to draw me into situations into which absolutely no one else could have drawn me. But this time I would not be seduced. I was *not* under any circumstances going to take Muggsbottom to Aftermath's rally at the Fifteenth Street Communion of the Holy Ghost.

The parking lot of the Fifteenth Street Communion of the Holy Ghost was already filled to the extent that, without banging against the automobiles on either side, doors could scarcely be opened wide enough for each car's occupants to squeeze out. So I drove on to the middle of the next block and parked behind a long black Cadillac with reflector-studded mud flaps and a bumper sticker that read, "Free South Africa." A portly black gentleman and his bejeweled wife were just stepping out of the Cadillac as we crunched to a halt behind them.

"That's Antonio Dalrymple," I said to Muggsbottom. "The black undertaker."

Dalrymple's face bore an unaccustomed scowl—in my few encounters with him, I had found him a genial fellow. I felt pretty sure that tonight, however, someone had taken his parking spot and had taken most of his geniality along with it. Also, Mrs. Dalrymple had clutched her husband's arm and lifted her right foot in the air. She was examining her shoe as if she might have stepped in something unpleasant beside the curb.

"Preachers and funeral directors are at the top of the black hierarchy," I pontificated, and then we got out of the car ourselves.

"Mr. Dalrymple." I smiled and nodded. "Mrs. Dalrymple."

The mortician flashed us a smile that never reached his eyes. "How y'all doin' this evenin'?"

Mrs. Dalrymple was aloof, giving us a look that fell just short of rudeness. Perhaps she was merely distracted—she would pause after every couple of steps and glance down at the offending foot.

"They think we're spies," I whispered to Muggsbottom.

"My dear fellow, if, as you say, we are to be the only Europeans in attendance, what kind of *spies* could we make?"

"I'm not a European, Muggsbottom. I'm . . . Oh, hell. Never mind."

Aftermath's opponent was—naturally—a white man, one who had also sought the office before.

John Bozeman was not a popular member of the Arcadian community. His principal advantage in the campaign was that he was not Abednego Aftermath. Having said that, one had enumerated all of Bozeman's assets. He was a tiny, frail, bald man of about fifty. He possessed independent means, and Arcadians were suspicious of any man under sixty-five who did not go off to work in the mornings. No one really knew the source of Bozeman's income, but rumors regularly made the rounds. The most exotic of these, and my personal favorite, was that he had an interest in a condom factory in Ohio. He lived alone. He had once been married, but his wife had divorced him and married Boyd Philpott, who had the Porky's Potato Chip route. She liked to pretend that she had never been Mrs. John Bozeman.

Although stiff and unfriendly by small town standards, Bozeman's behavior seemed relatively normal except in the single area of public affairs. He was the author of three books, with provocative titles like *Oligarchy in America: The Invisible Conspiracy against Democracy*. They were all published by The Wellspring Press of Shreveport, Louisiana. I had tried to read one of them but had soon lost the thread—or, to be more precise, I never found a thread. Bozeman's conspiracy was at least novel and eclectic. It linked international Communism, the Republican Party, Israel, the former Fascist powers, and Freemasonry in a shadowy web which had ensnared all of our Presidents and Congresses since World War II. Not content to be a mere theoretician, the author had sought public office on many occasions: county judge, county sheriff, county clerk. He had even run for municipal judge, despite the fact that he lacked a law degree. All his races—including his previous try for a city directorship—had ended in smashing defeats, or the Arcadian equivalent thereof, and he had become a joke candidate. But Drabny had dropped dead at a moment when no appropriate candidate was much interested in his job, the filing period had expired and, lo, either Abednego Aftermath or John Bozeman would be the new city director.

I did not wonder that Dalrymple and his wife were suspicious of the two white men walking along behind them. The Dalrymples were engaged in one of the few businesses in Arcady which, amidst all the changes of the preceding twenty-five years, had never been integrated—not a whit. Black funeral homes handled black corpses, and white funeral homes handled white corpses. I knew of only one notable exception . . . Sugar Ray.

Shortly after I came to Arcady, I heard stories to the effect that the local funeral parlor (white) had kept a preserved body (black) in the back room for years—the time span ranged from ten to twenty years, depending upon who was telling the story. It seems that at one of these points in the past, a black man in his middle thirties had been found dead of natural causes beneath the railroad trestle south of town. He was known to no one, and the body bore no identification whatsoever. For reasons not altogether clear, he was taken to the white mortuary, where he was embalmed, dressed in a new blue suit from the shroud department, and laid out in a modest pine casket. The body was held to be claimed, but it was never claimed. The longer the body remained unburied, the less urgent seemed the need to bury it. Gradually, the Arcady authorities gave up their efforts to identify the man, and he became a fixture in the back room of the funeral home. A widely believed rumor held that the undertaker, Mr. Cleghorn, used this opportunity to experiment with a revolutionary mummifying technique he had been working on for years. As time passed, the excellent condition of the anonymous corpse compellingly argued for the efficacy of Mr. Cleghorn's technique.

One day, an observer remarked that the deceased (whose handsome features added a nice dimension to the mystery surrounding him) resembled the famous boxer Sugar Ray Robinson. A second observer agreed with the first, and soon the deceased was familiarly known to all as "Sugar Ray." He became a local treasure, even something of a tourist attraction. Young Arcadians would take their visiting cousins from Little Rock to see Sugar Ray, then say to these smart alecks, "We've had him for ten years." Visiting Sugar Ray on a Saturday night was a cheap date for Arcadian teenagers. I, myself, never got to see the veteran corpse because just before I moved to town the State Health Department had discovered Sugar Ray.

Embarrassed by having lost track of a body long enough for it to become an artifact, the state officials ordered Sugar Ray's immediate burial. They instructed Mr. Cleghorn to turn Sugar Ray over to Mr. Dalrymple for that purpose. It was only then that Mr. Dalrymple felt secure enough in his newly won civil rights to complain that Sugar Ray really should have been his from the beginning.

The few steps leading to the entrance of the Communion Temple seemed a very long climb. With all my might, I willed myself to be a sophisticate, a cosmopolite. But it was no use—I felt conspicuous and awkward among all these black people. Muggsbottom, however, was at ease completely. As the saying goes, if you were to look up *insouciant* in the dictionary, you would find Muggsbottom's picture. Something about his carriage and his stride made me think of the white hunter entering a native village. I could almost see the khaki shirt and shorts, the pith helmet, the huge elephant gun cradled in the crook of his right arm. He scarcely took note of the people around him—they might have been his bearers. He craned his neck slightly to see over the crowd, to locate the thatched hut of the village chieftain.

Abednego Aftermath was at his pulpit, where preacher and politician were one. To our left, a lady with bright orange hair, whom I believed to be Mrs. Aftermath, was pounding a piano and, behind the candidate, the choir was swaying and leading the crowd in the campaign song.

The people gonna go
With Abednego.
He don't say no.
He don't go slow.
This time fo' sho'
It's Abednego.

The nave of the Temple was packed, as was the narthex. Mr. and Mrs. Dalrymple plunged into the crowd. I suspected that anyone sitting in their places, in their pew, would pay a heavy price for that presumption.

"There isn't a seat anywhere, Muggsbottom," I said. "Why don't we go?"

"Where do you suppose those stairs over there lead?"

"What? Oh . . . To the balcony, I suppose."

"My notion exactly. Shall we try the balcony then, my dear fellow? Old Muggsbottom has sat in the cheap seats for many a performance. No stigma attaches, old lad, none whatsoever."

Alas, a few seats were still vacant in the balcony, but I was cheered by the discovery that another white man was there as well. The reader will recall the Englishmen's next-door neighbor. He has made brief appearances in this narrative as my colleague in the English Department and as a socially conscious member of the Unitarian community. As a literary critic, I have long believed that inconsequential characters in a book should not be named. The act gives the reader heightened expectations—which may well not be met—for such a character. Thus, I leave my colleague in his anonymous state while making the craven admission that I had never once been glad to see him until that evening.

"Hey, fellows." He stood and waved. "Over here."

As we slid onto the bench beside him, he said to me, "I didn't know you were supporting Reverend Aftermath."

There was the slightest hint of skepticism in his tone. Everybody in our department knew everything about everyone else, so he was remembering my flirtation with the Republican Party. The black people around us were also regarding me with suspicion—and with hostility—I thought. Perhaps it was just my imagination. But they *were* regarding me—that was *not* my imagination.

"Actually, I've just brought Muggsbottom. He can never get enough of our politics, God knows why."

"Our discussion group has decided to support Reverend Aftermath strongly," said my colleague. "That man Bozeman is mad as a hatter . . . " Looking around, "I wonder where the rest of the group is. They were all supposed to be here."

At the pulpit below, Abednego Aftermath had begun to speak.

"Dearly beloved, tonight I'm asking for your help. You know that the rich and powerful of Arcady are dead set against my election to the City Board." Well, I thought, we don't have many of those. But, fair enough, the few we do have are formidable personages. "With all their money and influence, they would rather embrace a candidate who thinks he's Napoleon than see a black man join their lily-white board. Oh they say, 'Why, you're mighty fine . . . till you cross that line. Come shop in my store . . . but don't hang 'round the door. We want one of y'all here . . . but this just ain't the year.'"

"Here we go," I muttered.

"So tonight, old friends and new, we're not requesting a love offering for Abednego Aftermath. We're asking you to make an action offering for Arcady. Abednego Aftermath is the candidate of change for people of all colors." The crowd had long been into its rhythm, and they were talking back to him. "Tell 'em about it." "You the one, all right." So he threw them one more golden phrase. "If you like what you see, lay some green on me. What we sow we shall reap, so y'all dig down deep. It takes money to buy space in the *Harbinger*. It takes money to buy time on KARC. Sister Zelda's going to pass amongst you with the plate now. Brothers and sisters in the Lord, I need you. And you rounders out there, Brother Aftermath knows how you shake them bones Saturday nights at the Brothers Club. Old Nick can spare some of that money for a crusade like ours. And I ask our white friends to join hands—and pocketbooks—with us for the sake of our city."

As Aftermath looked up at us, the faces in the crowd also tilted up towards us.

He continued, "I'm especially delighted to see that Mr.

Mulberry, one of our visitors from England, has joined us this evening. Would you please stand, Mr. Mulberry, so that everyone can see you?"

Muggsbottom rose and took the few steps required to reach the balcony railing. I did not know how he would respond to Aftermath's mangling of his name. I never knew how Muggsbottom would respond to an offense. At times, he would mount his high horse over some slight that I could scarcely recognize as such. At other times, he seemed blithely impervious to what I would consider a grievous affront. But whatever his response was to be, he obviously took Aftermath's public recognition as an invitation to speak.

"I bring you greetings," he began in a stentorian voice which reached into every corner of the tabernacle, "from Her Most Gracious Majesty, Queen of England, Ireland, Scotland, and Wales. Though the Empire of blessed memory is no more, I know how pleased the sovereign would be if she were here with us this evening. 'Twas in the legendary reign of her great namesake that our sceptered isle achieved her first true greatness upon the world's stage. That Elizabeth's seamen smote and sank the huge Spanish fleet. She and her ministers forged a diplomacy which diverted and confounded her European rivals. And her clerics repelled the Roman effort to restore Britain to the Holy See. Thus it is that we are not meeting tonight in a Roman Catholic church and I am not required to address you in the Spanish tongue."

Muggsbottom paused for an appropriate response to this bit of levity, but all he got was blank stares. I could tell from Aftermath's expression that he was reassessing his decision to introduce "Mulberry" to the crowd. Too late now.

Muggsbottom continued, "Further, our present Elizabeth's great-great grandmother, I might make bold to say, is largely responsible for the spread of parliamentary democracy to the hot countries of our world. Thanks to her and to the ministering legions from Whitehall, the primitive rule of fang and claw has been somewhat temporized by habeas corpus and trial by jury. Whereas in the past rival factions might have grappled for dominance in the village with the aid of spears and blazing brands, today the Reverend Aftermath and his opponent appeal sans weapons to the electors of Arcady, some of whom are in fact literate. Fortunately, the English common law is no fragile flower that is blasted by the broiling sun of southern climes." Okay, Aftermath, what do *you* think of *this*? "I trust that soon elections such as this presently being contested will become such a common occurrence in the national life that they will cease to overexcite the electorate."

"I think what your damned Englishman just said may have been racist," whispered my colleague.

"He's in one of his Imperial moods," I explained. "He thinks he's Winston Churchill. It will pass."

"I serve in Arcady," Muggsbottom continued, "without portfolio. But as Luther argued that every believer is a priest, I assert that every Briton is a minister of the monarch's civilizing influence. As a foreign national, it would, of course, be highly inappropriate for me to contribute to the campaign of even so compelling a candidate as the Reverend Aftermath. Like yourselves, however, my companions have a crucial interest in this experiment in Arkansas democracy. I feel certain that they are prepared to contribute generously when sister Zelda appears before them with her plate.

"And by the way, the name is Muggsbottom, Charles P."

As Muggsbottom returned to his seat, there was a smattering of applause, but mostly there was silence . . . until from somewhere below a lone voice spoke for the multitude. "Say what?"

"Muggsbottom," I said, "what was all that pompous crap

about 'hot countries' and the 'rule of fang and claw'? This is not Kenya or Burma. Also, you may recall that we sent your 'civilizing influence' packing two hundred years ago with shot and shell." Then gratuitously, because I was angry, "And they're about to boot your butt out of the rest of Ireland as well."

"My dear fellow," Muggsbottom replied, "I am shocked. I never dreamt that you had this xenophobic streak in your nature. I fear it betokens a very narrow point of view. I could recommend some books that are quite good."

Three weeks later, on a day marked by heavy rain and a light voter turnout, Abednego Aftermath defeated John Bozeman for City Director, Position Three, 1,079 to 998.

My barber's comment summed up the election succinctly. "Lord, I never thought I'd vote for a n---x from Chicago. But I used to cut John Bozeman's hair, and he's as crazy as a bessie bug."

Did choosing a "n---x from Chicago" over a home grown nut signal an advance in Arcadian race relations? I suppose it must have.

Muggsbottom's observation was ambiguous. "This sort of thing happens pretty regularly now all through the Commonwealth."

8. Bards: Homer Joe and Twinksly Murk

Just before Thanksgiving, hostilities were resumed between Muggsbottom and Homer Joe Tennyson. The circumstances were curious as well as coincidental and will require some exposition.

I have previously mentioned Twinksly Murk, the British poet who was anathema to Muggsbottom both in his person and in his work. The coincidence was as follows. In our monthly departmental meeting, our chairman announced that we were in receipt of a grant from the National Endowment for the Arts. As usual, the grant money could not be used to subsidize anything we truly desired—e.g., our own writing, our own research, our own travel. It could, and would, be used to pay the salary of an artist-in-residence who would join us for the spring semester. This artist was a professor at one of Britain's redbrick universities, who happened also to be currently one of the hottest international gay poets. His name was Twinksly Murk.

"Murk's poetic preoccupation is not admirably suited to Arcady," said the chairman in one of his most triumphant understatements, "so I think we will avoid emphasizing it."

I thought immediately, of course, of Muggsbottom's reaction to this news. Next, I thought of the Ol' Perfesser, a notorious homophobe whose fag bashing—considered to be in poor taste in more sophisticated environs—was solidly in Arcady's mainstream. I did not for a moment think of Homer Joe Tennyson.

I had hoped to keep Muggsbottom in the dark about Murk's visit, if possible, until it actually came to pass. Ordinarily, I enjoyed the fruits of such antipathy as Twinksly Murk sowed in my friend. In this case, however, contrary poetic tastes were as much a source of ill will between the two men as were their different temperaments. And my poetic judgments were no more in accord with Muggsbottom's than with Murk's (except in the conclusion which any sensible critic would reach that Homer Joe's verses were deplorable). So, whereas Muggsbottom's railings on other subjects were usually highly entertaining, his quaint dissertations on poetic theory, acceptable prosody, and literary history were tiresome to me. They forced me either to suffer in silence or risk a quarrel which I was not sure our burgeoning friendship could withstand. Such matters had represented a large part of my professional training and, quite frankly, I felt I knew a hell of a lot more about them than did Muggsbottom. For these reasons, I hoped that the subject of Twinksly Murk would not surface for a while.

For Murk's part, he might not even remember Muggsbottom. The two had not seen each other since coming down from university. On the other hand, Muggsbottom was himself a memorable character. He remembered Murk; I expected Murk would remember him. Especially if there were any truth to Muggsbottom's tale of having once set fire to the young aesthete's trousers. It was clear enough to me that my friend enjoyed embellishing his reminiscences, but that was just the sort of prank he might actually have played.

My hopes were dashed when later in the week our public information office gave the story to the *Harbinger*. "Twinksly Murk, eminent British poet, will join the State College faculty as artist-in-residence for the spring term."

The newspaper fell from Muggsbottom's fingers, and these words fell from his lips: "Good God, is there no safe harbor anywhere?"

What none of us suspected, however, was the effect this news would have upon Homer Joe Tennyson. Homer Joe had never read a word of Twinksly Murk, but he had long yearned for converse with a fellow poet in the unpoetical territory of Dean County. His childlike mind seized upon the notion that he would find the visitor a brother under the skin. Homer Joe immediately initiated a correspondence with Twinksly Murk. We were to learn of this development only after that correspondence was well advanced.

Muggsbottom showed an admirable restraint for a couple of weeks but eventually renewed *his* correspondence with the editor of the *Harbinger*, to wit:

What ever happened to 'one if by land and two if by sea'? Now is the hour for you colonists to mount a watch in the Old North Tower. Twinksly Murk, purveyor of verse both vacuous and vile, is coming. The idea of exposing undergraduates to Twinksly Murk so that they may learn the value of poetry is rather like exposing them to bubonic plague so that they may learn the value of inoculation. Surely, there is some less dangerous course. Alas, the ignorance of modern educators tends to make them reckless. Remember, Muggsbottom has warned you.

C. P. M.

Muggsbottom's letter had a curious effect. Upon reading it, I had feared that my chairman might be moved to respond. I viewed a protracted public wrangle between him and Muggsbottom as a very unpleasant prospect indeed. I would be caught in the middle, since each man would view himself as the injured party and would expect some show of loyalty from me. My fears proved groundless, however. Perhaps my chairman felt that the less Murk's name

appeared in the pages of the *Harbinger* the better. At any
rate, he did not rise to the defense of Twinksly Murk or of
the decision to bring him to Arcady. Murk's champion
turned out to be Muggsbottom's old antagonist, Homer Joe
Tennyson.

In the next *Voices from the Vale*, this little ditty appeared,
under the title "Of English Bards and English Boozers":

An artist rare soon comes to Arcady.
We should heap garlands at this poet's feet.
This Virgil sails from far across the sea
To bring to us his vaunted verses sweet.

True folk of Arcady all bid him come
To share with us his wisdom and his art.
No strangers we reject, though there be some
Who've tried our patience from the very start.

One in particular presumes too much;
He'd tell us whom we may and may not host.
In Arcady the fair and friendly, such
A guest is rash at least, perverse at most.

If we must choose between our Englishmen,
Far better Twinksly Murk than C.P.M.

"Read this," said Muggsbottom, as he handed me the
offending page of the *Harbinger*.

I scanned the sonnet (more in the popular than in the
metrical sense) and, remembering that Muggsbottom had
once hinted at taking Homer Joe to court, remarked, "I
don't believe anything in here is actionable. Our libel laws
are far less stringent than Britain's, you know."

"Don't be absurd, dear boy. I would never sue that

loutish poetaster. We should both look the fool, and only the solicitors and the barristers would derive any satisfaction."

Muggsbottom had a convenient way of forgetting completely any immoderate remarks that he had made and of affecting astonishment when others made reference to them.

"I am merely directing your attention," he continued, "to those lines which are even more outrageous than his usual fare. What a mixture of obsequiousness and arrogance! You will note that in line three he applies the name of the great Roman poet to Murk, a cognomen equally as unsuitable as Homer Joe's own. Now, examine the third quatrain. To accuse a man of my circumspection of being presumptuous and rash is ludicrous enough. But to call *me* perverse in a paean to Twinksly Murk is to stand the English language upon its head. And the title, of course, quite unjustly portrays us as dipsomaniacs."

"Has that Homer Joe creature attacked us again?" inquired Smythe-Gardner, upon whom the context of our conversation had finally registered.

Ignoring the old salt (as was his customary practice), Muggsbottom said, "Finally, that pathetic attempt at rhyme in the couplet."

"Didn't I tell you?" groused Smythe-Gardner. "We should have given him a good biffing the first time."

I said, "Homer Joe's defense of Murk is a little surprising to me. I wouldn't think Murk would be his cup of tea."

"He's probably never read Murk," said Muggsbottom. "And if he has, my guess is that he's too thick to gloss the text of the lubricious passages. Poor booby."

Muggsbottom's mood appeared to be mellowing from anger to sadness. Could he be feeling genuine pity for his ignorant and deluded critic? I was moved by my friend's hint of unexpected magnanimity.

"I think it's time for Homer Joe and me to have a little

tête-à-tête. Where is one likely to find our bucolic trouba-
dour when he isn't in the woods slaying all creatures great
and small?"

"That's the ticket," said Smythe-Gardner triumphantly.
"Eyeball to eyeball. Give the blighter his choice—a public
apology or a public thrashing."

"He lives out along the Caddo River somewhere," I said.

I was being disingenuous with the "somewhere." I knew
precisely where Homer Joe Tennyson resided. He had a
mobile home on the river bank, two hundred yards off the
Underwood Road. Anyone seeking the bard turned right
just beyond an Indian burial mound, a landmark virtually
impossible to miss. I was sure that Muggsbottom intended
no such bellicose confrontation as Smythe-Gardner had so
rapturously envisioned. Still, knowing the eccentric natures
of the two men, I had no inkling of where a face-to-face
meeting between Muggsbottom and Homer Joe might lead.
Best not to contribute in any way to such an eventuality.

"I believe there are no phone lines out his way," I added,
hoping that my words and tone of voice sufficiently indicated that making personal contact with Homer Joe
Tennyson was a feat beyond the powers of mortal man.

"I know where you can find him about ten o'clock every
morning."

These words were spoken by Maynard. The Phlegm
Club's majordomo, like so many otherwise stupid people,
had a shrewd instinct for trouble making.

"Excellent," said Muggsbottom.

"At this time of year, the farmers come in and drink coffee all morning at Granny's. Homer Joe hangs out with
them."

"We'll take them all on," declared Smythe-Gardner, his
face growing redder.

"I'm unacquainted with this Granny."

"There ain't no Granny. That's just the name. It's on
Twelfth Street, two blocks down from the state college."

"Very well," said Muggsbottom. "Then I shall hie myself to Granny's on the morrow"

Ignoring the fuming Smythe-Gardner, he turned to Sir Monty and Reggie.

"What do you say, chaps? Shall I beard our agrarian adversary in his den?"

Sir Monty slept on, his silence apparently giving consent. Reggie, who had been sitting immobile and watching his cigarette ash grow to a length which defied gravity, started at the question.

"Beg pardon? I'm afraid I was thinking of something else."

"Ah," said Muggsbottom, in a gently chiding tone, "I shouldn't have wanted to interrupt *that*."

At the time, I did not know the cause of Reggie's uncharacteristic cerebration. In retrospect, I see that his usually empty head was filled with thoughts of love. However, therein lies the material for another story, to be recounted elsewhere.

"Waken me in time to accompany you," said Smythe-Gardner, who had sufficient insight to know that his warrior's instincts might not automatically overcome his customary early morning lassitude.

"I go alone, Biffy, as chargé d'affaires of our little outpost. If talks fail, I may have to resort to the heavy artillery, and you shall certainly have your role to play."

Another instance of Muggsbottom's using good sense. But I found him miscast in the role of diplomat, and the picture of him accosting Homer Joe among the soybean farmers of Dean County was an unsettling one. I faced the coming day with dread.

I was distracted the next morning by academic duties: teaching two classes, the members of which were far more interested in the upcoming Thanksgiving vacation than in *The Shepherd's Calendar*, marking papers, and adding my voice to the perpetual rumble of seditious talk in the faculty lounge. My afternoon was supposed to be devoted to office hours, but I knew from experience that before a holiday students are making preparations for a quick getaway rather than initiating conferences with their professors. I did not believe I could contain my curiosity until nightfall at the Phlegm Club, so by two o'clock I had slipped away to the old house near the Baptist college.

I found Muggsbottom alone on the front porch, his legs stretched out before him, his ankles crossed on top of the fluted railing. His relaxed posture announced that, at least from his perspective, the encounter with Homer Joe Tennyson had gone well. He knew immediately why I was there and began to tell his story without my having to ask for it.

"As you know, my intention initially was to take Homer Joe Tennyson to task. I was understandably offended by his unlikely alliance with the current Ariel of British letters, Twinksly Murk—the result of that alliance being a vicious personal attack upon C. P. Muggsbottom. However, I am happy to report that as of this morning Homer Joe and I have reached something of a *rapprochement*.

"This restoration of harmonious relations—perhaps 'inauguration' would be a more appropriate term than 'restoration'—began in rather an inauspicious manner. Upon entering Granny's at mid-morning, I found the establishment to be filled with chaps attired in blue denim trousers and what I believe are called bib overalls. They were engaged in boisterous, and frequently profane, conversation. I approached the fellow behind the counter—who, it seems, is the Granny of the moment—and asked him which of those worthies was the infamous Homer Joe Tennyson. 'Oh,' quoth he, '*that* turkey. He's the tall one at the end of the counter, the one with the National Rifle Association patch on his cap.' I pondered his reference to 'that turkey.' What was I to think? It *is* Thanksgiving, that uniquely American holiday. And here was Homer Joe being likened to that uniquely American bird. Once again, I feared that nationality had proved more powerful than taste and discrimination. Still, I quite understood. You may never have noticed, but I can on occasion be as xenophobic as the next fellow. It is my contention, however, that any Englishman who is not xenophobic shows an insufficient appreciation of his heritage.

"But, to return to my narrative. I strode up to Homer Joe and introduced myself. I was apparently known, at least by reputation, to his companions, for they immediately commenced to make comments both to and about me. The precise content of these remarks was by no means clear to me since they were, after all, uttered in your curious Arkansas dialect. But I was cognizant of the preference they showed for Homer Joe's position over my own.

"I was just upon the point of opening our colloquy with the admission that he had won the battle of public opinion, when Homer Joe clasped me by the hand and said, 'I'm sure glad to see you, Muggsbottom. I have something to show you. Excuse us, fellers.' He threw his arm around my shoulder in an astonishingly friendly fashion and straight-away ushered me out the door and to his pickup truck. He opened the glove box and drew out a lavender colored, nauseatingly perfumed letter. The simple exposure of this missive to the light of day instantly agitated the poor chap almost beyond measure. 'I have been writing to Twinksly Murk in London,' he declared, in a tone which clearly characterized the act as one requiring penance. 'I sincerely apologize for my little poem. You see, I had no sooner dropped it off at the *Harbinger* than I found *this* in my post office box.'

"He extended the letter, which one might easily mistake for an interior decorator's bill, and wordlessly bade me read it. It was a reply from Twinksly. It seems that in one of his more expansive moments Homer Joe had invited Twinksly to accompany him on a coon hunt during the latter's impending visit to Arcady. Twinksly had countered with a proposal so lewd and obvious that even Homer Joe's beclouded mind instantly apprehended the impropriety. Homer Joe was appropriately shocked and disillusioned. He *is*, you know, a child of Calvin, as the poet laureate of Antoine, Arkansas, must necessarily be. 'I would never go into the woods with a feller like that,' Homer Joe exclaimed, and I assured him he was quite right to demur.

"Well, that is the end of the Tennyson-Murk alliance— nipped in the bud by Twinksly's prurience, which he cannot master even in his correspondence—and Homer Joe and I are now on terms as congenial as the gross discrepancy in our intellects will allow. I have even subtly suggested that Homer Joe has reached an age at which he might consider retirement from the arts, so that he could devote himself full-time to his two principal avocations—the production of untaxed whisky and the slaughter of defenseless animals. But, alas, I fear I was not successful. He is adamant. He *will* continue with his 'pottery.'

"All in all, however, the affair could not have reached a more agreeable conclusion. I have but one regret. Smythe-Gardner's disappointment is acute. He has locked himself in his room and cannot be made to come out."

9. Christmas, 1980

It was a few nights before Christmas at the Phlegm Club, and two cozy gas space heaters were substituting for a cozy fire in the grate, since there was no grate. Muggsbottom, full of goodwill and hot buttered rum, was expatiating upon the season.

"During this, my first, yuletide in our quaint *ville provincial*, I have learnt that to the natives the Christmas goose is something that causes one to squeal and jump into the air. This meaning of the term was graphically illustrated for me by Maynard, our brain-damaged steward, one recent afternoon when he had been toasting the season with Mennen's after-shave lotion.

"Another of the curious holiday customs here in the colonies is the consumption of a thick, yellow, vile eggnog, which is not made by the lady of the house but is purchased, in hideous waxy pasteboard cartons. It is my belief that those who mix whisky with this nauseating potation are the same people who, like Maynard, will drink bourbon and black cherry soda."

I noticed that tonight Muggsbottom felt compelled to spice his soliloquy with more references to Maynard than was his usual want. I could see that the scamp was on his mind. I was to learn the reason later in the evening.

"But perhaps the most curious aberration is the profusion of football matches during the Christmas season. It appears that any team which during the autumn has managed to win at least one more match than they have lost is 'rewarded' with what is called a 'bowl,' for some reason not readily apparent to me. I understand that even our Razorblades, despite what their partisans consider to have been a most unsatisfactory performance, have been invited to participate in one of these contests. Of course, this synthesis of sport and the blessed season fits the football theology of Southern fundamentalism nicely. You know—the notion that Jehovah is that great coach in the sky, our Saviour is the quarterback, and the Apostles are his blockers, as he attempts to advance the ball into Satan's end zone."

These ramblings were familiar to the point of being well-worn. They had no bite at all to them. This was merely Muggsbottom's way of entertaining a company whose discourse, he had learned from experience, was all too drab when he did not take the conversational lead. My friend was really in an excellent humor.

I felt especially fortunate at this time to have been accepted as a perpetual guest of the Phlegm Club. The students and most of the faculty had abandoned Arcady for the holidays. I was not a native Arcadian, nor did I have close relations from whom I could wheedle a Christmas invitation. My former wife and I had been in the habit of visiting her parents (whom, even before the divorce, I had come to prefer to her) each yuletide. I believed that they bore me no ill will. Yet, under the circumstances, Christmas dinner at their house was no longer an option.

I have not mentioned my former wife previously for fear of adversely affecting the tone of this narrative. She is a beautiful and willful woman, totally devoid of insight—a lethal combination of attributes. She had long felt that Arcady was too small a pond for such an exotic fish as she. Her principal delusion was that she was a singer of extraordinary talent, and two years before the Christmas of which I write she had left me to pursue a musical career. Her decision was typically irrational.

Whereas most aspiring singers would have struck out for New York or Los Angeles, or perhaps, Nashville, my wife headed for Houston. Of course, I was aware that her old college boyfriend, Thurman "Slim" Snodgrass, resided in Houston, where he had amassed a fortune in oil and gas and real estate. I never actually heard that they got back together, but I confess that when recently I had read of Slim's bankruptcy proceedings I was not displeased. I am not always as big a person as I would wish to be.

But I am getting ahead of my story. I mention my failed marriage not to elicit the reader's sympathy but to concretize the circumstances under which I was spending the holidays in the company of my English friends.

Sir Monty broached the idea of a Christmas pantomime like those he remembered with such fondness from his Georgian youth, but he fell asleep before the subject could be thoroughly explored. Smythe-Gardner was, like Muggsbottom, in a mellow mood. In fact, his humor was as pacific as I had ever seen it, at least while he was conscious. Reggie was absent from the circle, as he had frequently been on recent evenings. He had developed a taste for solitary walks through the dark and deserted streets of Arcady, so he claimed. "Gives me a chance to get in touch with my feelings, don't you know." (He had also developed a taste for television's glib therapists.) Reggie's friends were skeptical of his story and even I, who did not know him as well as they, was also. They were especially suspicious on this night, for the wind was rising out of the north and had a bite to it. But four men cannot live together over a period of years without practicing tolerance, and they allowed each other their secrets.

Maynard brought a new round of drinks from the bar, ostentatiously cleared his throat, and fixed a conspiratorial eye upon Muggsbottom.

"Oh, very well, Maynard," said Muggsbottom. Then he

turned to the others. "Lads, Maynard has come to me with a request, and I promised him I would bring it before the membership."

"It isn't for a rise in salary, is it?" inquired Smythe-Gardner with alarm. "All Americans seem convinced that they are due a rise in salary."

"Out of the question," muttered Sir Monty, without opening his eyes.

"No," said Muggsbottom, "it isn't a question of wages. Maynard realizes that, considering his manifold and manifest shortcomings as steward, not to mention the character defects that would render him unemployable by most such clubs, he is well compensated here. Is that not so, Maynard?"

"I'm pretty well satisfied for the time being," replied Maynard—rather ambiguously, I thought.

"Rather," Muggsbottom continued, "it has to do with Maynard's cousin . . . "

"Billy Earl Hangar," Maynard interposed.

"Yes . . . Maynard's cousin, Billy Earl Hangar. Mr. Hangar is, I believe, some sort of commercial traveler. He is scheduled to spend the week between Christmas and New Year's Day in Arcady. And the long and the short of it is, Maynard has invited his cousin to stay with him."

Maynard had retained his daytime job as porter at the Caddo Hotel but had given up his room there. He was now bunking on a cot in the storage room of the Phlegm Club. He found these surroundings more congenial, enjoying especially the easy access to large quantities of liquor. I imagine that he considered the amounts he could purloin to be his chief fringe benefit. I assumed that this tendency toward theft was the major character defect of which Muggsbottom had spoken.

"Well, lads," said Muggsbottom, "what do you say?"

"Out of the question," rumbled Sir Monty, fending off

narcolepsy for long enough to voice his usual negative response.

"That pantry's scarcely big enough for Maynard," objected Smythe-Gardner.

"He says that he can fetch another cot in from the Caddo."

"I'm sure he can," said Smythe-Gardner with deep irony. "Maynard seems always to find what he needs."

Maynard smiled. The relative mildness of Smythe-Gardner's objection he had taken as a favorable sign.

"And I don't approve of setting this sort of precedent," Smythe-Gardner continued. "God only knows how many peripatetic cousins Maynard may have."

The conversation continued in this wise for a few minutes more, but the issue had clearly been decided. Muggsbottom did not seem unalterably opposed to Billy Earl Hangar's spending a few nights in the Phlegm Club's pantry, and Muggsbottom was the putative leader of the Englishmen. Smythe-Gardner grumbled on for a bit, his purpose being to put his dissenting opinion squarely on the record. Sir Monty lapsed deeper into sleep, his silence, as so often, ultimately giving consent.

When Billy Earl Hangar arrived in Arcady on Christmas Eve, we discovered that he was far more than the traveling salesman Maynard had represented him to be. To begin with, his arrival was less conventional than we had expected. He landed at the Arcady airport in a biplane of ancient vintage. The bottom of the lower wing and fuselage had been painted a bright red, so that viewed from below the craft resembled a fiery cross descending from Heaven over the bean fields. The Englishmen had every right to feel that their steward had misled them through his omission of several pertinent details. To their consternation, they discovered that they had invited into their sanctum sanctorum—albeit merely into the pantry thereof—a crop duster cum barnstormer cum revivalist. Muggsbottom manfully shouldered the blame, but he also said, "I shall ring Maynard's scrawny neck until his eyes pop out of his head."

Billy Earl Hangar was a short man, tending toward corpulence. His ruddy face was broad and flat. His small, watery blue eyes were intelligent (an observer less objective than I might have chosen the adjective *crafty*). His hair was thin, fine, and very blond—yet he had treated it with some tonsorial preparation that caused it to crest inches above his head. And so effective was this product that when Billy Earl removed his old-fashioned aviator's helmet, even after having worn it for several hours, his golden locks sprang instantly back into their haute coiffure. I imagined that had Chaucer's pardoner been traveling the evangelistic circuit in our own day, he would have applied something similar to his own "lokkes yelow as wex."

The flying revivalist had a deep, mellifluous voice, with that particular timbre which in our part of the country so effectively sells salvation and used Plymouths. From the very moment that he met the Englishmen, Billy Earl behaved just as if he had known them all his life. This presumption had various yet predictable effects upon his hosts. Muggsbottom was taken aback, temporarily immobilized by the impertinence. Sir Monty retreated into the state of selective senility with which he combatted most unwelcome occurrences—he affected unawareness of Billy Earl's existence. Smythe-Gardner grew red in the face and muttered about the "good biffing" that some people truly needed. The innocent Reggie was thoroughly charmed by the evangelist's brash and flamboyant manner. On his part, Billy Earl acted as if he could not have been greeted anywhere with a finer display of Christian charity.

Billy Earl allowed no winter grass to grow under his feet. On Christmas Day—which one might view as the least propitious time in the year to do business—he went through Arcady and its environs like a dose of salts (as the saying goes around here). Before ten a.m., he had rented the use of a field south of town for his "Giant After-Christmas Revival." What is more, he had rented the field for ten percent of whatever the offertory receipts would come to, from Jeroboam Jernigan, the hardest-nosed businessman in Dean County, never before known to have entered into a purely speculative deal with even his life-long friends. By noon, Billy Earl had struck another deal, whereby he would receive a week's use of a huge tent belonging to the Dean County Fair Association in exchange for his promise to provide, free of charge, one day of aerial entertainment at the Dean County Fair the following October. County employees would raise the tent for him first thing the next morning. Billy Earl announced that he would have wound up this phase of his preparations much sooner except that, of course, all the County offices were closed. At midafternoon, Arcady was blanketed with Billy Earl's preprinted posters with the dates, place, and time—multicolored and in Gothic script—of his local revival filled in. Clearly, in the person of Billy Earl Hangar, we were dealing with someone very special.

Before the week was out, Billy Earl had amazed us further still. He had secured a relatively permanent position at KARC by somehow persuading Newt Parker that Arcady needed an "Eye in the Sky." KARC is our three-thousand-watt radio station—country and western music interspersed with farm prices and canned news, all inexpertly manipulated by two fuzzy-cheeked announcers/engineers/college students. Newt Parker is the station manager. Newt drinks a bit, as I have noticed those dead-ended in the media tend to do. But I had never doubted his grasp of reality or his constant awareness of KARC's razor-thin profit margin.

"Billy Earl reminded him that it wasn't just Memphis and Dallas," Maynard reported with apparent tribal pride. "A Little Rock station has an 'Eye in the Sky' too. In fact, there ain't no market truly worthy of the name that don't have an 'Eye in the Sky.'"

The remarkable Billy Earl had seduced Newt into naming him the station's rush-hour (7:40 to 8:00 a.m. and 5:00 to 5:20 p.m.) traffic reporter. From his Christian biplane high above the city, Billy Earl would by remote broadcast survey and evaluate the traffic flow along Pine and Tenth Streets, our two intersecting major arteries. Any mention of KARC's newest employee would bring a flush of color to Newt's face and suddenly remind him of some business requiring his urgent attention elsewhere. For his part, Billy Earl would simply say, "It's a nice little contract—gives me a chance to do the Lord's work here in your fair city a while longer. Doesn't tie me down long-term, though. Jesus may call me to any place at any time, you know. And when the Savior calls, why, I just crank her up and I go."

Muggsbottom would later cynically remark, "I shouldn't expect the Savior to call him while a single Anabaptist in Arcady still has a nickel in the pocket of his overalls."

The membership decided unanimously that lodgings in the Phlegm Club pantry were totally unsuitable for a resident Billy Earl Hangar.

"That's all right," said Maynard, taking no offense. "He's moving into the Caddo in the morning. Miss Amanda's giving him a special rate. She got saved at his second meeting, you know. Course, she's been saved a time or two before, and none of 'em really took, far as I could see. But Billy Earl, well, he's a special instrument."

10. Dipswizzle in Love

During the first days of the new year, as during the last days of the old, Reggie was often absent from the Victorian house near the river. We had long since guessed that a woman was the occasion of these absences. The other Englishmen never mentioned this development but, whenever they spoke of Reggie *in absentia*, the tone of their remarks told me that they knew. I had come to the same conclusion quite independently. I recognized the air that enveloped Reggie as being identical to that which Iris had generated at the time of her affair with Seymour Schmidt, my colleague at the college. Seymour is a professor of behavioral psychology and, like most behaviorists, appears to have no concept of how human beings actually behave. Of course, as soon as Iris's head cleared, she saw that Seymour was not the answer to a matron's prayer. However, the collapse of her ill-starred romance had only served to make her less happy still in her marriage to me. At any rate, I recognized the signs. Reggie's every word and gesture spoke inadvertently of a liaison, of assignations in the shadows of Arcady.

Obviously, Reggie was attempting to keep his romance a secret because he feared that his comrades would disapprove. And his judgment was quite correct. By all objective criteria, his friends had no right to approve or disapprove of any of his actions. Despite his adolescent manner, he was a man past forty years of age. He was, himself, one of the most tolerant, least judgmental souls upon the face of the earth. And, finally, it was primarily his income upon which they all were living.

Let me try to explain the Englishmen's attitude toward any involvement with a woman. None was an out-and-out misogynist. None was homosexual. Sir Monty appeared to be asexual, although the absence of libido may simply have been another feigned facet of the hoary persona he had adopted. Muggsbottom and Smythe-Gardner were more in the mold of the confirmed bachelor of an earlier era. I do not believe that any of them opposed Reggie's entangle-ment with a woman for fear of losing their meal ticket. Their motivation was not so base as that. All three took the position that a woman was at best an inconvenience, at worst a positive danger to a man's peace and freedom. And, in Reggie's case, the latter circumstance would unhappily prove to be a reality.

In the first week of the new year, I received my initial concrete information regarding Reggie's innamorata. This information came from the ubiquitous Maynard. He sidled up to me one evening while we were all reading. On such occasions, the members of the Phlegm Club disposed themselves about the room, each man—in the current jar-gon—seeking his "own space." This arrangement made it possible for Maynard to converse with me in a tone that could not be overheard by my companions. From time to time, Maynard would approach me as a confidant—assum-ing, I suppose, that our shared status as outsiders had forged some sort of link between us. For obvious reasons, I was unwilling to acknowledge this link. But, today, it proved useful, for what Maynard told me was both extremely interesting and extremely troubling.

"When I was in Hot Springs New Year's Eve," he whis-pered, "guess who I seen."

Maynard often spent his nights off hanging about the

streets of Hot Springs, doing things I wished to know nothing about.

"Jimmy Hoffa," I said.

"No," he replied somberly, and waited for me to guess again.

"That's the only name that comes to mind. Tell me, Maynard."

"It was Mr. Dipswizzle. Goin' into the Arlington Hotel with a woman."

Maynard could see that my interest in his piece of intelligence had instantly shot up several degrees, and he was pleased.

"Did you know her?"

"Shore did." He paused, milking his part for several seconds more. "It was that woman plays the organ at the Presbyterian Church."

I confess that I was addled by Maynard's revelation. I had been pretty sure already that there was a woman in the case and, Reggie being the hopeless romantic that he was, I suspected that he would be thinking in terms of eternal love rather than a casual amour. But I would have thought Cecilia Luce the last woman in Arcady to stir thoughts of eternal love in Reggie Dipswizzle.

Cecilia Luce was an attractive ash blonde of thirty-eight to forty years of age. Aside from being the slightest bit heavy in the hips, she had retained a youthful willowy figure. She had come to Arcady in the mid-sixties as the wife of Wendell Luce, the local veterinarian. Wendell was a reticent, mild-mannered longtime bachelor, who had—to the amazement of all Arcadians—returned from a week-long veterinary conference in Kansas City with a bride. As the story went, Cecilia was a saleswoman for one of the pharmaceutical companies that sold horse pills and the like to the vets. Wendell had met her on the convention floor on Monday, and by Saturday she was Mrs. Luce. Cecilia was not actually disliked by her new neighbors, although she did come on a bit strong by Arcadian standards. Wendell seemed happy in his marriage, but he was clearly dominated by his wife's personality and became even more laconic than he had been before. Cecilia had artistic leanings. She immediately filled a vacancy as organist at the Presbyterian Church. She evinced few signs of an interest in theology, but she was a supremely self-confident woman who would certainly have considered herself one of the elect. In fact, she seemed to regard the Sunday services as her weekly recitals, within which the liturgy served as so much background and filler. She also had taken leading roles in several productions of the Arcady Community Players. Early on, there were rumors of liaisons between Cecilia and unnamed men of the town. She gained a reputation as a "hot number" but, if she was unfaithful to Wendell, she was so discreet that no one could substantiate the charges against her.

In the fifth year of their marriage, Wendell met a most unfortunate end. On a stormy April afternoon, he was attending one of Jeroboam Jernigan's horses, who had foundered far from the barn. As Wendell was laboring to entice the unwilling animal to its feet, a huge bolt of lightning had chanced to strike that very spot in the pasture, thus incinerating both Wendell and his patient. Jeroboam, always the businessman, was philosophical—he had lost the worth of the horse but had saved the amount of Wendell's fee. A number of the townspeople expressed the opinion that Wendell's was a most fitting demise, as he had been plying his trade up to the very second of his departure. A few of us, however, thought that this was perhaps an overly sentimental assessment of the incident.

To the surprise of many, the widow had remained in Arcady. Within six months' time—an interval considered barely decent by Arcadians—she was married again, this time to Maurice Bosshart, the drama teacher at the high school. Maurice was, as Wendell had been, a bachelor approaching middle age. The marriage did not surprise the town totally. Maurice had directed Cecilia in her most successful roles with the Arcady Community Players. They had both belonged to what was termed by a local philistine the "artsy-fartsy" crowd—a tiny and incestuous cell of aesthetes within Arcady's communal structure. This group felt besieged on the right and on the left. On the right was what they perceived as the predominant redneck culture of Arcady, always eager to expunge any alien influences. On the left were those of us at the state and Baptist colleges, who should have been their soul mates. But the aesthetes suspected, and probably with some justice, that any artistic endeavor which admitted people from the colleges would soon be expropriated by one or both campuses. The townspeople were actually more surprised by Maurice's marriage than by Cecilia's remarriage. There were winks and jokes and wide-eyed pronouncements such as, "I didn't know Maurice liked *girls*." The couple had been married only slightly more than a year when Maurice confirmed all these suspicions. Cecilia was playing the lead in *Tea and Sympathy*, under the direction of her husband. Performing the role of ingénu was Ralph LaFleur, a demure young man in his first term as biology teacher at Arcady High. On the morning after the final performance, Maurice Bosshart and Ralph LaFleur disappeared, never to be heard from again. It was generally supposed that they had left Arcady together and that someplace like San Francisco was their ultimate destination.

Cecilia took her abandonment very hard indeed. She had immediately taken back the name Luce, since Wendell had been faithful unto death. For a strong-minded and passionate woman like herself to lose her husband to another woman would have been a bitter enough pill to swallow. To lose her husband to a man was a pill she could not choke down. It was at this point that Cecilia had forsaken all discretion in her sexual practices. Furthermore, she henceforth allowed her natural aggressive tendencies free rein. Men began to tell stories. A favorite—and one with a probable germ of truth in it—was of Cecilia pasting herself against her partners at the Country Club dances, undulating against them, beginning to moan softly, and eventually experiencing, or pretending to experience, an orgasm on the dance floor. This performance dried the virility of some Arcadians right up. Some fellows it sent rushing to the men's room, others toward the parking lot. Cecilia gained a reputation as—to put it crudely—an easy lay, but also as a woman whose ferocious demands both during and after the act forced a man to pay dearly for his pleasure. Epithets like "maneater" and "ball buster" were commonly applied to her. This was the woman with whom gentle Reggie Dipswizzle had become romantically involved.

And there was another potential hazard for my friend. For the last year or two, Cecilia's frequent companion had been the Ol'· Perfesser, my former colleague and present enemy. He had made manifest his enmity for the Englishmen as well. He held no proprietary claim on Mrs. Luce—Cecilia, now totally liberated, would have allowed none. But he would certainly resent Reggie as a rival, and his well of resentment was deep, its contents ample.

"They were going into the Arlington?" I said.

"You know," Maynard prompted, "to that big New Year's Eve dance." Then he added with a broad wink, "What they done *after* the dance . . . ?"

Ah, yes. The Arlington held a Guy Lombardo-type dance each New Year's Eve. Iris and I had never attended one of these soirées but, as my imagination was unencumbered by any direct experience, I could see them clearly in my mind's eye. They were, I judged, patronized largely by superannuated Chicagoans. A phenomenon of the Hot Springs area was the large number of transplanted Chicagoans who, after having lived for sixty years in the biggest city in the Midwest, had inexplicably decided that they would be happier in a small town in Arkansas. Of course, they were not. They complained constantly about the lack of every sort of amenity and about the unintelligible dialect of the natives. In fact, they wished the sylvan hills and still lakes of Arkansas to be Chicago minus its inconveniences.

"Don't mention this to the others," I said in a conspiratorial tone. "When Mr. Dipswizzle wants them to know about the lady, he will tell them."

Maynard favored me with another ludicrously exaggerated wink and trundled off toward the pantry, I assumed to conduct yet another raid upon the Phlegm Club's liquor supply.

I determined to probe the extent of Muggsbottom's knowledge of this affair at my earliest opportunity. I spent the next evening marking papers, so two days had passed before I returned to the Phlegm Club. Once again, Reggie was elsewhere. Sir Monty was soon snoring noisily and, eventually, the gin and limes had overwhelmed Smythe-Gardner's sturdy constitution. I pulled my chair up alongside Muggsbottom's, determined to take advantage of this opportunity for discreet conversation. I had rehearsed my conversational gambit well and was confident that I had my lines by heart. Like Reggie, I had been absent from the Phlegm Club on New Year's Eve. I had attended a rare party. Every couple of years, my chairman would host a party for the members of the department and their spouses, mistakenly believing he was fostering togetherness and esprit de corps. He had most recently hosted such a party on New Year's Eve. Ours was a small and stable faculty—we had long been aware of and had grudgingly come to terms with each other's foibles and irritating mannerisms. Forced social contact was more likely to crack our fragile communal tolerance than to enhance it.

"How was your New Year's Eve, Muggsbottom?" I inquired blandly. "Mine was pretty ghastly. The high point of the evening—or the nadir, depending on one's point of view—came when we played 'Great Books I've Never Read.' The game is a sort of secular confession for English professors. I won with *The Consolation of Philosophy* by Boethius."

"We played charades," replied Muggsbottom. "Smythe-Gardner flew into a terrible temper when we couldn't guess that his man shaving was Prince Albert. Pretty damned oblique, wouldn't you say? But Biffy is so competitive that his judgment is easily clouded."

Here was precisely the sort of opening I had hoped for, and I was quite pleased with myself as I said, "Reggie should be awfully good at charades, what with his theatrical background."

"I'm not sure one can term the television 'theatrical.' Besides, Reggie wasn't here that night."

"Ah."

Muggsbottom gave me one of his piercing looks.

"My dear boy, you Americans are not by nature subtle creatures. And whenever you attempt to be so, you are thoroughly transparent. Are you asking me where Reggie was that night?"

"I think I know where he was that night."

"As do I, my dear fellow. Oh, I don't mean that I know his precise physical location on that evening, but I know he was somewhere with that woman."

"Then you know about her?"

"Of course. It's that awful Amazon who pounds the organ for one of the Nonconformist congregations. I've told you that I was once a ladies' man myself. I know all the signs of an *affaire de coeur* . . . Besides, I have an informant."

"I warned Maynard. I told him that whatever is going on between Reggie and Cecilia Luce is damned well none of his business. But I should have known . . . "

"Oh, it wasn't Maynard, my dear fellow. However,

since I didn't think Maynard could keep his tongue from wagging for two minutes consecutively, I am pleasantly surprised to learn otherwise. My informant was Homer Joe Tennyson."

"Homer Joe . . . ?" I was astounded.

"Ah, now *you* are surprised. But my newly forged alliance with Homer Joe Tennyson is not so strange. The horrid Twinksly Murk has brought us together. After all, my enemy's enemy is my friend, you know."

"But how does Homer Joe know about Reggie and Cecilia? I thought he lived in splendid isolation out there on the river bank."

"True, he leads an isolated existence, even by Arcadian standards. However, he visits the offices of the *Arcady Harbinger* every Thursday morning, alas, to deliver by hand his 'Verses from the Vale.' And on many a morning Homer Joe visits with his fellow bucolics at Granny's. I have taken to joining them there." Muggsbottom made this announcement with undisguised pride. "They listen with horrified fascination to my tales of the welfare state. I rather think they believe that God has sent me to put them on their guard."

I resisted the very strong temptation to probe Muggsbottom's performances among the farmers at Granny's, pursuing instead our original topic.

"I see. So you talked with Homer Joe at Granny's. But where did *he* learn about Reggie and Cecilia?"

"Why, at the *Harbinger*, dear boy. From that Ol' Perfesser person."

"Of course. Cecilia has sort of been his girlfriend for the last two years, as much as she's willing to be any man's girlfriend."

"Yes. According to Homer Joe, he's behaving like an aggrieved husband. I believe he has even threatened to do Reggie bodily harm. Imagine, poor gentle Reggie. Why, such a confrontation might well leave him totally devastated. Naturally, I dare not share this intelligence with Smythe-Gardner. He would first harangue poor Reggie for keeping secrets, then set sail immediately for the *Harbinger* office to start a frightful row."

"What do you suppose Cecilia sees in Reggie? She's what we Americans call a 'hot number.' I can't picture them in bed together."

"You hit the nail upon the head, my friend. I would be the very last person to denigrate our Reggie's manhood, but from what I have heard of this woman, they are supremely unsuited to each other." He was pensive for a moment before adding, "Most men and women are, of course."

"Then?"

"Money, old fellow. It has to be money. The natural acquisitiveness of the female species. They can smell riches at a great distance, I believe. Despite the most tremendous efforts of Her Majesty's government, the Dipswizzles of Hertfordshire have managed to retain much of their wealth. How, I do not know. Perhaps they have secreted it in Switzerland or buried it in strongboxes about the estate. At any rate, Reggie is the only Dipswizzle heir, and this woman has somehow learnt of his prospects."

"What will you do? *Should* you do anything?"

"Precisely the issue, old man. Reggie's a booby, but he is a freeborn Englishman. Puts me in a bit of a quandary at present. On the one hand, I can't allow this adventuress to ruin Reggie and, on the other hand, I can't go charging into a chap's private life like the Light Brigade. Bad form *and* bad strategy. I must mull the matter over a bit longer. I have no doubt that my ratiocination will eventually lead to the appropriate underhanded scheme . . . But let us turn our attention for the moment to yet another distressing matter."

He tossed that evening's *Harbinger* into my lap.

"Look at page two, under 'Campus Goings-On.'"

I knew exactly which 'Campus Goings-On' had distressed Muggsbottom. I had already seen page two and the announcement of Twinksly Murk's first public lecture at State College. The poet of "Greek love" had been exceedingly prompt, arriving at State right along with the new year. On the first day of registration, he was already building his nest in the office that had been placed at his disposal. I had spent no time with him, but we had been introduced. He was a short, pink, baby-faced man of indeterminate age. His very dark hair was thinning and graying, and he was always nervously patting it and maneuvering it about his skull, in the manner of women drivers stopped at traffic lights. He suffered from a tic whereby he would, every minute or so, cock his head ludicrously on his left shoulder for no apparent reason. He seemed inoffensive enough—scarcely the raging satyr of Homer Joe's experience. I had sampled *Water Skiing in Erebus*, the little book that had first called Murk back to Muggsbottom's mind. I found it routinely opaque, pretentious, and ugly—that is, what we academics call "postmodernist." It struck no sparks of indignation in my expedient being since, many years earlier, I had adopted in front of my colleagues and students the craven pretense that I liked that sort of stuff.

"We shall attend Murk's lecture, of course."

"What do you mean, 'of course'?" I liked neither the look in Muggsbottom's eye nor the tone of his voice. "You don't mean to disrupt a public lecture?"

"My dear fellow, have you ever known me to be a disruptive influence?" In accompaniment of this rhetorical question, a look of keen disappointment—in my judgment, I supposed—flickered momentarily in his rheumy eyes. "Read here." He did not, however, wait for my response to his injunction. He moved a forefinger through the last paragraph of the story and read aloud to me, as if I were a loved, but tiresome, idiot child. "'Local poets are encouraged to bring their own compositions to the lecture. As time permits, Professor Murk will critique work submitted by members of the audience.' Am I not a 'local poet'? Do you not recall my 'Ode to Arcady'?"

"Muggsbottom, you want to cause trouble."

"Trouble?" He affected incredulity. "My dear boy, I fly from trouble like Hermes of the winged feet. Now, Smythe-Gardner," gesturing toward his heavily sedated friend, "is quite another matter. I shall under no circumstances allow Biffy to accompany me to Murk's lecture."

11. Reggie and Cecilia

I am by nature shy and reticent. To this point in the narrative, I have found it easy enough to stand in the wings and report what took place on stage. I have remained essentially in the background for two reasons. First, as stated above, I am temperamentally disinclined to intrude myself into the scenes I have described. And second, this tendency to stand apart, to observe, and to record has resulted in my doing little that would have warranted such intrusions. In this chapter, however, I must step directly into the middle of my account. It is very painful for me because, in doing so, I reveal myself as the sort of person I most despise—an interloper, an eavesdropper, a voyeur. But this part of the story must be told, and it is precisely my dishonorable behavior that allows me to tell it.

The very evening after Muggsbottom and I had discussed Reggie's amour, I drove over to Hot Springs for dinner. The parents of one of my students from the autumn term operated the Lakeside Inn. Located on a scenic knoll overlooking Lake Hamilton, the Lakeside Inn was known as perhaps the finest restaurant in the city and had the prices to prove it. But on that particular evening, money was no object—or, to put it more correctly, fifty dollars or less was no object. The owners' son was one of the campus literati, a contributor of callow but promising poems to the literary magazine. He had taken a shine to me, as some students do to some professors, seeing me as brighter, better read, and more cultivated than I in fact am. At the end of the course, he had prevailed upon his parents to present me with a fifty dollar gift certificate. Since he was easily the best student in the class, there was absolutely no question of bribery. I had accepted the certificate with alacrity.

The Lakeside Inn occupied the former residence of a Prohibition era mobster who had wintered in Hot Springs, so the stories went. The restaurant had accommodated itself to the original structure of the house so that the rooms were still readily recognizable—the parlor, the library, the dining room, and so on. The maître d' showed me to a small table in the corner of a long, narrow space that must have been a sun porch. I faced a half dozen tables ranged along this space, only one other of which was occupied at the time I was seated. I could also pretty well see everything in the next room through the wide opening between, but a tall, bushy potted plant just across from me effectively blocked my view of the two tables closest to my own. I ordered a carafe of the house's red wine—wine lists break me out in a cold sweat—and finally chose a meal of onion soup, prime rib, and blackberry trifle.

I had just begun the entree when Reggie Dipswizzle and Cecilia Luce followed the maître d' through the adjoining room, out onto the porch, and to the table just beyond the potted plant. The most natural thing in the world would have been for me to rise and greet them with, "Hey there, Arcadians," or some such light remark. But they did not notice me behind my floral camouflage. Having learned of their romance only the night before, I was stunned by this Dickensian coincidence and could neither move nor say a word. Every minute that passed before I made myself known to them would make the situation more awkward when I finally did. Then, with horror, I discovered that I could hear their every word through the plant as if I were sitting at the table with them. The maître d' went away. A waiter came, took their order, and went away. Still I said nothing. Then, with even greater horror, I discovered that I had put my silverware down gently beside my plate and had even stopped chewing—I intended to do nothing that would send a stray sound wave from my side of the herb to theirs. In short, I was spying on them.

They were obviously continuing a conversation they had begun before arriving at the restaurant, for Cecilia said, "Well, *I* think Milton's accent has improved tenfold since you started working with him. You're far too self-critical, Reggie. Really you are."

"But he still hasn't read a single line in which he got the vowels right all the way through. And when he doesn't sound like an American southerner, he sounds like a parody of the Queen."

"Oh, my silly darling, our audiences will *expect* these people to sound like the Queen. You're doing a marvelous job, believe me."

"You're awfully kind, 'Cile, but I thought I could bring a certain authenticity to . . . "

"You have, my dear. Old Milton will pass muster, I assure you."

Of course, the Arcady Community Players. Those posters around town plugging the three upcoming performances of Noel Coward's *Private Lives*. Cecilia would be playing the female lead, or directing, or both . . . and Reggie, the old trouper, must have offered his services as diction coach or something of the sort. I had not been able to imagine under what circumstances a man like Reggie could meet and form a bond of intimacy with a woman like Cecilia. Here was my answer—the theater.

The lovers fell silent for a moment, and I imagined that Cecilia was leaning across the table to reinforce her encouraging words with a kiss. Mind you, during this little break in the conversation they could have been doing anything behind the leaves, but I was already embellishing the unseen scene in my mind.

When Cecilia spoke again, she said, "Reggie, have you ever made love beside a lake?"

After a short pause, Reggie said, "No. No, I don't believe I have. I think I should have recalled."

"Perhaps tonight."

"Perhaps." But I could hear a dubious note in Reggie's voice. "In the grass, do you mean?"

"Of course," Cecilia said with a snicker. "That's part of the fun."

"I shouldn't wonder . . . But your grass has so many unpleasant little creatures in it. I suppose one *could* become acclimated . . . eventually."

"And I thought you were a romantic, Reggie."

Her chiding words had no bite to them.

"You know I would do anything to please you, darling, but I'm so susceptible to rash."

She laughed.

"Next time, I'll remember to bring a blanket along."

"Oh, that would be very helpful . . . Is it quite common in America?"

"What's that, precious?"

"Making love beside lakes and things?"

"Oh, no. It's quite uncommon. That's why I like to do it."

"I see."

"The uncommon adds spice to an experience."

"Yes. It would, wouldn't it? Would you like to be tied up, then?"

"*Reggie.* What *have* you been doing?"

"The young women in Biffy's magazines are sometimes tied up. And I knew a television actress in London—not in the Biblical sense, of course—who was rumored to enjoy having her wrists and ankles bound with the bedclothes."

"What a delicious idea. Oh, Reggie, you *must* bind my wrists and ankles with the bedclothes this very night."

I was totally abashed by my performance as eavesdropper. At the same time, I found myself resenting the noise that issued from nearby tables. These were being rapidly filled with other diners, and the murmur of their conversations, the clink and clatter of their tableware were forcing me to strain a little to catch every word of the titillating exchange occurring beyond the plant. Besides being appalled at my behavior, I was physically trapped. It would be all but impossible to stand and walk past the lovers' table without being recognized. And if I were recognized, would they not suspect that I had overheard their conversation? I was like some sleazy private detective working a divorce case from the bushes. I had no choice but to remain in the bushes until the objects of my surveillance departed.

"You know, Reggie, you aren't like any man I've ever met."

"Oh, there are a lot of chaps like me. There certainly were at casting calls."

"No, I'm serious. Nothing about you is feigned or calculated. You're a true innocent, Reggie. Funny, I never thought innocence would appeal to me."

"Wouldn't Mama and Papa laugh to hear me described in that way. They always seemed to feel I was nothing but trouble."

"Innocent people often have more trouble than the wicked. They attract trouble. They all need someone to watch over them."

"You may be right. I sometimes think I lean on Muggsbottom too much."

"*You* lean too much on *him*? Reggie, he's been exploiting you for years, he and those other two parasites."

"Please, 'Cile, let's not quarrel about that tonight. I'm sure that if you knew them as I do, your opinion would be quite different."

"Oh, Reggie, how you exasperate me. You're so damned loyal. And that's appealing too . . . Pour me another glass of wine, will you? It makes me feel passionate."

"Isn't that curious? It makes me sleepy and gives me heartburn."

At that moment, the waiter came to inquire if I was ready for my dessert. Though Reggie and Cecilia still could not see me, they were aware for the first time of someone sitting behind them. From that point on, they lowered their voices so much that I could only pick up an occasional word or phrase, never enough to string together any meaning. I finished my trifle. To be more precise, I ate a bite or two and pushed the rest around my plate for a while. I had pretty much lost interest in my meal some time before. I was in an agony of suspense as I waited for them to go. I began to sweat in anticipation of the moment when one of them, for some unaccountable reason, would suddenly stand bolt upright and look down into my glazed eyes from above the potted plant. In near panic, I thought, "What if the maître d' should need this table? No, get hold of yourself. Tables are still open. You can see them." Diners who had arrived after I was served were paying their bill and leaving. I began to wish irrationally that the owners' son had taken that class with another professor.

Finally, after what seemed like hours, I heard the sound of their chairs being pushed back from the table. My plan was crude, but it was the only plan I had, so I put it into effect. I swept my fork off onto the floor, and I plunged beneath the tablecloth right behind it. I could hear their voices—I thought they were moving away. I grubbed around underneath the table like an idiot.

"I'll take care of that, sir."

I came out into the world, knowing that everyone within sight was staring at me. But Cecilia and Reggie were gone.

I placed my gift certificate on the little salver proffered by the young man. Flushed and shaken, I began to pull bills from my wallet. He stayed me with an upraised hand.

"This will be very satisfactory, sir."

"Oh? . . . Well . . . The meal was delicious."

"I'm glad you enjoyed it, sir."

In the foyer, an attractive female attendant brought my topcoat and made as if to open the outer door for me. I pressed a bill into her hand and waved her away, not rudely I hope. I gingerly cracked the door by about a foot, just in time to catch sight of the lovers pulling away in the Oldsmobile I had seen Cecilia drive so often through the streets of Arcady.

It took the very efficient parking attendant less than two minutes to fetch my car. What went on in my mind during those one hundred or so seconds is a testament both to the resiliency of the human spirit and to the essential baseness of human nature. A few minutes before, I had wished only to get out of that corner undiscovered so that I could head for home with my dignity, if not my honor, intact. Well, I had escaped undiscovered and now, having done so, I had lost all desire to return to Arcady. I suspected that Cecilia and Reggie were not returning to Arcady, and I was seized by the desire to know where they *were* going. They were less than two minutes ahead of me. Perhaps I could catch them.

The Lakeside Inn is located on the outskirts of the city. When I reached the highway, I turned right and headed for the downtown, driving ten to fifteen miles an hour faster than was my custom. I sped along, passing cars in both the inside and outside lanes. A couple of times I thought I saw them, only to realize as I drew closer that I was mistaken. The highway turned into Central Avenue, traffic grew heavier, and I was forced down to the speed limit by leisurely motorists who blocked both lanes ahead of me. Of course, upon leaving the Lakeside Inn, Cecilia could have turned south and headed for Arcady, in which case I was continuing to play the fool as I had at the restaurant. But, for some reason, I felt sure that she had not. Still, my confidence had begun to ebb away by the time I saw the blue

Oldsmobile stopped for a red light at the next intersection.

When I stopped also, they were two cars ahead of me. I had the lovers in my sights, with no intention of losing them. Cecilia eventually turned east on Grand Avenue. I stayed four to five car lengths behind and felt a growing excitement I had seldom derived from licit activities. Cecilia drove almost to the northeastern city limits before pulling into the Cytherea Motel, whose marquee boasted, "CABLE MOVIES IN EVERY ROOM—FULL RANGE OF SELECTIONS." I swung into the empty parking lot of Billy Bob and Bubba's Bang-Up Bar-B-Cue, situated just to the west of the Cytherea, and parked so that I could see the motel office. Apparently the public had spurned the bang-up barbecue, because the building was dark and a "For Sale or Lease" sign was displayed in the window. Cecilia had parked by the door to the office, and she entered while Reggie remained in the car. Five minutes later, she came out, and they pulled away out of my line of sight.

"What now?" I asked myself in disgust. "Will you search out the blue Oldsmobile again. Will you slip up to their unit and look for an uncurtained window so you can watch them watching dirty movies?"

I do not believe I would have done those things, but I was not put to the test because, at that moment, a car with a light on top turned into the lot and stopped immediately behind me. In my rear-view mirror, I saw a large uniformed figure step out of the car and approach my window. The face that appeared there was big and black and slightly familiar.

"Are you having any trouble, sir?"

"Why, no. I . . . Is this the Malvern highway?"

"No, sir. You passed the Malvern highway a way back there."

"Ah, well. I was thinking something doesn't seem right."

A very poor choice of words.

"So you don't come to Hot Springs that often then, Professor?"

"No. That is, I do. To the mall and that sort of thing. But I don't often get to this part of town . . . Are you Mr. Barnes, by chance?"

"That's right, Professor. Junious Barnes. You have a good memory. I was in your Freshman English One class about eight years ago. Made a D."

Uh oh.

"I'm sorry, Mr . . . Officer Barnes."

"Aw, that's all right, Professor. I wasn't no scholar no way. I never did read *Wuthering Heights*. Not even the first chapter."

"Many don't, I believe."

"I like being a police officer."

My recollection was that Junious Barnes had been one of State College's star offensive linemen until he severely injured some critical joint.

"What I like best," he continued, "is keeping people out of trouble in the first place. You know, keeping them from doing the things that will get them in trouble, instead of having to arrest them after they mess up."

As he said this, he cocked his huge head at me in an exaggerated manner. I supposed policemen learn they cannot be overly subtle.

"You wouldn't know this, Professor, since you don't come to this part of town. But prostitutes work this area right along here. Now, if they see a man sitting alone in his car in the middle of an empty parking lot, they might think he's looking for some action and solicit him. That's the way whores think, you see, 'cause some men do just that. We sure don't want a respectable citizen to be embarrassed by such a thing, especially one of our out-of-town visitors."

"Thank you very much, Officer Barnes. I always say, the policeman is our friend." By God, I wasn't going to be overly subtle either. "So I need to go back that way, do I?"

"Four or five miles. There's a big sign."

"I don't understand how I could have missed it. Probably distracted. Absent-minded professors, you know. Well, good to see you again, Officer Barnes."

"Good to see *you*, Professor."

As I drove back to Arcady in a deep funk, I thought, "Lord, I would sink even lower in his esteem if he knew what I was really doing there."

I never spoke of this to Muggsbottom or Smythe-Gardner or Sir Monty or anyone else. The reader is the first person with whom I have shared the mingled excitement and humiliation of that evening. It is said that confession is good for the soul. I hope so.

12. Ars Poetica

Like an appointment with the dentist, the evening of Murk's lecture had inevitably come despite all efforts to put it out of my mind. Muggsbottom and I sat down at the back of the room two seats away from Cecilia Luce and Reggie Dipswizzle. When Reggie saw us, he cast a nervous smile in our direction, but Cecilia stared straight ahead. Could she have seen me either at the Lakeside Inn or trailing her car through the streets of Hot Springs? No. This was my guilty conscience at work. Mrs. Luce had turned her cold shoulder to my companion, her lover's mentor, not to me.

I had tried to keep Muggsbottom from coming, but when I could not dissuade him I found that I could not stay away myself. Neither could I now abandon my friend and join my colleagues down front. So I sat beside Muggsbottom and hoped for the best while fearing the worst. My eye wandered back to Cecilia and Reggie, to whom I was very tempted to speak. Not to do so seemed unnatural, awkward. But Cecilia's demeanor discouraged—more precisely, forbade—conversation. Her posture was rigid, and she stared hard at the lectern, as if Murk were already standing there. Only her shallow, audible breathing and a barely perceptible quiver at one corner of her mouth showed her to be alive.

There were perhaps fifty people gathered in the tiered

lecture hall. The room could accommodate twice that number and had done so for several of the programs in State College's public service series. For example, the wine tasting classes and the short course in filling out income tax returns had virtually filled the house. Poetry was apparently not the same sort of draw. But the fifty members of the audience were spread down and across the fifteen rows of seats in such a pattern as to keep attendance from seeming too embarrassingly scant.

The assemblage, however, was neatly divided into two groups, as by an invisible rope stretched across the middle of the room. Scattered over the last several rows were: two dozen or so middle-aged to elderly women, who might as well have been wearing *Les Femmes Poétiques* T-shirts; a short, corpulent fellow with a full beard, about whom something looked very familiar; Cecilia and Reggie; and Muggsbottom and me. The front rows had been taken by the faculty and by a group of young people I recognized as students in the creative writing course. None of these students seemed older than the early twenties, and they were all male save one. She was a willowy young woman with long brown hair and a glittering eye. Her slender fingers writhed along her arm rests like a nest of snakes. She was the stereotype of the tormented young poetess, and I felt certain that her head was destined for the oven.

As we awaited the arrival of the distinguished visiting poet, the crowd from town hugged their Manila envelopes to their breasts and, whenever their eyes met, flashed each other nervous, sensitive little smiles. The entire membership of *Les Femmes Poétiques*, Arcady chapter, had obviously turned out for the Murk lecture. The chapter was exclusively female, as its venerable appellation proclaimed, and, for some reason, each lady seemed to require three names of her own. I could not remember if Cecilia was a member of *Les Femmes*—she continued to feign catatonia. I had heard from her own lips that she disapproved of Muggsbottom every bit as much as he disapproved of her. She thought him a leech, a parasite affixed to her beloved. The first moment she had seen him that evening, she must have determined to snub him.

The creative writing students laughed and smoked and generally asserted their status as insiders. Murk had already spoken in their class. A few evenings earlier, the department chairman had hosted a reception for Murk in his home. No doubt, all these aspiring young poets had attended. I was teaching a class that night, which met at the same hour. Thus I was able to establish an impeccable excuse for missing the reception.

We did not have to wait long. At only a couple of minutes past the announced starting time of seven-thirty, the chairman ushered the visiting poet into the room. At the same moment these worthies were entering from the adjoining room, the door at the back of the hall swung noisily open. A short, stout man in a baggy overcoat was standing there, examining the scene through thick spectacles. He pulled off his cloth cap and jammed it into the pocket of his overcoat, thus revealing a head of graying, spiky hair. From the other pocket, he withdrew a soiled and rumpled handkerchief and loudly blew his nose into it. The nose was red and veinous, not always—as on this occasion—from a cold. I knew that nose and the swarthy face behind it.

I put my mouth close to the ear of Muggsbottom, who had also turned to look at the late arrival.

"The Ol' Perfesser," I whispered.

"Ah," he responded ambiguously.

The Ol' Perfesser seated himself at the opposite end of our row—this noisily also—and glared at Cecilia and Reggie. I was dreadfully uncomfortable, but Muggsbottom appeared sanguine.

"Ladies and gentlemen." The chairman spoke as he ascended the steps, passing sheets of paper along each row as he came. "Before Professor Murk speaks and before he looks at the poems you've brought, let's spend a few minutes on this one."

The chairman's voice was trembling with excitement, and it was clear whose poem he held in his hands.

Murk stationed himself primly behind the lectern and gazed pacifically up at his audience.

"This," said the chairman, "is an original, unpublished lyric poem by Twinksly Murk. Professor Murk finished the poem only yesterday. Apart from the author, we are the first people in the world to read this poem."

There was something positively Gregorian in the chairman's intonation of this last sentence. For a few seconds, our contingent—the townspeople seated toward the rear of the lecture hall—bobbed and babbled over their duplicated sheets. The creative writing students up front nodded solemnly, knowingly, clearly implying that this was not the first unpublished masterpiece *they* had ever seen. Then the chairman gave his brief formal introduction of Twinksly Murk, and silence fell like an ax.

"Professor Murk has indicated," he said, "that he will begin by reading the poem I have just given you."

The chairman sat down. Murk opened his folder and commenced meticulously to arrange his papers. The silence was sepulchral, portentous. Having quickly read through the sacred text, we raised our eyes as one to the altar whereon Murk's transubstantiation was taking place. The diminutive figure, its balding head cocked on one side like a quizzical bird's, was gone. In its place stood a god of literature, trailing clouds of glory toward the blackboard.

When Murk finally began to read, our eyes fell again to the text of his untitled poem, and we followed along.

When last that lusty lissome lad
Lay leis of luxuriant lilacs

In languid layers, luminescent,
My heart let loose a lilting lay.
But, alas!
List, loved reader, hear my loss.
So little left
Of that pellucid light—
The lovelorn lament of the lonely loon,
Lying in his loamy lair . . .

Murk went alliteratively along in this wise for another twenty-five lines. As he concluded, silence again descended upon the lecture hall—a silence finally broken by the soft sound of familiar laughter.

"Jolly good," said Reggie to Cecilia in an artless stage whisper. "Jolly good."

Poor booby. His laughter was a sincere tribute to the reading. He innocently assumed that a performance so patently silly was intended to be so. Cecilia's expression of rigid self-control gave way to one of embarrassment. Reggie's puerile reaction to the great man's work clearly violated her sense of propriety. But, just as clearly, it mirrored her own first reaction to the poem, thereby throwing her into confusion. To add to her discomfiture, she appeared at that very moment to notice for the first time the glowering figure of the Ol' Perfesser. She shushed Reggie to show that his philistine behavior deserved no response—before tentatively endeavoring to respond.

"It's a lyric."

Reggie seemed to find this explanation singularly unsatisfying—as, quite frankly, did I.

"But . . ."

"*Please.*"

Cecilia's eyes clicked wildly about her. She might haughtily ignore the disapproving looks elicited by her flamboyant private life, but she would *not* be thought deficient in culture. Reggie, her middle-aged ingénu, was apt to say something perfectly dreadful, and she did not wish her artistic sensibilities to be equated with his. But before he could open his mouth again, another critic spoke up.

"It's tremendously moving, isn't it?"

These words were spoken, to no one in particular, by a little lady with blue hair, sitting three rows in front of us.

"It's a real cultural experience," responded another little lady from beneath her hennaed beehive.

The female creative writer with the suicidal eyes, her long fingers crawling through her hair and around her mouth, spoke next, revealing an unexpected and rather charming impediment.

"Alliterathion can thometimeth reenforth paradocth jutht ath well ath it can produth rethonanth."

The poet smiled and nodded. He seemed infinitely pleased with all the world. I reread the first several lines and found a *But*. Could that indicate paradox?

"We would so enjoy your sharing with us something of the creative process that produced the poem, Professor Murk."

This from Cecilia in a voice trembling ever so slightly. Her situation was not ideal—her current lover had publicly shown himself to be all at sea as a critic of serious poetry, while her former lover was staring daggers at her—but she had a reputation as one of Arcady's *artistes*, and she was reasserting it now.

"Unfortunately, madam," Murk replied, "only a distorted memory can reconstruct the creative process."

Murk's response was perfectly civil in tone, but it was plain that Cecilia felt she had been brushed off and was resentful.

Now the lisping creative writer spoke again (her attractiveness, once one got past her crazed expression and dirty hair, was really quite indisputable).

"Lineth theven and eight I find ethpethially effective. They thpeak to me ath a woman."

"What *can* that young person mean?" Muggsbottom whispered.

"Yes, my dear," said Murk. "That is precisely the effect I was seeking. In poetry the nuance is everything, isn't it? You read very perceptively."

"I just love the form of the poem, Professor Murk." It was the blue-haired lady again. "What form, exactly, would you say it is?"

"It ain't no haiku, lady," snapped one of the undergraduate writers.

"Form is meaning," growled another.

"Now, now," said Professor Murk, gently chastising the lads—neither of whom looked very lissome—with his mild blue eyes, "the good questions are always the basic questions." To the lady. "You will note, of course, that although my lines are largely iambic and anapestic they vary considerably in length. This is to avoid the deadly metronomic effect of sustained iambic pentameter."

"Like Pope's," muttered Muggsbottom, with heavy irony.

"And I have sought to synthesize these rising meters with the Anglo-Saxon line which, as I hope you all know, is accentual and alliterative rather than metrical."

"Why couldn't the son of a bitch have said that when *I* asked him a question?" Cecilia inquired *sotto voce*. Still, the comment was audible to people sitting several rows away.

At this moment, general discussion broke out.

From the front of the room:

"You notice, of course, that the run-on lines carry the poem's narrative element, just as one would expect."

"Depends on whether you always read a comma as an end stop."

"What?"

"I said, what if you don't always read a comma as an end stop?"

"For God's sake, who *doesn't* always read a comma as an end stop?"

"Lots of people. *I* don't always."

"Well, *you* . . ."

"I think you're both mithing the ethential unifying printhiple."

"Ah," said Murk contentedly, swinging his arm, the palm of his hand upraised, in a languid, expansive gesture. "I write for readers like you."

And from the back:

". . . a real cultural experience."

"Would you call it free verse, or what?"

"It does put you in a mood, doesn't it? I mean, sort of."

"I suppose he *gives* autographs."

"We will get to keep these, won't we?" inquired the lady with the henna rinse, clutching her copy of the poem as if in fear that someone might snatch it from her hands.

The bearded man folded his copy carefully and slipped it into an inside pocket of his jacket. Something about the way he used his hands, something about the way he moved his stout little body, was tantalizingly familiar to me. Where had I met this fellow before? Perhaps if he would speak, I would recognize the voice.

Muggsbottom reexamined the poem and whispered, "I feel certain Twinksly has already found a 'lissome lad' or two this side the Atlantic."

The chairman stood and said, "This discussion has proved very stimulating, but perhaps Professor Murk should continue with his . . ."

But *Les Femmes Poétiques* were just warming to the occasion. One of them, who was seated immediately behind the invisible partition, stood and said, "My name is Nelda Niblick, and I teach eighth grade English at Arcady Junior High School. Professor Murk, I would like to ask you how important you consider your teaching to be, that is, in comparison to your writing?"

"Ah, well, everything is one thing, really—if you understand what I mean. Writing, teaching, eating, drinking, singing, dancing . . . loving too. Everything is art and art is everything. Of course, as a teacher I can encourage young talent."

Murk smiled at an undergraduate litterateur poised intensely on the edge of his front row seat.

I ran the following gloss on the poet's response: "I don't especially give a damn for teaching, really, except that I meet so many boys this way."

Millicent Mortimer—the name, as I eventually learned, of the young woman with the faulty sibilants—was wrinkling her nose at the speaker. There are women, I have also learned, who believe that men like Murk have never succumbed to female charms only because they have not yet encountered *their* female charms. Millicent had clearly misinterpreted the poet's generous remarks to her.

Muggsbottom nudged me and said, "That young woman's certainly barking up an empty tree," as though he had just read my mind.

Suddenly, another *Femme Poétique* stood and said, "Sir, this poem reminds me very much of your early piece 'Lycidas at Leeds.' May we assume that it is to some extent autobiographical?"

"A perfectly understandable deduction," replied Murk, "but my work really should not be interpreted so literally. In the piece to which you refer, my interest was not so much in memorializing some Edward King of my own, as in returning to the long neglected pastoral elegy and exploiting whatever potentialities might still inhere. That is to say . . . "

As Murk's response soared into the stratosphere, my mind wandered elsewhere.

Reggie and Cecilia appeared to be arguing. That is,

Cecilia, wearing a very cross expression, was whispering nonstop into Reggie's slightly retreating ear, while he endured the murmured diatribe in silence. The Ol' Perfesser was attempting to glower at Reggie and Cecilia while at the same time blowing his nose incessantly. Neither effort was entirely successful since, really, each required his single-minded attention.

Murk completed his answer to the question none of us could remember.

"Professor Murk," said the blue-haired lady, "wouldn't you agree that women are simply more sensitive observers than men?"

"Well, I don't think we could state categorically . . . "

"For example, our last three state laureates have been women: Fannie Mae Dorsel, Lilly Pearl Prendergast, and Dinah Lee Drinkwater—all wonderful nature poets. Have you read Dinah Lea's 'Ode to the Yam'?"

"I don't believe I have."

"I think it's the best nature poem since 'Trees.'"

"Really? I must certainly try to read it then."

The undergraduates were laughing up their sleeves. Indeed, some were not even making this minimal effort to disguise their amusement.

The questioner pressed on. "When our Poets' Roundtable became ninety per cent ladies, we were forced to change the name to *Les Femmes Poétiques*. I don't mean to suggest anything invidious but, after all, you can't just ignore statistics like that, can you?"

Les Femmes Poétiques, though docile and awestruck in the beginning, were resilient ladies. They had apparently recovered their sangfroid, and this development had not gone unnoticed by Muggsbottom.

He leaned over and whispered, "These formidable females will not willingly surrender the bays to Twinksly, Homer Joe, or any other competitor."

The intense undergraduate at whom Murk had been smiling had heard quite enough from *Les Femmes*. He stood and said, "Professor Murk, would you say that in this poem you have developed some nexus of human experiences, or is every line scissile in its relationship to the whole?" He turned to give the blue-haired lady a look which said, "Dinah Lea Drinkwater, indeed!"

The relief showed in Murk's face. His normally placid expression reasserted itself as he said, "Let me preface my answer to that question with this little anecdote: My dear friend and colleague Bernard Postlethwaite of Glasgow University is easily the most original thinker among Renaissance scholars. He has devoted his life to proving—and has marshaled quite persuasive evidence, I feel—that Shakespeare's dark lady was neither dark nor a lady . . . "

"Another dotty don," explained Muggsbottom. "Postlethwaite was never sound."

After his anecdote had progressed to its ambiguous conclusion, Murk opaquely effected the transition to a series of scissile observations that eventually wandered off in search of a nexus. But not before the desired results had been achieved—*Les Femmes* were uniformly glassy-eyed. For the moment, Murk and his young man had quite taken the wind out of their sails.

My friend's eyes, on the other hand, were burning brightly, and it became clear to me that he was about to do whatever it was he had come here tonight to do. I knew it was useless to attempt to dissuade him. Besides, I was experiencing a tiny perverse thrill of anticipation.

Muggsbottom rose and said, "Professor Murk?"

"Yes?" Murk smiled broadly, for even in the four short syllables of address he had recognized the speech of a countryman. When Reggie had whispered his artless assessment of Murk's performance, that bit of criticism had not reached the front of the hall. And obviously, no one had told Murk that four Englishmen had been living among us for many months. "Am I correct in inferring, sir, that you are a fellow Englishman?"

"You are. I am a political exile but, since that subject is far too painful to broach on a joyous evening such as this, let us continue with our discussion of divine Poesy."

"Of course," said Murk, smiling even more broadly. He assumed Muggsbottom was being playful, and he was perfectly willing to play. "And what is your question?"

"Are you going to evaluate *our* poetry tonight, Professor?"

"Yes indeed."

This exchange must have finally convinced the chairman that he had lost the handle. He leapt back to his feet and said, "Twinksly—that is, Professor Murk—has not really begun his lecture yet. And despite the very exciting original composition we have just been discussing, it is, after all, the lecture that we have come tonight to hear. I will hasten to add"—a nod and a slight bow toward Murk—"that Professor Murk *has* several times today expressed his eagerness to see the work our local poets are doing."

"It's nothing," said Murk, somewhat ambiguously.

"In that case," said Muggsbottom, "might we begin with mine, please? I realize I'm being a bit forward—alien presence, and all that—but I think my poem is an excellent follow-up to Professor Murk's . . . creation."

Muggsbottom's familiarity had bred contempt. Murk retained his smile, but his eyes widened noticeably. Following a slight pause, he gave a little affirmative nod to the chairman, whose voice positively dripped sarcasm as he said, "Well, in that case, I suppose we simply *must* hear it, mustn't we?" After staring a few daggers at me, he sat down.

"Thank you."

From his jacket pocket, Muggsbottom drew a loosely folded sheet of note paper and, with a slight flick of his wrist, snapped it open. He cleared his throat. Then, several times, he moved the paper rapidly toward his eyes, away from them, as if playing an invisible trombone. This old bit of music hall business had the chairman seething, but Murk merely stared and massaged his upturned nose.

"An untitled poem by C.P. Muggsbottom." Recognition momentarily flickered behind Murk's pale little eyes, but the fire did not catch hold. Muggsbottom cleared his throat once more, and began to read:

Ah, fluent Thames, you call to me
Across the years, across the sea.
Your song of alma mater tells
Of vaulted rooms 'neath lofty bells,
Of punting in straw hat and whites,
Of languid days and rowdy nights.
;Mongst aged stones, we ruddy youths
Pursued our pleasures more than truths.
Amidst those spires, upon the nonce,
I found myself in College Ponce,
A place where I had never been
And fraught with sights I had not seen.
I had been told of curious rites
That kept young boys at home of nights,
Of handkerchiefs of silk and lace,
Of paint and powder on the face,
Of lovely satin underdrawers
That kept Ponce scholars home from wars.
These things I had been told, but I
Felt moved, myself, to verify
That scholars so unnatural
Trod Ponce's quad and Ponce's hall.

We could see that the flame of recognition was now kindling in Murk's doughy face, and his tic had become quite pronounced.

I chanced upon a little bard,
Declaiming shrilly in the yard.
He'd climbed a piece of statuary
(Some ancient Poncean equerry).
Oh, how he looked and what he said
Sowed thoughts of mischief in my head,
Till I forgot I was well bred.
I found a match, I took it out . . .

"*Muggsbottom*," Murk squealed, his memory now a conflagration. "I *knew* I knew that name. Charlie Muggsbottom—that's who you are."

Murk's consternation quite understandably propelled his audience into the same state.

"That man set fire to my trousers when we were at university." Murk addressed these words, in a clearly accusatory tone, to the chairman, as if the least he might have expected was that any person who had once tried to incinerate him should be barred from the lecture.

Reggie, his boyish nature much affected by the visualization of his friend's boyish prank, inquired in a loud voice, "I say, Muggsbottom, did you really? Top-hole!"

Reggie's exclamation appeared to embarrass Cecilia even more than had his first faux pas. The poor woman was terribly agitated. She had been humiliated by her escort and snubbed by the speaker. Where was she to turn? Scarcely had I posed this unvoiced question when Cecilia answered it. She rose abruptly and hurried to where the Ol' Perfesser sat glowering at all of us.

"Will you take me home?" she said.

The Ol' Perfesser's sour expression was instantly replaced by one of amazement, which was followed, in turn, by one of delight.

"Sure. This bunch . . . " He caught himself. He was an extremely bitter but not a stupid man. "Sure," he reiterated.

The former lovers marched out of the lecture hall, noses aloft.

Reggie, who had stood when Cecilia did, now slumped back into his seat, a dazed and despondent man. If even the most sophisticated boulevardiers could never truly understand women, what hope had poor Reggie?

At this point, despite the chairman's valiant efforts, the lecture, as a formal occasion, ceased to exist. The audience left their seats and clustered around the disconcerted Murk. *Les Femmes Poétiques* had wholly cast off their diffidence and, in their efforts to reach the great man, were briskly trading elbows with the students of creative writing.

"I believe I'll just step out into the foyer," said Muggsbottom with great satisfaction. "I'll fill my pipe while you collect Reggie."

As I made my way to where Reggie remained slumped in his seat, the chairman caught and fixed my unwilling eye. I lip-read, "I'll see *you* in the morning." I turned away from my chairman's flushed countenance and came face to face with the bearded man. At close range, I clearly saw that the whiskers were false. I also saw that the face I had found vaguely familiar belonged to Billy Earl Hangar.

"What the hell are you up to?" I inquired with deep interest.

"My next sermon," he replied, patting the pocket into which he had slipped Murk's poem. Then he slithered past me and toward the exit.

While I was still contemplating Billy Earl's curious impersonation, a singular voice rose above the general hubbub. "He may thend thome of my work to hith publithyer," cooed Millicent Mortimer, just before wriggling her way into the press of flesh around the poet.

"Slut," observed one of her classmates.

I touched Reggie on the shoulder.

He looked up at me and said, "Why is she so angry with me?"

"Women are like that. They explode when we least expect it."

I assumed what I thought was a sapient expression, designed to indicate that great depths of understanding lay behind the truism I had just uttered.

"It's something to do with Muggsbottom," Reggie said, as much to himself as to me. "Cecilia can't abide Muggsbottom, but I don't know exactly *why*."

Somehow, women can always spot their mortal enemies. I recognized this as a fact reliable as most, but I did not know how to communicate it to Reggie.

"Come on, let's go."

As we left the hall, Twinksly Murk was receiving solace on every hand. I thought I could almost smell a smoldering pant leg.

The footpath from the classroom building to the parking lot disappeared for a time into a cluster of dark pines. The State College campus was nearly deserted at this hour. The moonless night suited each of our several moods. We straggled along, never quite three abreast. Each man was sunk deep in his own thoughts, just as one ought to be after an evening of poesy.

13. Consequences

My chairman scrupled at guilt by association only as practiced by the House Un-American Activities Committee. In his everyday professional conduct, it was a prime *modus operandi*. Twinksly Murk was sulking, still very upset, and I was made to know that I was in large part to blame. My offenses were manifold. I should have stopped Muggsbottom from attending the lecture. Having failed to stop him from attending, I should not have accompanied him. Having accompanied him, I should have stopped him from reciting his rude poem. Having been unable to stop him from reciting the poem, I should have openly denounced him. Having failed to openly denounce him, I should at least privately denounce him. Being also unwilling to privately denounce him, I should admit that my chief loyalties lay not with the department but elsewhere. I was tenured, and it was a damned good thing I was. After this incident, my relations with the chairman were never again cordial.

Muggsbottom was outrageously pleased with himself. He had set out to publicly discompose the fraudulent (in Muggsbottom's eyes) Twinksly Murk, and he had succeeded admirably. For a week, he had been going about with a feline smile on his lips and canary feathers adhering to the corners of his mouth.

Reggie moped about for three or four days, cursing himself for the breakup with Cecilia. Then it suddenly occurred to him that a reasonable person might not find *her* behavior wholly blameless. As is so often the case in an *affaire de coeur*, once the jilted lover could finally conceive of wrongdoing on the part of his beloved, his guilt seemed to diminish and hers to grow. After all, what had he done? He had acted the teeniest bit rowdy in front of her affected artist manqué friends—an aberration in itself and quite out of character. He, who was a real artist. He, who had feelingly portrayed before millions the agonies of psoriasis, gumboils, and hemorrhoids. And what had Cecilia done? She had gone off with the Ol' Perfesser—a man she had earlier characterized as crude and loutish, a man for whom she said she had never truly cared.

Ultimately, Reggie announced, "I shall not speak to her again." Muggsbottom was delighted.

Within a week's time, Cecilia wished to make amends (perhaps she had regretted her impulsive action within minutes). After all, Reggie continued as heir to whatever Dipswizzle fortune existed in Hertfordshire, just as he had been before embarrassing her. And the Ol' Perfesser continued to exhibit those traits which had dampened her ardor in the first place. His column immediately following the poetry lecture contretemps was a scattershot attack upon effete poets, fawning poetasters, air-headed academics, and presumptuous foreigners, written in his usual style—clever but heavy-handed. Cecilia must have realized that the Ol' Perfesser was as much a philistine as Reggie, and had greater visibility to boot.

According to Muggsbottom, Cecilia telephoned their neighbor on at least three occasions. Reggie held firm, though direly tempted, and would neither go next door to take her calls nor return them. My informant was Muggsbottom, of course, so I do not know what role he played in the termination of this relationship. He represented himself as a mere passive observer, but I had my doubts.

Reggie had salvaged his pride, but the little spark Cecilia had momentarily struck in his timorous soul had gone out. He was more vacant and melancholy than before.

Billy Earl Hangar was active on another front. He was using his undercover experience at Murk's lecture as the linchpin for a month-long series of sermons on secular humanism. These were much dramatized by his account of attending the humanist meeting in disguise. It furnished the enemy with a mystique that enhanced its menace nicely. And when he told of coloring his hair and donning his fake whiskers, he implied his likeness to a primitive Christian infiltrating a conclave of Nero's agents. Billy Earl's "Giant After-Christmas Revival" in Jeroboam Jernigan's field had proved lucrative enough for him to lease the old Royal Theater, closed since the mid-seventies. In naming his new enterprise, he had employed his other vocation as a motif. The result was: The Runway to Heaven Ministry. What is more, in his role as KARC's "Eye in the Sky," Billy Earl was able to plug the ministry liberally from the cockpit of his Christian biplane as he described Arcady's twenty minutes of rush-hour traffic each morning and afternoon. Shrewd businessman that he was, he thus allowed his employer to daily subsidize his self-employment. In the early weeks of its existence, The Runway to Heaven Ministry was thriving.

I confess that I was curious to see Billy Earl in action, but I could not bring myself to join his congregation at the Royal Theater. Call it snobbery, fastidiousness, what you will—to be seen entering the Royal among the fanatical and the unwashed would have shamed me too much. I feel uncomfortable in making this admission for it reminds me that our religious tastes may be more temperamental and aesthetic than spiritual, and I would like to believe otherwise.

At any rate, events so ordered themselves that I did not have to visit the Royal in order to see Billy Earl perform.

Maynard fell ill with influenza and for several days was confined to his bed in the pantry of the Phlegm Club. He was in remarkably good health for a man of his irregular habits, and the case was not a serious one. However, he was temporarily too weak to rise from his sickbed, and he sorely required medication to ease the paroxysms of coughing and sneezing which racked his wiry little frame. His employers were of little immediate use to him, utterly dependent as they were for their own mobility upon Eddie Nunn and his taxicab. So Muggsbottom had me put through a call to Maynard's cousin at the Caddo Hotel. I left the message and, after receiving it, Billy Earl responded with the alacrity of a true Christian. He picked up Maynard's medicine at the pharmacy and within twenty minutes was at his cousin's bedside.

I did not know of this prompt response, and I will admit to doubting Billy Earl's commitment to the indigent ill. I thought, rather self-righteously, "I guess I'd better go back on out to the Phlegm Club and run whatever errands are necessary. Billy Earl will be off somewhere that there's a dollar to be made." So it was that I pulled up to the Phlegm Club right behind the big red sedan that Billy Earl was renting from Calvin McCall, the local Buick dealer. In only two months' time, Billy Earl had very comfortably settled himself in Arcady. Miss Amanda, as yet having experienced no relapse from her most recent conversion, had ensconced the Christian airman in the Governor's Suite, so called because Governor Ben T. Laney had spent a night there in 1946. We understood that Calvin McCall had rededicated his life after hearing Billy Earl preach an especially powerful sermon on avarice and sharp business practices. I suspected that Billy Earl's lease arrangement on the big red sedan had been one sweet deal.

I followed Billy Earl into the Phlegm Club, where I soon saw the proof of his errand of mercy. The evangelist seemed to have a genuine affection for his reprobate cousin and never, to my knowledge, attempted to reform him, despite the poor advertisement Maynard was for Billy Earl's beneficent influence upon those nearest and dearest to him.

"Let's get the details on that business of the phony whiskers at the lecture," I suggested to Muggsbottom.

"By all means, dear boy," he replied. "By all means."

When Billy Earl emerged from the pantry, I took him by the arm and guided him toward a chair that faced those in which the Phlegm Club was arrayed.

"Tell us what you were up to at Murk's lecture, you rascal," I said.

Billy Earl seated himself with aplomb and crossed his legs in a relaxed manner. His golden coiffure gleamed even in the soft light of the Phlegm Club. Muggsbottom and I leaned forward eagerly in our chairs. The story could not help but be a curious one. Smythe-Gardner eyed the evangelist with a mixture of hostility and suspicion (the same way, truth to tell, that he eyed everybody). Billy Earl pretended not to notice. Sir Monty snored softly and rhythmically. Reggie buried his face deeper in the *Reader's Digest* he was pretending to read. The memories of that night were still too painful to be looked squarely in the face.

"Well?" I said.

"I've preached on this subject, gentlemen. If you would only visit the Tabernacle . . . "

"It's an old movie house, Billy Earl. And if you can't get your own cousin to attend your services, you shouldn't expect more of us."

Billy Earl did not take offense. He shrugged and smiled.

"Okay. I had learned all about this Professor Murk from certain sources."

Muggsbottom caught my eye. He inclined his head back toward the pantry and smiled.

"I had learned that he was a notorious sodomite, although this information was being withheld from the good God-fearing folk of Arcady. What's more, you people at the state college"—here, he favored me with a disapproving glance—"who are supposed to be teaching our young people the best things that men have learned, were the very ones who brought that degenerate here."

Ah, the eye of the beholder, I thought, for I had often heard that last appellation applied to Billy Earl's own blood.

"Of course, the lecture was only one little ripple in the tide of godless secular humanism that has swept over our schools and colleges. In fact, Arcady is in desperate need of a good Christian academy. It would fill the spiritual void in our local educational system. Also, with God's help and twenty-five or thirty thousand dollars of capital, the right man could probably make it profitable in the very first term."

"Grab your wallet and cover your ears, Reggie," said Muggsbottom, apparently without giving much thought to the implausibility of his imagery. "Billy Earl, we quite understand your basic thesis that the Western world daily grows more vicious and debauched. In many ways, I share that conviction. But would you elaborate, please, upon the hirsute disguise you wore that evening?"

"I'm quite embarrassed to say this, but it's nothing more than the truth. Even though I have only dwelt in fair Arcady since Christmas, I am well known to my fellow citizens. The very nature of my three trades—aviator, radio personality, and, most importantly, minister of the gospel—gives me what is nowadays called a high profile. I would have been instantly recognized at the pervert's lecture. I had no desire to disrupt the proceedings, and, of course"—he gave Muggsbottom a look heavy with mock censure—"I had no idea that others meant to do so. I simply wished to reconnoiter the enemy camp. The Scriptures furnish ample precedent for such activity on the part of the faithful. Did not the Lord send two angels unto Sodom at even in search of ten righteous men, that the city might be spared? Genesis, Chapter Nineteen, Verses One through Twenty-nine. And did not Moses send twelve spies into the land of Canaan? Numbers, Chapter Thirteen. And did not . . . "

"Yes, yes," said Muggsbottom. "I believe I speak for all present when I say that we accept your precedents." He could see that Billy Earl was warming to his peroration. No doubt he was also concerned that the evangelist had progressed only to the fourth book of the Bible, thus leaving thirty-five more books of the Old Testament and all of the New Testament before him.

"As to the beard, I understand that many phony writers grow a beard because they think it makes them look more poetical. I thought I might fit in better with that crowd if I wore a beard."

"I saw scarcely a beard among *Les Femmes Poétiques*," Muggsbottom muttered. "Several striking moustaches . . . "

"I beg your pardon?"

"Nothing, Billy Earl. I was merely seconding your observation, after my fashion."

Billy Earl was accustomed to being momentarily interrupted by shouts of "Amen," "Hallelujah," and "Praise the Lord." So long as he remained the center of attention, he was not easily distracted from his narrative.

"I decided I'd better lightly color my hair because it's such a recognizable feature. I've often been told that it's unusual for a man of my age to still have such blond hair, you know. Oh, this is my natural color, I assure you."

"We never for a moment thought otherwise, Billy Earl," said Muggsbottom. "'Vanity of vanities, saith the Preacher; all is vanity.' Ecclesiastes, Chapter Twelve, Verse Eight."

"You may tease me, Mr. Muggsbottom, but the Lord blessed my efforts. Murk put an example of his foul writings into my very hands. I could have wished for nothing more than that. What better way to expose him than by his own words, in black and white? The poem is thoroughly pernicious. To those impressionable young people he clearly advocated that vicious practice which is a violation of both God's and nature's law. 'Thou shalt not lie with mankind, as with womankind: it is abomination.' Leviticus, Chapter Eighteen, Verse Twenty-two."

Billy Earl caught Muggsbottom's eye and held it with the unspoken challenge, "If you want to trade scriptures, I'll call and raise."

Muggsbottom said, "Murk's a great pansy, right enough."

At this point, Smythe-Gardner blurted out, "Damned pansies are trying to take over the world." He often lapsed into periods of alcoholic torpor, from which he would rouse himself with such an eruption. He continued, "We knew what to do with pansies in Her Majesty's Navy."

I suddenly recalled Churchill's observation that the three great traditions of the Royal Navy were rum, flogging, and sodomy. But, suspecting that Smythe-Gardner would not welcome this citation, I held my tongue.

"Better than my poor words could ever do it," Billy Earl continued, "that poem has alerted the faithful to the danger right here in Arcady. It's been the heart of every sermon I've preached since the night of the lecture. And there's still plenty of mileage left in it, believe me. The Lord does work in mysterious ways, bless His holy name."

Well, I thought, as Maynard once said, Billy Earl is a special instrument.

"Thank God there is *another* college in Arcady, one dedicated to Christian principles." Billy Earl had fixed his watery blue, but now glittering, eyes on me. "In fact, I've been invited to speak there next week, at chapel."

Well, well. The Baptist college was naturally our arch rival. We competed for students and for prestige in our part of the state. The Baptists would certainly be enjoying our discomfiture over the Murk flap—the Ol' Perfesser's hostile pieces in the *Harbinger*, Billy Earl's sermonizing, the light that was being thrown upon precisely the kind of poetry Murk wrote. But what in the world were they up to? Chapel was a compulsory morning exercise with a huge attendance. The school was decidedly evangelical in tone, but why would they furnish Billy Earl—more an Elmer Gantry than a Billy Graham—such an audience? Now I would not have to visit the Royal. I determined to be at Bunyan Chapel on the morning of Billy Earl's address.

"Best keep an eye out for Murk disguised as a homely coed," said Muggsbottom. "Tit for tat, you know."

14. Among the Anabaptists

On the day appointed for Billy Earl's testimony, I had no early class and was thus free to observe him before an audience. I was even able to feign a motivation more worthy than morbid curiosity. The State College Administration had long encouraged us to "participate" and "interact" with our opposite numbers on the Baptist College faculty. Although we paid lip service to Arcady's "community of scholars," as a practical matter we had little to do with each other. The two student bodies, on the other hand, interacted vigorously. The previous autumn, the Baptists had slipped onto our campus under cover of darkness and attired the statue of the Founder in a bra and garter belt from Frederick's of Hollywood. Our lusty lissome lads had retaliated—to excess, some said—by bombarding the Baptists' homecoming parade with water balloons. For the purpose, a guerrilla crew had commandeered a helicopter from the R.O.T.C. department. I, however, would contribute to good institutional relations by reverently and unobtrusively attending a morning chapel service.

Muggsbottom accompanied me to Bunyan Chapel. I felt sure that on this occasion he would behave himself. The minute that Maynard's cousin ended his temporary residence in the Phlegm Club's pantry, Muggsbottom had adopted an attitude of complete neutrality toward the evangelist. He even seemed to take pleasure in Billy Earl's antics and to admire his confidence man's skills. No one else from the Phlegm Club was present. Sir Monty was not a "morning person." Smythe-Gardner could scarcely tolerate Sunday services—to him, a religious exercise early of a weekday morning smacked of fanaticism. It was clear to me that Reggie was still depressed over his breakup with Cecilia, and that he badly needed assistance from Above. But at such moments of spiritual crisis, he was more apt to turn to Joyce Brothers' column than to God. Maynard was barely recovered from his bout with influenza and, besides, he saw his cousin only socially, never professionally.

To the rear of the Baptist campus was a bluff overlooking the river. The newer buildings lined this bluff. Bunyan Chapel was located in what had once been the center of the campus but was now on its periphery. The building faced but was set well back from the narrow street which encircled the campus until it met the arc of the river. From the street, the chapel was, except for its steeple, effectively masked by old, wide-branching trees. A series of walkways radiated out from the building in all directions, attesting to the fact that it was still the spiritual hub of the campus. Muggsbottom and I ascended the three marble steps and passed through the wide double doors in the company of clean-cut Southern Baptist youth. I saw no one who appeared capable of dressing our Founder so suggestively. The Spartan interior seated several hundred, and its high, vaulted ceiling gave it about as much grandeur as a Protestant chapel can achieve. It was certainly a long step up from the Royal Theater. We found seats near the back of the room.

Three high-backed chairs were ranged behind the simple pulpit, which was really hardly more than a lectern. In the middle chair, the one with the highest back, sat a tanned and handsome man of sixty, whom I recognized as the college president. My goodness, I thought, on this leg of his pilgrim's progress Billy Earl is traveling first-class.

Our flying evangelist occupied the seat of honor to the president's right. Billy Earl had a way of elevating bad taste to a sort of art form, and this morning he had chosen to make himself the caricature of a television preacher, right down to the minutest detail. He wore a suit of some shiny synthetic material which seemed to be pulsating. Its color fell somewhere between wine and a deep purple. His tie was in a busy print that matched the huge handkerchief overflowing his breast pocket. An immense gold watch gleamed from his wrist, and diamond rings sparkled on at least four of his fingers. From top to bottom he was magnificent—his pompadour had never been more splendid, and his expensive loafers caught the light and shot it back at us.

On the president's left sat a young man of dazzling beauty. He was everything that Billy Earl was not—tall, lean, athletic. His teeth were straight and white, his eyes were a bright blue, his sandy hair was cropped neatly short. He had to be the student body president. After receiving a nod from the college president, this young man rose and stepped up to the lectern. Even before he spoke his first word, I had said to myself, "He will one day hold high office in our evangelical commonwealth."

The young man said, "I want to welcome you all to this morning's service, especially those who are visitors to our campus."

His voice was rich and full. His dialect featured the soft vowels and liquid consonants of the delta. I was confirmed in my prediction.

"In a few moments, Dr. Littlejohn will introduce our special guest, who will bring us the message. But first, let us go to the Lord in prayer. Every head bowed and every eye closed, please."

I felt Muggsbottom slide forward in the pew, preparing to kneel. But he caught himself—there was no bolster for the knees in Bunyan Chapel.

"Heavenly Father, Thou who art always with us, even unto the end of the world, we ask that Thou wilt be mindful of each one of us this morning. Grant us open hearts and receptive minds. Bless him who brings us Thy message. And, Father, if there are those among us who knowest Thou not as personal Savior, as Lord of their lives, may they come to feel the power of Thy presence and the balm of Thy loving grace. Knowing that Thou hearest our words even before we speak them, we ask all these things in Thy precious name. Amen."

I remarked, not for the first time, that it is God only whom we address in seventeenth-century English.

Next, we were directed to "Onward, Christian Soldiers" in the hymnal. This rousing old call to arms had been banished from the song books of the more effete Protestant sects as too militaristic and provocative for an enlightened age. Not so in Bunyan Chapel. Muggsbottom sang out as lustily as Smythe-Gardner might have done.

Then the young man turned and said, in precisely the same reverential tone he had used with God, "Dr. Littlejohn." He would indeed go far.

Dr. Littlejohn sprang lithely into the pulpit. Whoever said that the forties are the old age of youth and the fifties are the youth of old age, surely had someone like Dr. Littlejohn in mind. He was a grand advertisement for the efficacy of Christian living. His bronze face spoke of trips to the Bahamas or the tanning salon. He seemed impervious to midwinter in Arcady, a season which had always had a rather stultifying effect upon me. He radiated good health and self-satisfaction.

"Colleagues, students, guests," he said, "we live in trying times. There are wars and rumors of war. There are drugs and divorce and promiscuity."

"Dancing and mixed bathing," I whispered to Muggsbottom. Since he was behaving himself so well, *I* felt a little mischievous.

"All around us, we see our young people bowing down to the false idols of the world. At no time, perhaps, since Paul took up his cross to follow the Master, has the Lord demanded so much of his people."

From all outward appearances, Dr. Littlejohn was suffering from no debilitating thorn in the flesh. In the midst of these troubled times, he was thriving.

"At no other time in history has the intellectual growth of young people required a firmer grounding in spiritual values. At no time have our state and our nation had a greater need for the Christian institution of higher learning."

Ah, now I understood why the president—who anyone could see was an optimist by nature—was willing to grant Maynard's mountebank cousin a platform on his campus. True, Billy Earl's charisma might draw a few students with a taste for the tacky away from the mainline Baptist churches of Arcady and to the Royal Theater. But his Chicken Little testimony might also scare up a few dozen more freshmen for the coming term or a few hundred thousand dollars more from apprehensive donors. A fair exchange.

"This morning, Brother Billy Earl Hangar of the Runway to Heaven Ministry will share with us his own recent encounter with the forces of secular humanism right here in Arcady, Arkansas. His witness may at first chill you to the bone. But I know you students on this campus, and I know that your next impulse will be to gird your loins for the long twilight struggle to come."

"Baptist moms and dads especially want the coeds' loins girded," I whispered.

"Get thee behind me, Satan," replied Muggsbottom. "I am striving to maintain an appropriate gravity."

"Our guest," continued President Littlejohn, "has led hundreds of revivals, from Virginia to West Texas.

Although his ministry in Arcady has been comparatively brief, Brother Hangar already plays a vital role in the spiritual life of our city. We also know him as a radio personality, the 'Eye in the Sky' for our own KARC. And he tells me that come spring, when the Lord's stewards are again making preparations for the bounty to come, he and his plane, the *Flaming Cross*, will be available for crop-dusting work. He also tells me that, although he does not claim to be the only Christian crop-duster in America, no crop-duster is *more* Christian than he."

An approving twitter of laughter ran through the congregation.

"Now I welcome to our pulpit Brother Billy Earl Hangar."

Applause was inappropriate to the sacred premises, but a chorus of "Amens" greeted the pastor of the Runway to Heaven flock.

Muggsbottom permitted himself his first wry observation. "That glowing introduction seems a bit more than Christian charity demands."

Billy Earl rose and shook Dr. Littlejohn's hand heartily as the president gave way to his guest. So grand had been Brother Hangar's predecessors—the first the very embodiment of vital, virile Christian youth, the second of vigorous yet serene Christian middle age—that the purple suit and pompadour seemed even tackier than they had earlier. Billy Earl would have to be very good indeed not to seem insubstantial by contrast.

I need not have worried.

Billy Earl wasted no time or energy on felicitations. "Brothers and sisters in Christ," he began, "I have been called to fly over the length and breadth of this great land, aiding the tillers of the soil in their age-old task of bringing forth God's bounty. 'Thou shalt eat the herb of the field; in the sweat of thy face shalt thou eat bread, till thou return unto the ground.' Genesis, Chapter Three, Verses Eighteen and Nineteen. And I have also been called to seek out the lost and lead them unto salvation. 'Go ye therefore, and teach all nations, baptizing them in the name of the Father, and of the Son, and of the Holy Ghost: teaching them to observe all things whatsoever I have commanded you.' Matthew, Chapter Twenty-Eight, Verses Nineteen and Twenty. I could have asked for no greater challenge and no greater joy than to nurture simultaneously men's bodies and men's souls. In this dual labor have I, like the Apostle Paul, wandered far and wide for many years through a wicked world.

"And, brethren, this *is* a wicked world, wicked and blind to the will of God. Men seek only wealth and power and the pleasures of the flesh. Women have abandoned all modesty. Children defy their elders and scoff at righteous instruction. The pernicious doctrines of Satanism and Marxism and humanism are to be seen at work on every hand. But every man and every woman and every boy and every girl will one day be called to account before the throne of God. 'Be not deceived: neither fornicators, nor idolaters, nor adulterers, nor effeminate, nor abusers of themselves with mankind, nor thieves, nor covetous, nor drunkards, nor revilers, nor extortioners, shall inherit the kingdom of God.' First Corinthians, Chapter Six, Verses Nine and Ten. But I can hear you saying, 'Hold on, Preacher. This is not Sodom. This is not Gomorrah. This is Arcady. Christian Arcady. Righteous Arcady.'

"But I say to you—Satan's legions are on the march. And do not delude yourselves that it is only through the streets of New York and Los Angeles and Chicago that the tramp of their cloven feet resounds. These demons are right here in sweet Arcady, using as their pawns the willfully perverse and the unwitting pseudointellectuals who support them."

"I believe," I whispered, "that Twinksly Murk is numbered among the 'willfully perverse,' while I am merely one of the 'unwitting pseudointellectuals.'"

"Please, dear boy," Muggsbottom replied. "Billy Earl is not speaking in tongues. I do not require a gloss."

"Very recently," said Billy Earl, "I attended a *lecture* [voice heavy with sarcasm] at your sister institution [laughter here, for the oft used term 'sister institution' excited nothing but derision on either campus], given by a foreign professor whose claim to fame is that he writes poems about men who lust after young boys. Only a hundred years ago, Oscar Wilde was sent to prison for the very behavior that this *poet* [even heavier sarcasm] eulogizes. That's just one measurement of the decline of the so-called Christian nations."

Having been chastened by Muggsbottom, I would not speak again, but I thought: And only three hundred years ago, John Bunyan could be thrown into prison merely on the charge that he was a big pain in the ass. The hazards of citing precedent. If I were to take Billy Earl and his ilk for my sole reference points, I might argue that we have been in decline ever since the reign of the Caroline kings.

"And friends, this man's perverse and pornographic verses are not merely countenanced by other college professors—which would be shameful enough. They are *praised*. What is more, my brethren, he was brought here, all the way from England, at *government expense*. That's right, apparently no *American* poet would do. Now, as he spreads his noxious doctrine of hedonism, you and I, the God-fearing, Bible-believing taxpayers of America are being asked—nay, compelled—to pay his salary. I have not mentioned his name. I will not mention his name. His name is of no importance [and, who knows, he may have a litigious nature]. What *is* important is the attitude found on college and university campuses all across the land-—except, thank God, on campuses like this one—that his case points up.

"Secular humanism now dominates America's public

institutions, and the hiring of perverts to teach young people the joys of literature is just one inevitable result of that abominable philosophy. All ideas, say the secular humanists, may have some validity—except, of course, religious ideas. Therefore, the student should be exposed to everything—except, of course, religion—no matter how absurd or outrageous. Today, we sit and listen politely to speakers that our parents and grandparents would have chased right off the stage."

Amen, I thought.

"The people who run our public colleges and universities are not evil people. They are not stupid people. They are misguided people [a benevolent glance—at least, I imagined so—in my direction]. They have allowed the Marxists and the evolutionists and the extreme feminists and the other agents of Satan to persuade them that tolerance is always good. That tolerance of *everything* is always good. But tolerance of everything is *not* good. Tolerance of everything is just another way of saying, 'I don't care.'"

A smattering of amens.

"As you might imagine, not many secular humanists visit our sanctuary at the Runway to Heaven Ministry [it was, however, a regular hangout for them during its incarnation as the Royal Theater], so I determined to seek *them* out. I read of the aforementioned lecture at State College and was made aware of some very disturbing facts about the lecturer. I decided I would attend, after having disguised myself as a secular humanist."

I began to giggle. I was imagining that I had gone to the Beaux-Arts Ball costumed as a secular humanist. Muggsbottom smiled benignly upon me, for he knew roughly what was in my mind. But a young lady sitting in the pew immediately in front of us—who did not know what was in my mind—turned, pursed her lips, and waggled her head at me in the manner of a schoolmarm.

Billy Earl drew a folded sheet of paper from the inside

pocket of his iridescent jacket.

"I obtained a copy of the poem the lecturer read that night to a *public* audience [so much more dramatic than 'I was given a copy . . .']. I can not and would not read it to you, certainly not here in the House of the Lord."

Here's a parchment with the seal of Caesar. 'Tis his will—which, pardon me, I do not mean to read.

"But, I assure you, there's no doubt as to its meaning. An older man is clearly stating his infatuation with a younger man. I do not say, since I can not *know*, that the older man in the poem is the *author*. But I can say that, no matter who that older man is, the poem *advocates* an unnatural relationship between him and a boy. Imagine—such a poem recited by a *professor* at a public institution, which asks the mothers and fathers of Arkansas to send it their children."

I wondered if Billy Earl knew those sonnets Shakespeare had written to the third Earl of Southampton. No matter, that was ammunition Billy Earl would never use. I happened to know that he considered Shakespeare sort of holy, because the Bard always sounded just like the King James Version. "This sad little story illustrates the disappearance of those Christian proprieties that, not so many years ago, were practiced in all of our colleges and universities. Yet, blessed of the Lord, we can't give up. We can't say, 'Lord, the task You've given me is too great.' We can't say, 'Lord, the world has won.' We've got to just pray *harder* and work *harder*." Pause. "My ministry is responding through an outreach mission to State College. My hope is to establish, adjacent to the campus, a place of recreation for our Christian students over there. A place where they can escape from the atmosphere of secular humanism for at least a few minutes each day. Where they can play a little ping-pong or a quiet game of chess or checkers. Where they can read their Bibles undisturbed or, if they prefer, fellowship with other Christian young people—the way you-all do over here. Since this will be one of the gathering places for the children of the Lord on their journey to Heaven, I thought we might call it 'The Loading Zone.'

"Of course, a project of this sort naturally costs money, and to find that money we must look to our God and to His people. So, beloved of the Lord, if your heart has been warmed this morning, if you have been moved to help us fight the good fight against this plague of secular humanism—you will find envelopes marked 'The Loading Zone' in the foyer. Remember, the forces of Satan are powerful and well financed. Every dollar, every hundred dollars will help us so much in this battle. The stakes are high indeed. They are nothing less than the souls of the next generation."

Well, I thought, we should have known that Billy Earl would arrange his own honorarium.

Billy Earl turned to look at Dr. Littlejohn. The president smiled and nodded, as if to say, "You're doing fine. Finish her up."

"For our closing hymn this morning, let us sing that wonderful old call to salvation 'Just As I Am.'" Billy Earl found the number and announced it. "If there are those of you who do not know Jesus Christ as your personal Lord and Savior, won't you come forward at this time and accept His wonderful gift of eternal life. Won't you say, 'Jesus, I know I can't do it alone. I'm placing my life in Your loving hands.' Won't you come forward this morning. Don't say, 'I'll do it tomorrow,' or 'I'll do it some other day.' There may not be a tomorrow. Won't you come now, as we sing."

As we finished the first verse, I heard Muggsbottom say, "Excuse me, old boy." He eased past me and out into the aisle. My first thought was, "Why is he leaving now? We only have a few more minutes until the benediction." But Muggsbottom did not turn toward the exit. With a spring in his step, he headed straight toward Billy Earl.

The reader can imagine how flabbergasted I was to see

my friend Muggsbottom responding to the altar call, but Billy Earl Hangar was no less amazed than I. He momentarily lost the words to the familiar hymn, and for a split second his jaw went slack. But Billy Earl was a seasoned performer—he recovered quickly. Still, as he and Muggsbottom stood side by side waiting for us to finish two more verses, I thought he could not completely conceal the look of suspicion in his eyes.

At the conclusion of the hymn, Muggsbottom spoke first, in a full, though not quite declamatory, voice.

"This is the point in the service, is it not, at which one may offer one's testimony?"

"It is, brother."

Neither could Billy Earl totally conceal the suspicion in his voice.

"I thought so. I have pertinent testimony to offer." Muggsbottom faced the somewhat bemused congregation. "Ladies and gentlemen, I must begin with a caveat. I am not recommending a specific tactic in the war against secular humanism and would not wish to be understood as doing so. But I am moved to acknowledge in this public forum that I once set fire to the trouser leg of the pederast so prominently featured in Brother Hangar's homily.

"Here we have, if not a theological, at least a moral conundrum. My action, upon its very face, was neither intellectually nor ethically defensible. In fact, I will stipulate that it was *sinful*—you see, I do not shy away from that word which passes so few lips in our benighted century. The possibility of young Murk's actually being turned into toast as a result of my little prank was extremely remote. However, here you will find me a moral absolutist—one must accept the unlikely consequences of one's actions as well as the likely. Also, I can anticipate further censure from a group of good Anabaptists, such as that assembled here this morning. I have now heard enough of your sermons, I believe, to identify the basic tenets of your faith. And one of these is that God takes an inordinate delight in setting sinners afire. The flames in question went out within seconds, despite Murk's wild expostulations to the effect that the grave was yawning before him. Had I accidentally and prematurely cremated the young sodomite, I should have added to my offenses the sin of pride . . . since I would have usurped one of the Creator's basic prerogatives and chief pleasures.

"But now to the conundrum. Despite *knowing* that what I did was wrong, despite *admitting* that what I did was wrong, I still feel rather pleased with myself for having struck that match. As a matter of fact—how oft, amid the fretful stir unprofitable and the fever of the world, has the memory of my rash act produced in me an emotion that can be described only as . . . joy! In the C. of E., we lean heavily upon form, and form is invaluable in solving the thorniest theological and ecclesiastical problems. However, you Anabaptists, I know, set such great store by the answers provided by the human heart. My Christian conscience tells me that my persecution of Twinksly Murk, tepid though it may be, is wrong. But my heart continues to speak its shameless, amoral, delighted assent.

"It is within what little illumination this murky moral light can shed that you must judge the worth of my testimony this morning."

A long silence ensued, which was finally broken by the resourceful Billy Earl.

"If I understand Brother Muggsbottom correctly, I believe that he wishes to rededicate his life to Christ."

"What a good idea, Brother Hangar," replied Brother Muggsbottom.

President Littlejohn and I were chatting on the steps of Bunyan Chapel.

"Brother Hangar might have laid it on a little thick," he said. "I hope you folks at State can take his remarks in the right spirit."

I shrugged and smiled and tried to look like a good sport. I also changed the subject.

"The president of your student body is an impressive young man. He can be pious without seeming sanctimonious."

"Barry? Barry Sanderson is his name. Yes, he's a very special young man."

"I certainly foresee a successful political career for him."

"Is it so obvious to everyone? It's been obvious to us ever since he arrived. Yes, Barry's a political science major and plans to enter law school next fall. I'll be surprised if he doesn't make his mark . . . And your friend's an extraordinary person as well." He nodded toward Muggsbottom, who stood about twenty feet away, regaling a group of undergraduates with some lengthy anecdote. "I've been hearing tales about the Englishmen in town for a year now, but this is my first experience with any of them. He's quite a character, isn't he?"

"Yes," I said. "He's quite a character."

"Muggsbottom," I said. "You're an unpredictable rascal. You were behaving so well right up to the very end."

"Anabaptists enjoy lay participation in their services. Indeed, they invite it."

"I believe they found your testimony a little . . . cryptic. I overheard some people expressing the opinion that you had been 'saved,' while others were dubious."

"If multiple interpretations are possible, might we not embrace the more agreeable one? But my thoughts have been running along somewhat different lines. You took note of Billy Earl's appearance this morning—his hair, the suit, that awful tie?"

"Of course. Those are Billy Earl's working clothes."

"Precisely, dear boy. An astute observation. One Sunday, not long after our arrival in Arcady, our landlady took Sir

Monty and me to church with her—I believe I have told you of that experience. The preacher on that occasion had teased his hair in precisely the same manner. He wore just such a fluorescent suit and nauseating tie. And then, there's you, old fellow."

"I?"

Muggsbottom had taken another of his sudden leaps, and I was left behind, searching for the transition he had neglected to provide.

"Yes. I've noticed that you dons, British and American alike, often have a certain shared look and air about you. Patches on the sleeves, pouches under the eyes. Enervation masquerading as a sort of fashionable world-weariness."

"Now, hold on, Muggsbottom . . . ."

"The point is this, dear boy. One wonders if stereotypes, far from being fallacies, aren't the inevitable products of natural law. There may be a very interesting monograph here. I must subject the idea to a more rigorous examination."

I was eager to turn the conversation away from my enervation masquerading as fashionable world-weariness, so I said, "Speaking of Billy Earl, you saved him some embarrassment anyway."

"How, pray?"

"You saved him from striking out at the altar call. When a hotshot evangelist doesn't get a single convert or rededicated life at the altar call, it's very damaging to his reputation."

Muggsbottom smiled broadly.

"So, dear boy, you see that my instincts were entirely right. As they usually arc."

15. Homer Joe and Muggsbottom at the Festival

That April, just as she had for many Aprils before, Arcady polished herself until she gleamed and donned her finery in preparation for the Twin Rivers Festival. Arcady is situated just below the confluence of the Caddo and Ouachita Rivers, for which our festival is named. Being a river town, Arcady is quite an old town, at least by the standards of a frontier state like Arkansas. Dean County was well settled by the 1830's, and by the next decade Arcady had become its trading and financial center, also the seat of county government. During the latter part of the unfortunate misunderstanding all Arcadians above the age of forty had been taught to call the War between the States, Arcady had been a hub of Confederate military activity, the Rebel forces having been driven out of Little Rock and to the south. To celebrate this proud heritage was one reason for the festival.

There were other reasons as well. The Twin Rivers Festival drew tourists into Arcady. There was a sanctioned 5K race which attracted runners from all across the state. And because the exhibits, contests, and entertainment— along with one large block devoted to carnival booths and rides—were held in the middle of downtown, many apostate Arcadians were drawn back to the business district for the first time in many months. Yes, not even Arcady is so idyllic as to have escaped a shopping mall on the outskirts of town. Our mall is not much by the standards of Dallas or Houston, but this irresistible phenomenon of modern mercantilism had already, by the time of which I write, begun to bleed our downtown merchants white.

In stark contrast to the beleaguered businessmen of downtown Arcady were my English friends. From all appearances, things were going swimmingly at the stately old house on its tree-shaded street.

Muggsbottom was in excellent spirits. I had heard him recount his performance in Bunyan Chapel at least a dozen times, with some improving embellishment on each occasion. Everyone enjoyed the story immensely except Sir Monty, who allowed, "One should never give the Puritan element encouragement of any sort. They hover constantly on the brink of fanaticism, you know." But for the rest of the household, "the day Muggsbottom got saved" became a recurrent term of jocularity. Muggsbottom also continued to cement his friendship with his one-time enemy Homer Joe Tennyson. He kept up the habit of meeting Homer Joe and his coon hunting buddies for coffee each Thursday morning at Granny's. One of my profoundest regrets is that, because of my teaching schedule, I could never sit in on one of these coffee klatches. They must have been something to see and hear.

Smythe-Gardner was more placid than I had ever seen him. He had made a wonderful discovery. For only a few dollars more each month, the local cable television company would pipe in a channel which featured films with titles like *Sex-Starved Stewardesses in Seattle*, *Love Me till It Hurts*, and *Young Vixens at School*. Smythe-Gardner was now able to supplement the dirty books—I always assumed they were dirty—which came to him regularly through the mail with these nightly films. Their only drawback was that they began rather late in the evening, and not even the naked cavorting of nubile actresses, their squeals and moans, could indefinitely retard the effects of gin and lime.

Reggie, as usual, kept his own counsel. But he had brightened up a bit, and he gave his friends the decided impression that he was slowly getting over Cecilia Luce. The only melancholy note in the colony had been sounded by Sir Monty. The old gentleman had stirred from a nap one evening to mutter, "Oh, to be in England now that April's there," before lapsing back into unconsciousness.

Other characters in our story, however, were not so sanguine as the members of the Phlegm Club.

Of late, we had seen little of Billy Earl Hangar. Billy Earl was not exactly in a snit, but his guest appearance at Bunyan Chapel had clearly put him out of countenance. It had been less than a success in two ways. First, Muggsbottom's dramatic "witnessing" at the altar call had stolen some of Billy Earl's thunder. And second—and more importantly—the contributions toward his dream of a "Loading Zone" at State College had totaled only $27.40. The awkwardness with Muggsbottom could scarcely have been avoided. After all, when a preacher pleads, "Won't you come," *anybody* is liable to come down that aisle, and in *any* frame of mind. The preacher takes the luck of the draw. But with a little research, Billy Earl could have saved himself the embarrassment of his puny love offering. For many years, State College had had a very active Baptist Student Union on campus, and few in Bunyan Chapel that morning had felt the need to fund a competitor.

Twinksly Murk had settled into the lumbering daily routine of our department and had attracted a number of disciples from among the creative writing students. But Muggsbottom had put him out of countenance as well. Murk worked hard at playing the affable don, but I could see that he had never fully recovered from Muggsbottom's disruption of his lecture. He would suddenly become irritable and querulous. His tic would become more pronounced. These brief mood swings always exaggerated his effeminacy and made him appear shrewish.

The on again, off again relationship between Cecilia Luce and the Ol' Perfesser was currently off. (In Arcady, we consider any romance within the city limits to be a form of public entertainment, and there are *no* truly secret affairs.) Apparently, Cecilia had soon recalled her reasons for breaking it off before with her bitter and jealous paramour. The depth of the Ol' Perfesser's unhappiness could be gauged by reading his column. It moved rapidly from satire to sarcasm to invective as he lashed out at everyone and everything, on both left and right. Cecilia busied herself as director of the talent revue which would serve as the principal entertainment for the final night of the festival. Did she continue to think about our Reggie, and about his prospects? I suspected that she did.

One evening during the week before the festival, Muggsbottom sighed and said, "Alas, I bring sad news from Granny's."

"Someone's dog died?" I inquired.

"An excellent conjecture, but at least from my perspective, an even more dolorous situation has arisen. Homer Joe has decided to participate in the talent revue for the upcoming fete. He will recite a poem—naturally of his own composition—commemorating the Battle of Slackwater Slough, an unpleasant rencontre I understand you experienced with the real Yanks some one hundred and twenty years ago."

"More of a skirmish, really," I said, in the interest of historical accuracy.

"It puts me in rather an awkward position," Muggsbottom continued. "In my former role as objective literary critic, I was free—no, *bound* would be the more correct term—to point up Homer Joe's repeated offenses against sweet poesy and the mother tongue. To be sure, these offenses are committed in all innocence, for no creature on this earth is more innocent than Homer Joe Tennyson. But now that I have come to see in Homer Joe the finest qualities of your native yeomanry, now that he has so graciously sponsored my membership in his club of bluff but greathearted woodsmen, now that, in short, he is my friend—I can no longer with serenity of spirit tell him that his work has so far failed to rise to the level of tripe. I do not wish to reopen old wounds. And nothing can dislodge from Homer Joe's head the fantastic notion that he is a literary artist of some consequence."

"I have heard," I said, "that Cecilia Luce is directing the talent show. I wouldn't have thought Homer Joe was quite her cup of tea."

"According to my informants, the seductive Mrs. Luce has also been compromised, and I do not speak now of her amatory excesses."

"How so?"

"It is her intention, I believe, to perform a scene from *Antony and Cleopatra*. She, of course, will portray the alluring Queen of the Nile. Queen of the Nile, Twin Rivers Festival—you see how one can justify the choice of dramatic material if one stretches the connection to the outermost limits of apposition. In any event, she will be supported by several of the Community Players with whom she customarily treads the boards. Certainly, the male members of the Festival Committee were intrigued by the prospect of Mrs. Luce attired in the scanty costume ordinarily associated with the Egyptian queen. But both they and the distaff members of the committee have serious reservations about Shakespeare's being performed on a platform on Main Street as semiliterate fun seekers surge past on every side. In other words, the committee fear that *Antony and Cleopatra* will come a cropper no matter how ill concealed Mrs. Luce's breasts may be during the performance.

"But she could not be dissuaded. Thus, the committee felt that they could not then deny a place on the programme to other less conventional acts who were clamoring to inflict themselves upon the public. One was a group of geriatric square dancers called the Oldfangled Arcadians. These spry and sprightly oldsters enjoy their hobby extravagantly and have developed the curious notion that everyone else does as well. A second unorthodox performer was the Bard of the Bayou, Homer Joe Tennyson. The Festival Committee pressured the director into adding to her bill of locally popular singers and musicians the Oldfangled Arcadians and Homer Joe Tennyson."

"Muggsbottom, you amaze me. I've lived in this little town for years, and I don't have your sources of information."

"It pains me to say so, old fellow, but I have noticed that pedagogues are usually very poor listeners. They are so accustomed, I think, to imparting information to others— often information, it also pains me to say, of the most dubious character—that they are oblivious to the intelligence to be had from others. I sit unobtrusively by and, as loquacious Arcadians pass in pursuit of their daily affairs, I gather rumors like the ripe fruit from a heavily laden tree whose branches are drooping almost to the ground."

This from a man who had obtruded himself, usually in a highly melodramatic fashion, into the cultural, political, artistic, and religious life of Arcady almost from the day of his arrival. This from a man for whom pontification was the natural mode of conversation, for whom fact and fancy seemed largely interchangeable. In the early weeks of our friendship, I was often irritated by Muggsbottom's more outrageous observations on America, Arcady, and me. But, like a man whose beautiful wife's exquisite elegance is marred only by a laugh like a donkey's bray, I had come to accept my friend as I found him. After all, if Muggsbottom's sense of irony about himself had been as strong as it was about everyone and everything else, he would have scarcely dared speak a word on any subject.

"Perhaps," I ventured, "if the Community Players' rendition of Shakespeare is dreadful enough, Homer Joe's recitation will profit by the comparison. The Battle of Slackwater Slough *is* Dean County's Acre or Agincourt, you know—well, maybe Dunkirk would be a better analogy. Anyway, few Arkansans still come to the show with rotten fruit and dead cats in their pockets, as Mark Twain represented them in *Huckleberry Finn.*"

"I am much relieved to hear it, dear boy."

The Twin Rivers Festival was now only two days away, and a great deal was happening.

Two square blocks of downtown had been closed to all but pedestrian traffic. The Apex Entertainment Co. of Winter Garden, Florida, was setting up a carousel, a tilt-a-whirl, and a half-dozen more suchlike attractions. The grimy employees of the Apex Entertainment Co. went about their work stolidly—or, in a friendly little town like Arcady, one might better use the term "sullenly." Their world-weariness could have served well as an exemplum for the darker side of show business, but how many stagestruck young Arcadians took note I can not say. Artisans from the northernmost reaches of the state, and even some from Texas and Louisiana, had joined area craftsmen in reserving every inch of space in the booths lining one side of Main Street. By Friday afternoon, these would be filled with dolls and ceramic pots and ashtrays and glazed coasters—artifacts that would someday testify to one aspect of the 1980s. The local running club was marking the route for Saturday morning's race with hand-lettered signs. A couple of members were inscribing the distances of the various legs on the pavement with yellow paint.

Cecilia Luce had called a final rehearsal for the talent show. As Muggsbottom and I arrived on the scene, the participants were milling around in front of the platform stage, construction of which had finally been completed earlier in the day. Upon learning of the rehearsal, we had come downtown to hear Homer Joe recite his poem. Neither of us felt that we could bear to wait until Saturday night.

Muggsbottom had said, "Homer Joe ostentatiously neglects to *mention* the poem to me, much less allow me to read the text. Alas, I fear my former references to his 'wretched rhymes and mangled metrics' caused wounds that have not as yet completely healed."

I had then reminded Muggsbottom, "You called his work 'execrable doggerel,' I believe."

"I may have done, my dear fellow, but he took my remarks in a more deeply personal way than ever they were intended, I assure you."

So we were anxious to hear the poem. There was absolutely no possibility that Homer Joe's performance would be "good," or even "OK." Our only hope was that his composition might not be as stilted and lachrymose as a poem on the Battle of Slackwater Slough conceivably could be.

Imagine our disappointment then when Cecilia clambered up onto the stage and announced, "I won't keep you long this afternoon. This is a technical rehearsal, so you won't actually have to go through your numbers again."

They were assembled there, as it turned out, solely for the benefit of the technicians now busily positioning the light stanchions and setting up the sound system. In their assigned order, Cecilia had each of the acts-—the country and western band, the rock band, the female vocalists, the male vocalists, the Community Players, the Oldfangled Arcadians, Homer Joe Tennyson—scramble up the steps to the stage, fix the precise spot from which they would perform, "block" any movements about the stage to be made during the act, then scramble back down the steps again. With solemn faces, the musicians discussed what portions of their equipment would have to be hauled onstage with them, what portions could function effectively below them, at street level. They estimated the maximum length of time they would require to properly amplify themselves. An earnest looking young man, whom I took to be Cecilia's technical director, made notes furiously on a big yellow pad. Cecilia herself was everywhere, making a suggestion about the lighting here, asking a question about the sound there. To my layman's eye, she appeared quite theatrically sophisticated.

One of the acts was a trio of young men in their very early twenties.

"See the one in the middle there?" I said to Muggsbottom. "Do you know who that is?"

"He is our handsome young Anabaptist friend from Bunyan Chapel, is he not?"

"Yes. His name is Barry Sanderson."

I noticed nearby a young man methodically untwisting a tangle of cables. He wore a Baptist College T-shirt.

"Pardon me," I said. "Can you tell me the name of that group?"

"Sure. They're Solid Rock."

"Solid . . . ?"

"They do Christian pop-rock. Have a good sound, too."

"They sing rock-and-roll songs with Christian lyrics," I reported to Muggsbottom, who did not seem nearly so scandalized by this intelligence as I had expected. "Apparently, young Sanderson has a good singing voice in addition to his many other attributes. Oh well, that won't do him any harm in Southern politics. Louisiana once had a singing governor. He wrote 'You Are My Sunshine.'"

"For you Americans, and Southerners especially, politics is mostly entertainment. But believe me, old dear, I do not posit this as disapprobation. If the behavior of British politicians had been more entertaining and less malignant, I should not have had to emigrate."

At that moment, Cecilia Luce noticed us for the first time since we had walked up. As the nineteenth-century novelists like to put it, a dark cloud passed over her countenance. This was not the first time I had observed Muggsbottom's provoking such a nineteenth-century response from others.

Cecilia strode over to where we stood and, her dark countenance only inches away from Muggsbottom's placid one, said, "This rehearsal concerns only the people involved in Saturday night's performance. May I ask you to move along, please?"

"You may ask me anything, dear lady. But I must remind you that this is a public street, and we are members of the public. Thus, whether we go or stay is not a matter of your instructions but of our inclinations."

Cecilia's dark countenance turned red. She wheeled and, as she marched back to the platform, snapped at her poor technical director with such sudden fury that he dropped his yellow pad. I believe both his feet may have left the ground.

"She is angry with me because she believes I turned Reggie against her," said Muggsbottom. "But, as you well know, I would be the last man on earth to interfere in an affaire of the heart."

We stood there for another three or four minutes, silently asserting our right of assembly, or whichever inalienable right it was. Then we turned and walked slowly back to my car.

We had learned a bit more about the mechanics of putting on a show, had experienced an exciting little adventure with Cecilia Luce, but still had not heard a word of Homer Joe's ode to the Battle of Slackwater Slough.

Saturday dawned cool but with intimations of the Arkansas heat to follow.

The first afternoon and evening of the festival had proved a marked success. The rides of the Apex Entertainment Co. were operating at near capacity. The craftsmen and craftswomen were doing a brisk business, despite the fact they were all selling pretty much the same stuff (there are fashions in the arts and crafts line just as in hair styles and footwear). The downtown retailers had moved the hoariest portions of their inventories out onto the sidewalk, had cut prices just a tad here and there, and were selling many items they had feared they were going to have to eat. Street vendors were selling hot dogs and corn dogs as fast as they could heat them up. On the whole, the Twin Rivers Festival was going very well for all those who *needed* for it to go very well.

Only a few Arcadians had suffered disappointment.

One of these was Billy Earl Hangar, who had experienced another of his infrequent setbacks when the committee had declined to designate his "Down by the Riverside" Revival an official festival event. But Billy Earl was as resilient as ever. He boasted that a majority of his Friday night crowd had been out-of-towners despite his absence from the published schedule of events. I should add that the "Down by the Riverside" Revival was not in fact conducted on the banks of the Caddo or the Ouachita but at the old Royal Theater. At least the revival's cognomen was in harmony with the motif of the festival, and in the use of figurative language evangelists are granted quite as much license as poets.

Another Arcadian not sharing in the general fun and frivolity of the weekend was the Ol' Perfesser. He had scarcely seen Cecilia since she accepted the directorship of the talent show. And even before she acquired this excuse for putting him off, she had made it clear that they had not reestablished a "relationship." Oh, she had not told him that she never wished to see or hear from him again—nothing of that sort. Despite her love for the theater, histrionic partings were not her style. At some time in the future, if the need were there and the circumstances were favorable, she might go to bed with him again. But she made him know that it would not *mean* anything. He was made even more miserable because he blamed himself for the current state of affairs. Reggie Dipswizzle's callow behavior at the Murk lecture had been pure serendipity, and he had squandered it almost immediately. Gradually his melancholy was turning to anger, with Cecilia and with himself.

Naturally, I did not know these things at the time, since the Ol' Perfesser had not confided in me for many years. I drew these inferences in light of what he did later on—but I must not get ahead of myself.

Saturday's activities had, if anything, gone better than Friday's. For example, the race that morning proved to be the most successful in festival history, and that by a wide margin. Even the problems resulted from a surfeit of riches—e.g., so many more contestants than expected showed up for registration that the organizers did not have enough T-shirts to go around. The harried registrars took down the name of every disappointed runner and assured him/her that this important item of memorabilia would soon follow in the mail. The light blue T-shirt, by the way, was quite handsome. Above a representation of three trim, good-looking runners, matching each other stride for stride, was the legend TWIN RIVERS FESTIVAL 5K and below, ARCADY—THE ATHENS OF ARKANSAS. Arcadians were generally suspicious of us, frequently exasperated with us, but proud and boastful of us too. The top division of the race was won for a third consecutive time by a high school football coach from Little Rock who had run the Boston Marathon the year before. He was heartily congratulated and thoroughly despised by his fellow competitors.

Although the official program made no mention of an address by the governor, rumors had circulated throughout the day that he would make an appearance. Shortly after three p.m., the rumors turned out to have come from reliable sources.

State policemen cut a swath through the crowd, and the governor followed along, smiling, waving, and calling out to some people whom he appeared to know by name. He was flanked by our state senator and state representative, each playing the role of beaming sycophant, and trailed by camera crews from the Little Rock TV stations. The governor eventually made his way to the platform and delivered an address of some fifteen minutes' duration. "Unmemorable" is the most charitable adjective one could apply to the speech, and I believe the reader will not be too disappointed if I do not cite passages from it here. At the conclusion of his remarks, the governor plunged into the crowd where he kissed dozens of cheeks and shook hundreds of hands. In those days, the governor's term of office was only two years, so there was never a day when the incumbent was not campaigning for reelection. Thus, though our governor might be a rotten administrator, he was likely to be an excellent candidate.

In point of fact, the governor's appearance could have been omitted entirely from this narrative without doing it the least injury, but I chronicle it by way of impressing upon the reader the substantial nature of our festival.

The Englishmen had chosen to spend Friday evening at the Phlegm Club rather than at the Twin Rivers Festival. They had risen late on Saturday and spent a leisurely day at home. When I called for Muggsbottom at a quarter of seven, they were still appraising the pros and cons of the festival and trying to determine which of them would attend.

"Do we really *want* to hear Homer Joe's threnody for the fallen rebels?" inquired Sir Monty.

"I can not resist," Muggsbottom responded. "I am a moth, and Homer Joe's composition is the flame. Besides, it may not be *that* kind of poem."

"Of course it will be, Muggsbottom. You know how lugubrious all his pieces are . . . Shall we have someplace to sit?"

Muggsbottom turned to me. "Is any seating provided?

No, I thought not. But we can take our folding chairs."

"I think I shall stop in tonight," said Sir Monty. "Feeling a bit rocky, you know. That chop I had at luncheon was decidedly off. Which reminds me, Maynard is growing more and more careless with . . . "

At this point, Sir Monty's disquisition was interrupted by a huge, prolonged, openmouthed yawn. By the time he recovered the power of speech, he must have decided that he had said quite enough. I could not see that he looked to be any rockier than usual.

"Precisely what's on for tonight?" said Smythe-Gardner, appearing to have profited little from the preceding discussion.

"A talent show," I said. "Begins at seven-thirty, I believe."

"Ah . . . And it will last how long, do you suppose?"

"About two hours probably."

"I see," said Smythe-Gardner. "Actually, there's this film I've been wanting to see. Comes on the telly at nine. I shouldn't like to miss the beginning, you know."

"I'll come along," said Reggie.

Immediately I wondered if Reggie knew that Cecilia was scheduled to perform. I supposed Muggsbottom was wondering the same thing. As always, it was difficult to read Reggie's face. He was wearing his customary expression, equal parts of abstraction and melancholy.

"Well, let's be off then," I said.

As the three of us piled into my car, I felt the ambivalence always produced by accompanying Muggsbottom to a public gathering. I was fearful the whole time that he would do something irregular but felt slightly let down when he did not.

Main Street was still crowded with people of all ages. Tonight Arcady reminded me of Saturday nights in the little Arkansas towns of my boyhood. When things were hopping until late because farm families came in to spend the day and often put off shopping for their staples until the last thing before going home. When there were two or three pharmacies with soda fountains in every town, and they stayed open until ten o'clock. When from ten in the morning until midnight the movie house ran continuous showings of a double feature, a cartoon, and a serial, and we kids usually stayed to see everything twice. I was almost moved to share these nostalgic thoughts with my English friends, but then I realized I could never properly set for them a context in which my musings would seem other than trite and maudlin. Reggie would have smiled pensively and feigned interest, but Muggsbottom—imagining all the time that he was handling me very deftly and gently— would have let me know I was boring him stiff.

Because we were a few minutes early, we were able to stake out a good spot close to the raised stage. The show began exactly on time, with the minister of the First Methodist Church serving as master of ceremonies. This ebullient cleric was a leading light in the local Toastmasters Club. He had perfected a line of patter which made him everyone's first choice for assignments of this kind. And, in point of fact, he was an excellent m.c. His jokes and anecdotes were well chosen and brief. He kept things moving. He had a reputation for consistently getting his congregation out to Sunday dinner ahead of the competition.

Thursday night's technical rehearsal had apparently been very useful. There were few delays between acts, and only once or twice was our Methodist master of ceremonies required to "stretch." The lighting was good in general and, specifically, the spot was able to locate the performers after a minimum of wandering about the stage. The sound system functioned with scarcely a glitch, although the volume was set far too high, as was the case with sound systems everywhere during the 1980s.

I knew, of course, that Muggsbottom would hate the

country and western band and that his reaction to the rock band would be, if possible, even more negative. He seemed able to satisfactorily tune out their performances by closely studying the reactions of the men and women around us. Muggsbottom was a keen observer of his fellow man, notwithstanding the often fanciful conclusions he drew from such observation. The audience was as attentive and courteous as could be expected in such a fluid situation. Here and there, people broke off from the crowd and wandered away to be replaced by the newly arrived.

A group of black girls, of high school age, sang and were very well received. Their lead singer had a fine, strong, even stirring voice, but she abandoned the melody after a few bars and never returned to it.

"I thought for a moment I knew that one," said Reggie.

Next, Solid Rock took the stage. They performed a song whose title I missed but which contained the following lyrics:

> *Help me, Lord, I need you.*
> *Yeah, yeah, yeah, yeah.*
> *Help me, Lord, I need you.*
> *Yeah, yeah, yeah, yeah.*
> *It's true.*
> *I do,*
> *Truly do*
> *Need you.*
> *Yeah, yeah, yeah, yeah.*

The crowd gave Solid Rock a big hand, and they responded with a second number. It was more up-tempo still, and "Jesus" was one of the few words I could catch. Barry Sanderson performed with movements and gestures that were studied but not distractingly so. I was not surprised to find him poised on stage just as he had been in the pulpit, and as I imagined him to be on the stump.

As the applause died away, I said, "Well, make a joyful noise unto the Lord."

Muggsbottom's reply was, "I'm sure the psalmist had more demanding criteria in mind than he actually stated."

We had been looking forward to the next act almost as much as to Homer Joe's recitation—Reggie, I suspected, even more so.

Cecilia Luce mounted the stage in regal splendor. How authentic was her costume, I had no idea. It *looked* Egyptian. In any event, few men in the audience would have quibbled over historical accuracy, since much of her back and belly were showing, and her breasts were ill-concealed by some pasties (they were scarcely more than that) bearing a vaguely Middle Eastern design. I noticed several sets of parents glance first at their children, then furtively at each other. O.K., it was Shakespeare, but maybe it was also Parental Guidance Suggested. At his first sight of Cecilia, Reggie had drawn his breath in so sharply that the people next to him had jumped.

Following Cecilia up the steps were two women of early middle age. Even in their flowing robes and elaborate headbands, they continued to look like what they were— high school English teachers—rather than what they were supposed to be—Cleopatra's attendants, Charmian and Iras. Behind these ladies came two men, one of whom was unmistakably costumed as a guard. The other I recognized as a local florist named Milton—I believe his last name was Melton. He appeared to be made up as Raggedy Andy, but I assumed he was playing the Clown. He was carrying a basket within which, of course, lurked the deadly asp.

Cecilia had naturally chosen to do the last ten minutes of the play, because it was Cleopatra's big death scene. The play actually ends with Octavius Caesar's assessment of the situation after coming onstage to find the queen dead, but Cecilia was not about to be upstaged, even by the first Emperor of Rome. Octavius Caesar had been cut. Cecilia was not a bad Cleopatra, the scene was not overly long, and the crowd did not get as rowdy as the Festival Committee had feared. There were several strained moments, however, when the thing came close to going seriously wrong.

When Cleopatra (Cecilia) first asked the Clown (Milton) about the "pretty worm" he had brought her, two teenaged girls to our right began to giggle. Unfortunately, this archaism recurred frequently (I counted eight times) during the next two minutes of dialogue. The girls' giggling had impressed the double entendre upon other members of the audience who, having once recognized it, could not thereafter completely put it aside. The alternate reading for every line became increasingly difficult to ignore—so that when the Clown said, "I wish you all joy of the worm" and "The worm is not to be trusted" and "There is no goodness in the worm," the snuffling and snickering grew to embarrassing proportions.

Adding to the volatility of the situation was the fact that Milton was not known as one of Arcady's more virile citizens. In fact, he had over the years been the butt of many a tasteless joke. Any fleeting consideration of Milton Melton's worm was inherently funny.

After the sixth or seventh mention of "the worm" and the ensuing sniggering, a lady down front—another high school English teacher, I would have wagered—turned and hissed, "It's the *asp*." But her clarification merely served as a straight line for a teenaged boy who, doubtless in an effort to impress the girls who had started it all, whispered, "Milton doesn't know his asp from a hole in the ground." Happily, the Clown exited before there was a general upheaval in the audience.

The next part of the scene posed a different sort of difficulty. Cleopatra called for her robe and crown, and once she was covered, launched into a fairly long speech. For the first five minutes of the scene, the audience had had Shakespeare and Cecilia Luce's tits. Now they had only Shakespeare. A young man standing close to Muggsbottom was holding his four- or five-year-old daughter on his shoulders so she could see.

"Daddy, what is this?" she inquired, with all the heartfelt curiosity of youth.

"Culture," her father replied grumpily, as he began to work his way out of the crowd.

The Queen of the Nile had to navigate other hazardous waters as her demise drew near. The asp which she drew out of the basket and applied to her breast, now completely covered by her robe, was a rubber snake of the novelty shop variety. In all fairness, we could not reasonably have expected a real asp, but the rubber snake did so look like a rubber snake. Its appearance reminded the teenaged girls of the Freudian fun they had had a few minutes before. It set them off again, and they had the same undesirable effect upon their neighbors, especially the teenaged boys in the audience.

Eventually, Cleopatra wrapped another rubber snake around her arm, made her speech, and expired with Antony's name upon her lips. The tittering had been widespread but never approaching full-scale disruption. I would have given the production a C+, the audience a C-. As Cecilia rose from the dead, she received a good hand. In acknowledgment, she raised and spread her arms, thereby causing her robe to gap open. Applause increased noticeably.

As the Community Players were leaving the stage, I said to Muggsbottom, "I wonder if Mark Twain wasn't right when he had the duke tell the king and Huck, 'These Arkansaw lunkheads couldn't come up to Shakspeare; what they wanted was low comedy.'"

Muggsbottom appeared to give my facetious remark

careful consideration before saying, "Just as in the novel, dear boy, there was much guilt on both sides."

"Well, Reggie, what did you . . . ?"

But Reggie was gone.

I could see in Muggsbottom's eyes that he and I were leaping to the same conclusion. The Queen's stately entrance had featured four retainers, her egress five. An old saw came to mind that would certainly have fit Cecilia and Milton in the present instance: an actress is something more than a woman, and an actor is something less than a man.

"I fear the worst, but let us hope for the best," said Muggsbottom.

Meanwhile, the Oldfangled Arcadians had taken the stage. They experienced a couple of false starts when the taped music to which they danced developed a hiccup. But they quickly overcame that malfunction with a sangfroid which said, "This is among the tiniest of the difficulties we have encountered in our long and trying lives." Their caller was soon calling, and they were soon clogging, do-si-doing, and forming squares and stars up a storm. The young people in the audience seemed most enthralled by the performance of the Oldfangled Arcadians. After the first few minutes, they must have expected the old folks to begin dropping dead one by one. But when the old folks thrived instead, the kids were mesmerized.

"My Baptist friends don't believe this is really dancing," I said. "I tell them that St. Peter will set them straight."

"It will not be the greatest of their surprises, you know. Perhaps they will not be too distressed, there amidst the generally favorable circumstances . . . I believe I shall go for a pee before Homer Joe gets on."

"What a good idea," I said, and we each headed for one of the portable chemical toilets so kindly furnished by the festival's sponsors.

When we returned, the Oldfangled Arcadians were

receiving a round of applause which proved they were far more popular than I had expected them to be. But then, I have never been good at guessing what the public will like, and I have six unpublished novels to prove it.

"And to conclude this evening's entertainment," said the master of ceremonies, "we are so pleased to have with us the poet laureate of Dean County [at this point, a significant portion of the audience began to ease themselves away from the stage], who will recite for us his own composition 'The Gallant Garrison at Slackwater Slough' [here the effects of centrifugal force upon the audience became even more pronounced]. Ladies and gentleman, the renowned Homer Joe Tennyson."

As Homer Joe came from out of the darkness behind the stage and mounted the steps, the impending dispersal of his audience was instantly arrested. A brief outbreak of gasps and low whistles was followed by absolute silence on the street.

Homer Joe was wearing the butternut uniform of a Confederate rifleman. His muzzle-loader was cradled in his left arm, and on his right shoulder rested the staff of a huge Stars and Bars. Where had the Minstrel of the Marshes found that getup? He looked absolutely authentic: the gangling, rawboned body, the sun-browned face jutting forward atop the long neck with its prominent Adam's apple. He might be a Scotch-Irish backwoodsman stepped right out of the 1860s, ready to fight for the Confederacy, whatever that was, or more likely just for Arkansas. A tape recording of the elegiac cadence of a snare drum—it must have been a recording, since I saw no drummer—furnished the background for Homer Joe's deliberate progress to center stage. The folks who, only a moment before, had been drifting away came drifting back.

"I had no idea Homer Joe was such a showman," I said.

"Perhaps we are seeing Mrs. Luce's fair hand in this," Muggsbottom responded.

Homer Joe "had" the audience, and he knew it. He allowed the flagstaff to slide down from his shoulder, and he braced it against the toe of his right boot. He lowered the butt of his muzzle-loader to the floor of the stage and thrust it out from his left boot at a forty-five degree angle. He was now standing at parade rest—sort of. He began to recite from memory. Homer Joe spoke with the nasal intonation and thick-tongued articulation characteristic of his dialect, but his voice was by no means unpleasant, at least to the Arkansas ear. And he declaimed with a certain proficiency for, after all, he had over the years recited, both bidden and unbidden, many a poem.

Before going further with this account, I must pause to state for the reader my intentions. A generation of my students has gone solidly on record against the unreliable narrator. In terms of artistry, I can not agree with them, but as a practical matter I am sympathetic to their position. We live in an age in which the government systematically lies to us, our spiritual leaders habitually oversimplify and misrepresent, and the media have obliterated every distinction between news and entertainment. So if, when we have settled down for a few quiet moments with what we hope will be a good book, we begin to suspect that the narrator is not being straight with us . . . well. It may just be the straw, etc. I have been scrupulously honest with the reader up to this point and will finish as I began. Thus, since some of you are unlikely to be completely familiar with our Battle of Slackwater Slough, I feel bound to interrupt Homer Joe's declamation occasionally to provide a gloss for his more romantic embellishments.

'Twas on one autumn morn in 'sixty-four [Homer Joe began],
A Yankee force struck south to rape the land.
[A mounted patrol of about thirty Union soldiers came

drifting toward Arcady, foraging for provisions.]
They little knew what Ares had in store,
For this day they would face a doughty band
Of Southern boys defending hearth and home.
Today these Johnny Rebs would make the stand
That is the subject of my humble poem [for Homer Joe,
an exact rhyme with 'home'].
These golden lads—most from the county, too—
Were guarding horses so they would not roam.
[A band of guerrillas had stolen two dozen Union Army
mounts in Missouri, driven them south, and sold them (for
gold) to a Confederate procurement officer, thus turning a
nice one hundred percent profit from their patriotic
exploit.]

"I say, can Homer Joe be using . . . ?"
"Yes, he can," I said. "Terza rima."

Right well their charge the boys from Dixie knew:
'Defend with life and limb these noble steeds,
Oh, gallant garrison at Slackwater Slough!'
[The "garrison" was a detachment of perhaps fifteen men
under the command of the procurement officer, a Captain
Galbreath. The main body of Confederate troops was
bivouacked further to the south, near Camden, poised to
move north in a probe for the enemy. Until this regiment
arrived, Homer Joe's heroes were to guard the remuda
beside a marsh called Slackwater Slough, located some six
miles from Arcady.]
'Twas in this spongy land of pads and reeds
Marauders came upon our boys in gray.
'Surrender's not a word a Rebel heeds,
Though Yankee force o'erwhelming comes his way.
Great-Grandpa talked of those brave men long dead.
We boys would sit and listen all the day
And wish that this day was those days instead.

Gramps told us at his slow, accustomed pace
Of hiding family heirlooms in the shed.
He ran to town and soon made known the case:
The Northern foe was met hard by the slough.
Capitulation meant one thing—disgrace.
Strength numerical possessed the Blue,
But strength of will and purpose had the Gray.
Which strength would win the day nobody knew.
The Yankees charged, and thus began the fray—
Our boys stood fast, their captain cool as ice,
His orders, 'At discretion, fire away!'
Their yardage and their windage figured nice,
The boys in butternut took aim and fired.
For marksmen's skills, three Yankees paid the price.
Soon men and horses in the bog were mired,
And cold steel, hand to hand, did each man face—
But let us turn to Gramps for what transpired:
'The gunfire rumbled so it shook our place.
My oldest brother fought like hell until
His musket's hammer blew off in his face.'
We thought ourselves to be heirs to a will
Like Gramps', not found in any northern clime.
That gallant stand—makes me a dreamer still.
Their courage far exceeds my pow'rs of rhyme.
The day was lost—undying fame was won,
And they will be remembered for all time.

[The skirmish lasted a quarter of an hour. Best estimates are that the Union patrol lost five men, killed and wounded, and the Confederates four. Our boys escaped with most of the horses.]

My poem of homage now is nearly done.
Their fabled fight is fought, their race is run,
Their glory's like the radiance of the sun.

[Perhaps, in the years that have passed since that night, some of Homer Joe's tercets have left me, but I have recorded his threnody as perfectly as memory allows.]

Homer Joe paused for a moment, a moment of precisely the right length (I did not know he had such timing). Then he snapped to attention, the muzzle-loader and flagstaff snug to his hips in soldierly fashion. Now the audience paused for a moment—before breaking into tumultuous applause, punctuated by wild shouts of approval.

"It ain't Gettysburg, but it's ours," I said. "We're still suckers for the old Lost Cause."

And as a Southern boy, when I said "we," I meant "we."

Muggsbottom's reaction was more analytical.

"Homer Joe's powers are not great, but he was working at their peak tonight."

Homer Joe was basking in the limelight, bowing slightly in the manner of a seasoned performer.

"Shall we look for Reggie?" I said.

"He will come home eventually, with his tail tucked between his legs." Then, as an afterthought, "Or perhaps wagging it merrily."

16. Murk Strikes Back

On Monday afternoon, the *Arcady Harbinger* and I arrived simultaneously at the Phlegm Club. Eddie Nunn was just leaving, and Maynard was just arriving. Eddie was very solicitous of the Englishmen. Arcady is not Los Angeles, but we are a mobile society with few adult nondrivers. Eddie was assured of a fare out to the old AMVETS Club every day just before sunset, a fare back to town about four hours later and, not infrequently, a fare sometime earlier in the day as well. The English goose was laying several little golden eggs a day, and old Mrs. Davidson and Eddie's other regulars simply had to rework their schedules around the Englishmen's.

Maynard usually arrived at the Phlegm Club well ahead of his employers but, today being Blue Monday, he trailed them by a few minutes. The Englishmen, of course, were accustomed to Maynard's decreased efficiency immediately following the weekend. On many days, he would bring fresh supplies of drink and other provisions. Every day except Sunday, he brought the *Arcady Harbinger*, which came out at roughly four p.m.

The perusal of the *Harbinger* then proceeded according to a ritual observed as punctiliously as any practiced by Muggsbottom's beloved Church of England. In recognition of his age and station, the paper was put first into the hands of Sir Monty. He would riffle through its few pages, choose some arbitrary point between front page and back, and fold the pages back then over. This act asserted Sir Monty's primacy, for the next fellow would be forced to undo the old baronet's handiwork before he could properly attack the paper himself. This next fellow was always Muggsbottom, who would pluck the *Harbinger* out of Sir Monty's lap as soon as the old gentleman nodded off— Muggsbottom's wait was seldom a long one. He would read the paper with great care, pointing out to his companions those articles which might prove interesting to them. Smythe-Gardner's turn came next. He was little interested in local affairs, to which, after all, the *Harbinger* was largely devoted. He could, however, always discover some development at the levels of city, state, nation, or world (sometimes at all four) to infuriate him. He would rail for a couple of minutes against the modern world, enumerating several statesmen in need of a good biffing, then pass the paper along to Reggie. Reggie usually made quick work of the *Harbinger* since, as he once pointed out to me, "I'm not a great reader, actually."

As I walked into the Phlegm Club only seconds behind Maynard, the ritual described above was already under way. Sir Monty riffled through the pages of the *Harbinger* and, inverting the crease along its spine, folded it open at the middle. The Phlegmatics nodded their unspoken greeting, and Muggsbottom waved me idly to a chair.

"Anything in this evening's gazette, Sir Monty," he inquired.

"There is, actually—appears to be a piece about that woman . . . and another dealing with those poet chaps. The lot of them, frankly, bore me quite stiff. *You* might find this interesting, though."

Sir Monty passed the paper to Muggsbottom. Reggie had been leisurely fingering his way through the men's wear section of a department store catalogue. At the mention of "that woman," his head had popped up like a hound's when the scent is in the wind. In this household, "that woman" could only be one woman.

Generally speaking, Muggsbottom would read aloud portions of any article he found especially interesting, apparently upon the assumption that anything which interested him would—or should—interest his companions. In this instance, however, he shared not a word with us, despite the intense interest betrayed by his features. His silence derived from Reggie's presence in the circle, and Reggie knew it.

I was soon able to read the article for myself. It was the Ol' Perfesser's column, the entire text of which I now reproduce:

"On Saturday night, Arcadians and their guests was treated to a spectacle not often seen in south Arkansas. And, unless the Ol' Perfesser misses his guess by about three and a half miles, it will not be seen again right soon. The Ol' Perfesser refers, of course, to the Community Players' excerpt from Shakespeare's *Antony and Cleopatra*, a segment of the otherwise entertaining Twin Rivers Festival Talent Show.

"Naturally, the Queen of the Nile was portrayed by Arcady's own theatrical queen bee, Mrs. Cecilia Luce. Mrs. Luce sure done her historical research for the role all right, and she come up with some danged interesting facts. For example, the Ol' Perfesser did not know that Cleopatra went around half naked all the time. And, for some reason, he had got it into his hard old head that she was younger and a little less heavy than Mrs. Luce's version of her. Well, sure enough, when he turned to the encyclopedia, the Ol' Perfesser found that Cleopatra was nearly forty when she died. So Mrs. Luce had that about right, give or take a year one way or the other.

"Now, the Ol' Perfesser never could find a real good description of Cleopatra anywhere, but he did read that she had had one child by Julius Caesar and three by Marc

Antony. Childbearing, so the Ol' Perfesser is told, plays the very devil with a woman's shape. That is surely why Mrs. Luce took the part herself rather than selecting some slender, willowy actress.

"But the Ol' Perfesser has not yet mentioned the most fascinating feature of Mrs. Luce's performance. According to Plutarch and them other Romans, old Cleopatra was a real plotter and schemer, who even poisoned her own baby brother. Also, Will Shakespeare claims—and Plutarch backs him up—that Cleo would hop into bed with any dog-goned man who could be of the least benefit to her. You would not suppose that the organist at the Presbyterian Church could do justice to such a wanton woman, but dang burn it if Mrs. Luce was not completely convincing in the part.

"Unfortunately, the audience did not appear to enjoy the performance as much as they should have. There was a right smart of laughing and even some rude remarks. The Ol' Perfesser is not an expert on Shakespeare, and he could be wrong. Still, he is pretty sure that *Antony and Cleopatra* is not a comedy."

Later, Muggsbottom would say, "Hell hath no fury like a columnist scorned and needing to fill six inches thrice weekly."

Eventually, of course, Reggie laid claim to the paper and read the Ol' Perfesser's column. Immediately thereafter, he hurried out of the Phlegm Club without a word of farewell for any of us. But he was back within thirty seconds, very shamefaced and flustered.

"Maynard," he said, "will you give me a ride?"

Maynard, who was washing glasses, glanced quickly in Muggsbottom's direction. Muggsbottom nodded affirmatively. Maynard dried his hands, untied and hung up his apron with the Confederate flag on it, and he and Reggie went out the door together.

"He is going to comfort Mrs. Luce," said Muggsbottom,

"to assure her that she is neither too old nor too heavy, that she is still a femme fatale. I am sure that he spent some time with her on Saturday evening, her provocative costume having overcome all his good intentions. But she is a highly unpredictable woman, and whether it is 'on' again between them I do not know. Well, lads, in my own subtle way I have done what I could. We can hardly lock Reggie away in the pantry. If he is determined to pursue this perilous course, we can do little more than pray and hope for the best."

Smythe-Gardner, who was scanning the offending article, said, "You don't suppose Reggie has gone off to give this Ol' Perfesser cad a good thrashing?"

"What a romantic notion," Muggsbottom replied, looking at the old sailor askance. "I do not suppose that for one moment . . . But if I may?"

He reached out for the newspaper, and Smythe-Gardner handed it back to him.

Muggsbottom said, "The Ol' Perfesser's is not the only diatribe in tonight's paper. Here is a letter to the editor."

And he began to read.

"'Dear editor:

'I was in attendance on Saturday last when the Twin Rivers Festival concluded with its talent revue. As a visitor to Arcady, I naturally hesitate to comment upon any of the decisions made by the organizing committee. Still, in one instance I am impelled to do so.

'I admit that the music did not stir me, but I am not a musician. The singing seemed, to me, of a middling quality at best—but I am not a singer. I could say no more of the dancing than that it was high-spirited—but I am not a dancer. I did not expect a performance of Shakespeare worthy of Stratford, and I did not witness one—but I am not an actor. However, I *am* a poet.

'I am also a teacher of poetry and, as such, have been subjected to much bad poetry over the years. But I am bound to say that Homer Joe Tennyson's recitation at the end of the programme on Saturday was the worst travesty I have encountered in three decades of listening to bad poetry on five continents. And matters were made worse—if that *can* be possible—by the appalling theatrics and jingoism with which Mr. Tennyson sought to mask his dearth of talent.

One deeply regrets the necessity of such comments on so joyous an occasion, but when one's art is abused one must defend it. I observe, in conclusion, that there are several delightful poets currently in residence at the State College. Any one of these young men, had he been granted use of the platform, could have done the festival as much honor as Mr. Tennyson did it harm.

Twinksly Murk
D.Litt. Oxon.

After a pause, Muggsbottom said, "You will recall that Homer Joe Tennyson, who is as righteous as Mrs. Luce is lewd, also rejected the unnatural advances of Twinksly Murk."

I should have known better, but I said, "You know, Muggsbottom, you once criticized Homer Joe's poetry just as harshly yourself."

"Not a bit of it. My criticism was in no way informed by the venom displayed here." He gave the page a backhanded slap and let the newspaper fall from his fingers as if it were a thing unclean. "Really, my dear fellow, sometimes I find your memory quite unsound."

In a moment, he added, "Murk is still smarting from my disturbing presence at his lecture. He's not found the means to strike back at me, so he's vented his spleen on poor Homer Joe. This is also a transparent device for promoting his protégés at the college. You see how the old bugger bends over forwards to aid these latest lissome lads."

"Six of one, half a dozen of the other," said Smythe-Gardner, who had never warmed up to Homer Joe.

"I don't recall seeing Murk at the talent show," I said.

"When the grass is tall," Muggsbottom snapped, "one often does not see the snake."

I could do nothing but hope that this incident would not spark another confrontation between the two old Oxonians. So I hoped.

The longer I considered the matter, the more I came to share Muggsbottom's opinion. Murk had acted out of spite. He had reasons for holding grudges against both Muggsbottom and Homer Joe, and now the two had come together as friends. What is more, his behavior was clearly not that of a disinterested critic. Homer Joe had read on Saturday night, there was no mail delivery on Sunday, and Murk's letter had appeared on Monday afternoon. Therefore, Murk must have delivered it to the *Harbinger* by hand—the act of a man in the throes of passion.

Later in the week, my chairman was complaining loudly of something that, I observed with satisfaction, he could not blame on me.

"I've been getting calls all week long from outraged townspeople. The President has been getting calls. Those baboons on the board of trustees have been getting calls. Why, for God's sake, did Murk have to attack a poem honoring the Confederate dead?"

"Perhaps he considers a scrap leaving only four Confederate dead insignificant."

"He should keep his nose out of local affairs."

"Murk is *your* Englishman," I said with relish.

The chairman had often characterized Muggsbottom et al as my Englishmen, and fair is fair. His look indicated that he both acknowledged the truth of my observation and resented my making it.

"Well," he said, "if we could keep everybody's Englishmen from writing letters to the local newspaper, we'd be a hell of a lot better off."

I could do nothing but nod my head in concurrence.

When Homer Joe's "Verses from the Vale" came out on Thursday afternoon, the editor of the *Harbinger* preceded this latest contribution of "pottery" with a signed paragraph. The paragraph was panegyric in tone and spirited in its defense of the poet laureate of Dean County. Homer Joe had taken wise counsel from some quarter and made no mention whatever of Murk. He did not need to do so, for all of Arcady was rising to his defense in a way they had not during his rencontre with Muggsbottom. Fortunately for Muggsbottom, the War between the States had not become an issue in that confrontation.

It has been my experience that most passions, no matter how deeply felt at the moment, are short-lived. Therefore, the controversy would surely have faded away within a couple of weeks except for an unfortunate happenstance. Later in the month, NOUNS AND VERBS, a literary society in Little Rock, announced that this year's recipient of its prestigious Broadhead Prize was to be none other than Twinksly Murk. Murk had given a couple of readings in Little Rock. These had put him in contact with the literati of central Arkansas. They, always eager to prove themselves more progressive and cosmopolitan than their benighted brethren in the state at large, found Murk just the ticket—a homosexual foreigner. Their announcement rekindled the fires of anti-Murkianism. Letters went flying to the *Harbinger*, and to the Little Rock papers as well, protesting any Arkansas award to a man who had sullied the fair name of Dixie. This criticism was, of course, grossly unfair to Murk, who had condemned Homer Joe's versification and histrionics, not his subject matter. But I had my hands full with explaining the behavior of

Muggsbottom, Smythe-Gardner, and Sir Monty (Reggie never gave offense to anyone, except to Cecilia). The chairman could stand up for Murk.

But let me return to the week following the festival, for I also learned at that time of interesting developments on another front.

One evening, Reggie drew me aside and asked, "What do you know, if anything, about a young fellow named Barry Sanderson—a pupil at the Baptist college? He is, I believe, president of the student body."

"Yes, he's one of their shining lights—the brightest one probably. Has all the Southern virtues. He's good-looking, seems to be reasonably intelligent. He's also gregarious in a composed manner and pious while still seeming manly. It's the Robert E. Lee syndrome. I expect him to be one of our up-and-coming politicians before very long. Oh—he sings too. Remember that group in the talent show called . . . Solid Rock?"

"I do remember," Reggie said mournfully. "And he's also quite rich."

"Oh? I don't think I knew that. Well then, there are no advantages the young man lacks, are there?"

"I am told that his father is a planter with immense hold-ings in the eastern part of the state . . . Forgive me, my friend, for pumping you for information but, as you see, I have also been pumping others."

"I'm happy to share what little I know about Sanderson, but why . . . ?"

"I have seen Cecilia again . . . three times, to be precise, since her performance."

"Yes? Well, Reggie, I've never really thought that was any of my . . . ."

"She's through with that Ol' Perfesser person, you know. Utterly."

"Ah . . . well, I thought she might be when I read his . . . "

"Now I'm afraid she fancies this Sanderson chap."

Patrick Adcock

"What? Why, she's twenty years older than Sanderson—fifteen, at the very least."

"I'm afraid age has little to do with these things, especially from the perspective of the older woman."

I was momentarily chagrined when poor Reggie's assessment of the situation proved wiser than my own.

"They were thrown together at rehearsals, you see," he continued.

"Ah. And young Sanderson—how does he feel about her?"

"Who would not return Cecilia's love?" He turned his palms up, as if in supplication. "What shall I do?"

"I'm hardly the man to tell anyone how to handle a woman, Reggie. I can say that Mrs. Luce's infatuations always seem eventually to pass."

Reggie said sorrowfully, "My dear fellow, I don't relish waiting for yet another one to pass."

"Of course."

I could see that any woman might be attracted to Barry Sanderson. And now that I knew he was heir to a fortune, I could see how Cecilia Luce especially might be. But for the boy, such an affair would be disastrous. Certainly, the young Robert E. Lee would never have been tempted by a grass widow, no matter how sexy.

"What am I to do?" he asked.

I knew that his distracted question required no answer, and I had none to give him. If Reggie had judged the case aright, this rival not only possessed a future legacy but also youth, vitality, physical beauty, and charm. What indeed was Reggie to do?

"What do you know about these people who are giving Murk the award?" Muggsbottom asked me one evening.

"NOUNS AND VERBS? They're a Little Rock literary society. Actually, they claim to have a statewide membership. The nucleus of the organization is a crowd of upper

212

middle-class sixties types with literary pretensions. They all live in western Little Rock, but to avoid the appearance of a central Arkansas clique they do some recruiting out in the hinterlands. In fact," I said, affecting a conspiratorial tone, "I myself am a member of NOUNS AND VERBS."

"Are you indeed? And did you have a hand in selecting Murk for this signal honor?"

"You know I didn't. A selection committee determines the recipient each year. Murk must have really impressed them, or perhaps his reputation did. They usually give the award to one of their friends."

"This party mentioned in the press, the party at which Murk will receive the prize—you will be invited to attend, I take it?"

"Yes," I replied, and I heard the suspicious connotation with which I had loaded that single word.

"And is the member of . . . GERUNDS or whatever . . . is he allowed to bring a guest to this party?"

"Yes," I said, and this time I heard my word filled with dread.

"I have never attended a literary soiree in America. I wonder if they can be as awful as those in Britain?"

"Muggsbottom, you can't expect me to take you? After those performances of yours at the Communion of the Holy Ghost, the lecture, and Bunyan Chapel? Why, the minute Murk saw you he would go right through the roof. And my chairman would be right behind him."

"My dear fellow, I should never dream of forcing myself upon you. If you do not wish to invite me, the matter shall never be mentioned again."

I sputtered a response in which I could recognize no sound that was actually a word.

"I sense that you are not entirely comfortable with the idea of my accompanying you to the party. I have noticed these attacks of timidity on other occasions, but I do consider them aberrations. You are at bottom a stout fellow, I know. Now, let us put the matter aside for the time being. Several weeks remain before the evening of Murk's lionization. We will speak of this again later, when I trust I shall find you stouter of heart."

I left the Phlegm Club that evening not entirely comfortable in my mind.

17. Smythe-Gardner to the Rescue

Nightingale Nook is situated on the extreme western verge of Little Rock, and I located it only after some difficulty. After much meandering about, Muggsbottom and I finally stumbled upon a narrow little street which was essentially a private drive, extending some two hundred yards to the gates of the lone house it served. On either side of the lane, closely packed greenery grew to within ten to twelve feet of the pavement. The street sign was so shielded by the enveloping branches of a big sweet gum tree that at first glance it read "ale No," like an error the spell check on your computer will not catch.

"Is the nightingale indigenous to Arkansas?" Muggsbottom inquired with feigned innocence.

"No."

"I thought perhaps not."

Near the gate, several cars were parallel-parked on each side of Nightingale Nook. A boy of about sixteen was standing in the middle of the road. He approached us with a diffident hand signal which seemed to say, "Halt . . . if that's O.K. by you."

"We're full up inside," he said. "Will you pull in behind that car over there, please?"

One of the young man's eyes was covered by a shock of sandy hair, and he wore an incipient moustache of a slightly darker color. He also wore dark slacks and an open-necked white shirt with a blue ascot blousing at his throat. On his feet were sandals and socks to match his ascot. I thought, irrelevantly, that any kid showing up at my high school in socks and sandals would have gone home with a bloody nose.

As we parked, Muggsbottom said, "A bloodless youth, but polite."

"One of our host's progeny, no doubt," I replied. "He'd probably rather be up in his room reading Proust."

Lorenzo Sandcastle was a doctor of osteopathy who had obviously made a great deal of money doing whatever doctors of osteopathy do. As we passed through the gate bearing a bronze plaque reading CASTLE WEST in scrolled script, an immense landscaped and manicured lawn stretched away on either side. We followed a wide path, laid in worn red brick from another era, up toward an equally immense house. Castle West somewhat belied its name, however, as it was a sprawling Tudor structure, apparently intended to suggest Hampton Court. This remote and affluent section of Little Rock was known as Happy Valley or Paradise Valley or something like that—I could never remember. I do not forget streets named for presidents or trees or even abstractions like State, Commerce, and Victory. But streets and, in this case, developments with names that are all connotation and no denotation, I can never recall.

Dr. Sandcastle often appeared in the Little Rock newspapers. The good doctor's interests extended considerably beyond and well to the left of his lucrative practice. He was active in social, political, and artistic (as evidenced by tonight's party) circles. He belonged to every organization a membership in which proves that one's heart is in the right place in regard to race, gender, and the planet. He had even run for a couple of minor constitutional offices. The electors of Arkansas are of a conservative turn of mind and are deeply suspicious of the wealthy. Thus laboring under two such debilitating handicaps, Dr. Sandcastle had finished dead last in both his races.

I had been a member of NOUNS AND VERBS for three years. Every year, I was required to file a report with the Office of the President outlining my activities outside the classroom. During the year just past, my principal activity had been hanging around the Phlegm Club with Muggsbottom and the boys—not the sort of thing, I was sure, that the President was attempting to encourage. But, in addition to my AAUP and MLA union cards, I was now able to list membership in NOUNS AND VERBS, the Literary Society of Central Arkansas. My professional life was made to seem more active when, in fact, I only attended this one big do each year, slipping unobtrusively away as soon as the wine bar closed and the speeches began.

The Board of NOUNS AND VERBS was composed, with a few exceptions, of former classmates at the University of Arkansas. Dr. Sandcastle was one of these exceptions, being an émigré from some remote northern point. But he had lived in Little Rock for so many years that his English was, on the whole, comprehensible to the natives. Each year, the Board of NOUNS AND VERBS chose a recipient for its Arlene Broadhead Prize for Excellence in Letters. As well as being the hugely wealthy widow of a cotton and rice broker, Mrs. Broadhead had been the author of haiku without number and a verse play entitled *The Dolorous Death of Hernando de Soto*. Thus, in her declining years, NOUNS AND VERBS, *Les Femmes Poétiques*, and the Repertory Theatre of Central Arkansas had courted the poet-playwright in a spirited competition. I did not know which organization had finally prevailed, but I did learn she had left something to each of them. NOUNS AND VERBS had obviously competed well enough, for their endowment funded a prize that was substantial.

In the first four years of its existence, the Broadhead Prize had been thrice awarded to members of the Form and

Patrick Adcock

Theory of Fiction class at the University of Arkansas during Autumn, 1971. The fourth recipient was the teacher of the class. This year, however, the presence in the state of the poet Twinksly Murk and the prestige to be gained by awarding the prize to one so eminent had caused the selection committee to slightly modify their criteria. Under ordinary circumstances, my chairman would certainly have been there to see his distinguished visiting professor receive the prize, and he would have viewed my presence with Muggsbottom at my side in a most unfavorable light. Fortunately, certain circumstances had kept him at home in Arcady. The previous spring, he had published his first book, *God's in His Heaven: The Strain of Optimism in Victorian Verse.* His counterpart at Little Rock University had panned the book in our state philological journal, calling it—in an alliterative onslaught—"trivial, tendentious, and turgid." My chairman felt, and I agreed, that "if you can't expect a good review in your own professional journal, what's the point in belonging to the goddamned organization in the first place?" He had then added the adamant footnote, "I will never speak to that son of a bitch or even be in the same room with him again." The reviewer was a member of the Board of NOUNS AND VERBS.

As a matter of fact, we encountered this gentleman soon after our arrival. He was in charge of the registration table, situated immediately beside the front entrance to the house. Under his direction, two bespectacled young women of unprepossessing appearance were registering the guests. I assumed they were junior members of his department. I handed my invitation to one of them and, gesturing toward my companion, I said, "This is my guest, C.P. Muggsbottom."

While the young woman consulted her list, then searched for our name tags, I introduced Muggsbottom to the Little Rock academic. I knew him very slightly, not only from NOUNS AND VERBS affairs but also from the annual

218

meetings of our state philological society. I had once been a member of his audience as he read a long, incomprehensible paper on the clarity of Twain's prose style.

"I am delighted to meet you, Professor," said Muggsbottom. While still pumping the man's hand, Muggsbottom clasped the right forearm with his left and, drawing the startled scholar toward him, said as though he were a spy imparting crucial intelligence to his contact, "Avoid uncooked fish. Salmonella will be the Black Death of this generation."

My chairman's enemy was flustered for just a moment but, having attended many a literary and academic affair, he was no stranger to irregular conversational gambits. He recovered himself quickly and said, "None on tonight's menu, I think. And speaking of food, there's a snack table in the garden. Also a wine bar. That's where everyone is gathering."

He directed us around rather than through the house. As we walked, I said to Muggsbottom, "What was that raw fish business all about?"

"A matter of genuine concern. I read that the practice has already reached epidemic proportions in California." Muggsbottom patted the side of his nose with his right forefinger, smiled, and continued, "As I told you, I have attended parties of this sort before. The guests are prepared to match aphorisms until dawn. That's always the game, old boy, and I have not come empty-handed."

On any occasion that presented Muggsbottom with an audience, he was not prepared to behave himself. I had never really believed, of course, that he would be.

We followed a path of attractive, irregularly shaped stones around to the rear of the house. The "garden" was a courtyard too spacious to be called a "patio." It was constructed on two levels and appeared to be floored with large squares of white marble. The buffet and the wine steward were situated on the upper level. Three steps led down to a large swimming pool which ran at a right angle to the upper courtyard. Well manicured trees and flowering shrubbery sheltered the garden on three sides. Perhaps as many as one hundred people were in attendance. Some were currently acquiring food and drink, others were clustered in tight conversational knots, and still others had taken their wine and finger food down to the side of the pool. I saw many vaguely familiar faces, but I did not see Dr. Sandcastle or Twinksly Murk.

The president of NOUNS AND VERBS, seeing that we had just arrived, approached us. He was a handsome man in his late thirties, both a poet with a regional reputation and a successful Little Rock tax lawyer. I found him witty and affable, and over time I had established with him, if not a friendship, an agreeable acquaintanceship.

"Glad you could come," he said. "Our host is showing the guest of honor through the house. So I'm filling in, like the usher greeting the faithful at the church door."

I introduced Muggsbottom who, after having voiced the standard felicitations, said, "You need not attempt to formulate a philosophy of life, you know. So many other people will kindly offer you theirs."

The president scarcely missed a beat. As a poet and a lawyer, he was adept at verbal games. He replied, "Yes, tonight probably. Especially after they've had a few more glasses of wine . . . Excuse me. Here's someone else who's just come in. Help yourself."

He gestured toward the buffet and left us.

"Cut that stuff out, Muggsbottom," I said. "You don't plan to play Oscar Wilde all evening, do you?"

His beaming smile did not reassure me.

We turned to the young fellow manning the carafes of wine. An older sibling, I thought, of the youth who had directed our parking. Muggsbottom chose a white, I one of the several reds. For me, some wine is sweet, some is sour, and some splits the difference. All of it tends to give me a headache.

We picked up little plastic plates and tableware, as well as napkins ornamented at the corners with tiny pictures of books, and began to work our way around the buffet. I loaded up on fish paste sandwiches and cookies because they were easiest to handle but, while attempting to juggle my plate and glass, I spilled half my wine into a bowl of congealed salad. Fortunately, it was red also. I moved right along without looking up from the table. I hated to commit a faux pas in Little Rock, but I invariably would do so. Ours is a small state with only one city of any size at all. Thus, the residents of this one city have developed a grossly exaggerated notion of their urbanity. They tend to treat their country cousins with kindly condescension. So, naturally, the country cousin hated like the very devil to spill wine in the congealed salad. I turned to discover if Muggsbottom had witnessed my misadventure . . . and discovered instead that he was gone.

In the brief moment that I had failed to keep him under surveillance, Muggsbottom had descended the steps and attached himself to a group of young women at poolside. They had the look, ineffable but unmistakable, of public school teachers—in the present instance, since this was a literary do, probably English teachers. A couple of them were very attractive. Not surprisingly, Muggsbottom was speaking as I approached, and his remarks confirmed my hypothesis.

"Ah, dear ladies, I have recently lectured in the public schools of Arkansas myself. Are you at all familiar with the Arcady High School? No? Let me share with you what I learnt there . . . Never file any sort of complaint against a teen-ager whose deprived childhood has been succeeded by a depraved adolescence. You should heed this admonition no matter what dreadful things the creature has done to you. You will only earn the enmity of school counselors and social workers everywhere, and will be fortunate to escape incarceration yourself . . . Ah, ladies, here is my dear friend—another denizen of fair Arcady, that delightful hamlet to the south."

I was introduced to the young schoolmistresses whom, without exception, Muggsbottom had already enthralled. Then a pretty little blonde asked, "Are things very different in your English schools, Mr. Murk?"

Muggsbottom was not wearing his name tag. I supposed he had stuck it in his pocket or simply thrown it away. Murk was inside, being shown the house by Dr. Sandcastle. And here was an Englishman who had launched into a peroration without pausing to identify himself, a not uncommon practice with my friend. His remarks clearly suggested that he had come this evening from Arcady. Not surprisingly then, the young women— some of them, at least—had assumed that he was Twinksly Murk.

"Our state schools gave up the attempt to teach anyone anything about a decade ago. Now they simply declare everybody equal to everybody else in every way, and send the pupils out to play football in the schoolyard all day long . . . Also, my dear, I must correct your impression . . . "

But before Muggsbottom could correct the young woman's misapprehension, a formidable silver-haired lady had dislodged herself from a nearby group and confronted him vis-à-vis.

"Did I hear you addressed as Mr. Murk?" she inquired abruptly.

"Madam, you did hear me so addressed. However, . . ."

"Allow me to introduce myself, Mr. Murk. I am Matilda Deauville Danforth. I am president of *Les Femmes Poétiques*, Capital City chapter. I am also recording secretary of the Arkansas Daughters of the Confederacy."

"Two most estimable organizations, I am certain, but I should say . . . ."

"Mr. Murk, it is not my nature to dissemble. I feel oblig-

ed to tell you straightforwardly that I come tonight to
deliver a strong protest against your receiving the
Broadhead Prize. I am acting as spokeswoman for both
organizations—which, by the way, voted almost unanimously in favor of this protest. We voice no judgment on
your *poetry*, Mr. Murk. In fact, none of us are familiar with
it. But many of us knew Arlene Broadhead quite well, and
we are certain that she could not have approved of your
recent denigration of our state's heritage and of one of its
best loved poets. Perhaps you do not know that in 1935 the
Arkansas Daughters of the Confederacy arranged for an
historical marker to be placed at Slackwater Slough, and
we have physically maintained the site since that time.
Your attack upon Mr. Tennyson's commemorative poem is
akin to writing a bawdy parody of the Gettysburg Address
if you were a guest in the North. Furthermore, Mr.
Tennyson has long been a friend of *Les Femmes Poétiques*
and has read at our annual Poetry Day on more than one
occasion. Therefore, we cannot believe that Mrs.
Broadhead would support the selection committee's choice
when so many deserving Arkansas writers have yet to
receive the prize."

"Madam, was this, in fact, your protest? Or can we have
merely heard the prologue?"

"I beg your pardon?"

"Your organizations are, I assume, of the large, far-flung
sort? That is very good. One should never entangle oneself
with a small organization."

"I'm afraid I don't understand . . . "

"For example, one should never join a minor political
party, such as the Libertarian or Prohibitionist. One will be
expected to do some of the work, you see."

"Mr. Murk, I . . . "

"For that matter, one should avoid the major political
parties, as well. This is my humble observation as a visitor
in your wonderful country. One should not join the

Democratic Party unless one aspires to become mayor of New York City. And, of course, no sane person aspires to become mayor of New York City."

"Mr. Murk . . . "

"On the other hand, one should avoid the Republican Party, since being a Republican seems never to be a rewarding experience for a person."

Matilda Deauville Danforth had had enough. She turned on her heel and marched erectly back to rejoin her group of dowagers.

Muggsbottom's (or Murk's) young admirers had stood stunned and silent during the exchange, but they now rushed to his defense.

"How *can* she have spoken to you that way?"

"This is disgraceful, Mr. Murk. We're so sorry a thing like this has happened."

"Really! The poor woman must be deranged."

"She must need psychiatric attention."

Muggsbottom stilled their cries of indignation by raising his hands in a benevolent gesture.

"Ah, ladies. May I voice a cautionary note? Never see a psychiatrist. If you are truly mad, he will be unable to help you but will probably wish to do something to you you would rather not have done. If you are not mad, he will still expect you to visit him at three-month intervals until one or the other of you is dead."

"Excuse us, will you please?" I said and, catching Muggsbottom by the elbow, steered him up the steps and away from both groups, now staring icily at each other.

"Muggsbottom," I said, "How do you manage it? Immediately getting involved in a controversy that isn't even about *you*."

"I protest my innocence in the strongest possible terms. You heard my attempts to disabuse friend and foe alike of the fantastic notion that I was the abominable Murk. But you know the female mind—when an idea somehow lodges itself there, man is usually powerless to alter it."

The president of NOUNS AND VERBS came hurrying over to speak to us again.

"There's a disturbing rumor circulating through the crowd," he said. "Have you heard it? Supposedly, some of those old bags from *Les Femmes* are going to kick up a fuss during the presentation ceremony."

Muggsbottom nodded solemnly and said, "All too true, old man."

"This is damned awkward," the young man said. "The society editors from both papers are here with their photographers. We've always gotten such excellent press for our Broadhead Prize. Do you think they've found out he's queer? I wouldn't think any of them have read Murk, would you?

"No offense," he said, directing his next remark to Muggsbottom, "but I've just assumed all you English guys were queer to one degree or another. No big deal."

Muggsbottom smiled, indicating that no offense had been taken.

"I think something else is at issue," I said, in an attempt to be helpful.

"I hope so. If those old broads call Murk a fag in public, Lorenzo may just order them off the premises. *Those* pictures won't wind up on the society page. Lorenzo is so damned intolerant of bigotry, you know."

"Never try to save a left-winger from his own good works," Muggsbottom intoned. "Unless he happens to be among the elect, he cannot be saved."

The young man was lost in thought and appeared not to profit from Muggsbottom's homily. As he moved away from us, he mused, "Maybe we should get Murk out here to mingle with the guests until time for the ceremony. But he's hardly the endearing type, is he? Such a cold carp. And that damned tic puts a person off immediately."

As if these reflections were an incantation to summon

him up, Murk appeared. He and Lorenzo Sandcastle emerged from the rear of the house, looking rather stiff and uncomfortable together. Dr. Sandcastle was a slender man of early middle age, whose pale face wore a practiced caring look. He and Murk were trailed by the insipid teen-ager who had told us where to park.

Dr. Sandcastle's eyes registered no recognition as they met ours, but he smiled and said, "Lovely evening, isn't it? Have you seen the house? Lars, show these gentlemen the house, why don't you?"

The doctor scarcely paused as he spoke these words. Murk said nothing when he saw Muggsbottom, but he flushed a deep red and his tic was frantically activated. Sandcastle caught sight of an attractive young woman, whose soft blouse displayed a pair of prominent nipples. He waved, caught Murk by the arm, and hurried him away towards her.

"Will you gentlemen please follow me?" the boy said wearily.

I was glad for the excuse to get my aphoristic friend away from the crowd and, at least for the moment, he seemed content.

On our tour of the first floor, we met a half dozen other guests wandering through the house. An observer with a better eye for furnishings and ornamentation might give the reader a definitive description of "Castle West." I, however, can recall only that it was self-consciously eclectic. One room was furnished in an Oriental motif, the next in Colonial American, and the next in Louis Quatorze—that sort of thing.

My clearest memory is of the little entryway at the front of the house. On one wall was a life-sized portrait of our host, and the smallness of the space really made it seem larger than life. Dr. Sandcastle was represented as holding a closed book, his place marked with a forefinger, while he chewed pensively on the ear piece of his eyeglasses. He was, I assumed, thinking sympathetic thoughts about the downtrodden masses. I was reminded of portraits of Victorian and Edwardian ancestors on the walls of old Hollywood movie sets. I was certain that I had never before seen such a painting in anyone's home. The opposite wall was empty, but the blue paper bore a rectangular shadow of identical size.

Our young guide, noticing my expression of curiosity, said, "My parents were divorced last year." Then he glanced at his wristwatch and added, "It's about time for the ceremony. Shall we return to the garden?"

We made our way back through the house to discover that in our absence a podium had been set up, facing several rows of folding chairs spread across the courtyard. While the chairs were rapidly being filled, other guests were situating themselves along the low stone balustrade that surrounded the upper level of the "garden." Clustered around the podium were Dr. Sandcastle, Murk, the president of NOUNS AND VERBS, and Matilda Deauville Danforth, who was waving a sheet of paper under her host's nose.

I could hear exasperation in Sandcastle's voice as he said, "But, Matilda, this *is* Professor Murk."

"I don't understand . . . Then where is the *other* Murk?"

"There is no other Murk, Matilda."

The rising voices had caught the attention of the members of the press, and strobe lights began to flash.

"Do you remember the way back to the front door?" I asked my friend.

"I believe I can reconstruct it," he replied.

We made our third trip through the first story of Castle West, this one at double time. We went right out the front door and down the red brick path.

As we pulled onto Interstate 30, heading south, Muggsbottom said, "A pretty diverse group, your GERUNDS. I suppose they eventually sorted out that little mix-up without too much rancor, don't you?"

We learned upon our return that there had also been a little mix-up in Arcady, one characterized by considerable rancor.

"Well," said Sir Monty, whose knitted brow gave evidence of the effort he was expending in marshaling his thoughts, "Maynard came bursting in here about an hour ago, babbling this story which I suppose is true or, at least, very nearly true. The blighter learns everything that happens in Arcady, you know, usually within five minutes' time.

"Apparently, poor Reggie has not, after all, been able to break the spell cast upon him by the Luce woman. He went to her home tonight—bidden or unbidden, I do not know. While he was thus in her company, that Ol' Perfesser person turned up. Despite what he had written about Mrs. Luce in the newspaper, the booby had got himself drunk enough to believe that he might heal the breach between them.

"Mrs. Luce would not admit him. Learning somehow that Reggie was inside the house, the Ol' Perfesser went quite mad with jealousy and frustration. He began to pound upon the door and loudly to threaten Reggie with bodily harm. Reggie, having that sense of propriety which comes only from one's upbringing, chose not to telephone the police. Instead, he telephoned our neighbor. I do not recall hearing that gentleman's rap at the door—I may just have been taking a little catnap at that moment. Smythe-Gardner apparently took the message and, learning of Reggie's distress, flew to his assistance on wingèd feet. Fortunately, as you know, Mrs. Luce's house is not too far distant.

"According to Maynard, when Smythe-Gardner arrived he found the Ol' Perfesser attempting to throw rocks through the woman's windows. They had words, and—you know Smythe-Gardner—the words soon led to fisticuffs. Our truculent companion has been spoiling to biff somebody for months now, and my report is that he gave a good account of himself indeed.

"I mentioned, did I not, that Reggie, hoping to avoid notoriety, chose not to call the police. A neighbor, understandably disturbed by the affray in Mrs. Luce's front yard, was not so circumspect. Maynard tells me that Biffy, Reggie, the Ol' Perfesser, and perhaps Mrs. Luce as well have been taken 'downtown.' I was, naturally, deeply concerned but found that I lacked the energy to take decisive action."

By God, I thought, Sir Monty *can* talk when he has a tale to tell. Quantitatively, this speech very nearly equaled everything I had heard the old man say in more than a year's time. And qualitatively, it was certainly his finest hour.

Muggsbottom put his hand on his old friend's shoulder, then turned to me.

"Could I impose upon you for just a bit longer, old man? If you *could* run me down to the headquarters of the local constabulary . . . ? I have, I think, evolved into the closest thing my country has to a diplomatic presence in Arcady. Now is surely the time to act in that semiofficial capacity."

"I'll take you on one condition," I said. "No more of those non sequiturs you've been peppering everyone with all evening. You start that stuff at the police station, and you'll wind up behind bars with everybody else."

Muggsbottom smiled indulgently.

"My dear fellow, I have come to love you like my own brother, but I am bound to say it—you are decidedly deficient in a spirit of fun."

18. The Flaming Cross

My reference to the lovers' triangle plus one as being "behind bars" proved hyperbolic. Our police chief adheres to the customary small town practice of arresting strangers and members of the working class, while giving citizens of Mrs. Luce's standing "a good talking-to." I do not know if Muggsbottom's diplomacy was helpful—it apparently did no harm. I dropped him off at the police station and went on my way. I had seen quite enough of his performance for one night. No charges were filed by anybody, and the disputants were eventually returned to their several homes by squad car.

The row cooked poor Reggie's goose once and for all. I have no idea how much progress he was making in rekindling the flame. But for a second time he had been party to an incident which deeply embarrassed Cecilia, and that was that. Had the brawl been between the two suitors she might have experienced some gratification—I am told that, despite their protestations, women still enjoy the spectacle of men fighting over them. In this case, however, one of the suitors had remained behind locked doors, wisely but unromantically declining to face his adversary. And one of the combatants had been defending his countryman's honor, not hers.

The incident turned out to be disastrous for the Ol' Perfesser also. The "Police Report" was a daily feature in the *Harbinger*. So when the paper's star columnist turned up in that very report, right alongside folks arrested for passing hot checks and soliciting at the truck stop, the editor was every bit as embarrassed as Cecilia Luce. He was not a proponent of the "New Journalism." Rather, he held tenaciously to the old-fashioned principle that journalists wrote the copy, were never part of the copy. Despite the fact that the columnist appeared in the "Police Report" under his name rather than his cognomen, the editor fired the Ol' Perfesser on the spot.

Smythe-Gardner was the only participant who seemed to have suffered no ill effects from the fracas. To the contrary, for the next several weeks he was positively rejuvenated. The only physical sign of the encounter was a slight abrasion above his left eye, which he made no effort to conceal. His conversation grew more nautical, sometimes distractingly so. He took to issuing commands to Maynard such as, "Belay all that gabble, steward, and secure the ship's stores, or I'll throw you in the hold and give that job to some boy who steps lively." Maynard appeared to enjoy Smythe-Gardner's cheerful abuse. In fact, we all welcomed the old sailor's good humor. We knew that his golden glow must inevitably fade away, but for the time being we basked therein.

I never saw my former colleague, the Ol' Perfesser, again. We academics are probably more subject to inertia than most people. He had been unhappy in Arcady for many years, but it is likely that only such a personal calamity could have induced him to leave town. Well, it had occurred, and he had left. Strange, I thought, how illogically we human beings react to the behavior of our fellows. The Ol' Perfesser's jaundiced view of mankind and its institutions was not objectively different from Muggsbottom's. But whereas his attitude had long seemed peevish, unpleasant, and basically unhealthy, Muggsbottom's struck me as essentially innocent and charming. Perhaps my Anglophilia made all the difference. But, on the other hand, Murk was an Englishman too, and I did not like him worth a damn.

And speaking of Twinksly Murk, it was also time for him to leave Arcady. Summer had come, the spring term had concluded, and Murk's tenure as poet-in-residence had ended along with it. I sensed that he was happy to be going. How could he have imagined that Muggsbottom would materialize out of his past to haunt him? In actuality, their contact had been scant, but Murk must have viewed my friend as a sort of evil doppelgänger who might reappear at any moment.

And then there had been the fiasco at the Broadhead Prize ceremony. The papers on the following morning had not played up the controversy—much to the relief of the Board of NOUNS AND VERBS—but they had run pictures of people whose faces clearly revealed their anger. A story originated in Little Rock, then made its way around the state, that the exchange between Matilda Deauville Danforth and Lorenzo Sandcastle had finally grown so heated that the former had clubbed the latter over the head with her purse. I was sure the story was apocryphal. *That* would have been in the newspapers—besides, my recollection was that Dame Danforth had carried no purse. Another story out of Little Rock—this one I was able to verify— told of the mass resignation of the mesdames holding joint membership in *Les Femmes Poétiques* and NOUNS AND VERBS. They vowed to boycott the Broadhead Prize until such time as an Arkansas poetess with three names should receive the award, "as Arlene Broadhead would certainly have wished."

Reggie returned to his former state of deep melancholy.

One evening, before I could stop myself, I blurted out a piece of gratuitous advice. "Reggie, you should take up a hobby, do something to distract yourself."

To my amazement, his response was, "I have done. Billy

Earl is teaching me to fly."

"Billy Earl . . . ?"

"Another string to his bow, you might say. The fee seems quite reasonable."

"But does Billy Earl have a license to give flying lessons?"

"I'm sure I don't know."

"Reggie, you can't drive an automobile. At least, I've never seen any evidence that you can."

"Billy Earl says it isn't the same thing at all."

When I next saw Billy Earl Hangar, I confronted him.

"What's this business about your giving flying lessons to Reggie Dipswizzle?"

"Well, I'm not 'giving' them exactly, but he is receiving a special discount."

"You know what I mean."

"We must all work. We must earn our daily bread. The Master said, 'Which of you shall have an ass or an ox fall into a pit, and will not straightway pull him out?' Luke, Chapter Fourteen, Verse Five. And, believe it or not, Brother Dipswizzle shows some promise as a pilot."

"I believe it not," I said.

"Each of us must use those talents the Lord has given us for the benefit of others. Which reminds me—do you remember the young man who shared the pulpit with me that morning at Bunyan Chapel?"

As transparent as this effort to change the subject was, I allowed it to succeed.

"Barry Sanderson? Yes, I do remember him. As a matter of fact, I've heard quite a lot about him lately."

"Have you?"

Billy Earl framed the question so archly that I caught myself. I would hold my tongue and hear what he had to say.

"What about Sanderson?"

"He came to the tabernacle Wednesday night for prayer

meeting." He waited for me to respond to this announcement, but when I did not he continued. "And at the altar call, he came forward and rededicated his life."

O.K., I thought, I'll let you crow a little.

"Well, that must have been quite a coup for you, all right. But I should think a mainstream type like Sanderson could rededicate his life perfectly well at Bunyan Chapel or at the First Baptist Church."

"That is exactly the point I'm making," said Billy Earl, obviously warming to his topic. "God gives us each the means to be of service. In cases like this, my ministry can meet a need that the mainstream churches cannot meet. You see, Barry had become involved in an illicit relationship with an older woman. He was too ashamed to confess his sin to anyone at the college or his home church, but the Lord—praise His holy name—had provided the Runway to Heaven Ministry to which he might turn."

"And he made a public confession at the Runway to Heaven?"

"No, no. He confided the details to me privately, after the service."

"Then, should you be telling me this? What about the seal of the confessional, that sort of thing?"

"That is a superstition of the papists, as you well know. I only shared this information with you to illustrate the point that God always leaves a door ajar for the sinner somewhere."

I am not one of those people who always know the latest gossip, so I am not usually required to feign ignorance. On this occasion, however, I knew a good deal and thought it would be fun to probe the extent of Billy Earl's knowledge.

"Who is the woman?"

Billy Earl made a long, sanctimonious face, but his eyes twinkled as he said, "Now, that *would* be betraying a confidence, wouldn't it? I'm not saying that I *know* the lady's identity, mind you, but I would not reveal it even if I did. I can assure you of one thing, however. The affair is over, done with. Naturally, Barry's Christian conscience was bothering him, but I think his mistress had him a little scared too. You know how aggressive these older women can be. God's ways of mending the errant human heart are many and varied."

Poor Cecilia seemed to have missed the gravy train once again. But the game was still afoot, and Cecilia was no quitter.

As Reggie's flying lessons progressed, he spent more and more time in the company of Billy Earl Hangar. Soon he was accompanying Billy Earl on his twice daily "Eye in the Sky" flights over Arcady. One morning, probably on a whim, Billy Earl decided to "mike" his pupil as well as himself. Thus debuted the Billy Earl and Reggie Show. Although destined to be short-lived, it quickly became the most popular locally produced show in the history of KARC.

Billy Earl's traffic reports from his Christian biplane, the *Flaming Cross*, had attracted an audience from the first, but the addition of Reggie Dipswizzle doubled the show's listenership almost at once. On the air, the two men had a chemistry that nobody could have predicted but that everybody could recognize. Local sponsors who had before been wary now clamored to get their thirty second spots on board. Newt Parker came out of hiding. Initially, he had taken so much ribbing over a rush-hour traffic report for Arcady that he was ready to crow a bit.

"The smartest thing I ever did was hire Billy Earl Hangar," Newt said to me one day after I had broached the subject of the "Eye in the Sky."

"And the smartest—or luckiest—thing Billy Earl ever did was recruit Reggie Dipswizzle."

"People just like that damned Englishman. Hell, *I* like him. He's the only one of them who's the least bit approachable." Then Newt remembered my well-known relationship with the Englishmen. "Of course, I know *you* like all of them a lot. All I meant was . . . "

I took him off the hook by saying, "Reggie should be good on the radio, you know. He was in show business in England."

My intention was subtly to suggest, by changing the subject, that Newt's remark had not offended me and he needed to make no amends. I had, however, inadvertently hit upon a point that made him even more defensive.

"My contract is with Billy Earl. I don't have any agreement with Dipswizzle. Now, if Billy Earl wants to subcontract a spot on his show to Dipswizzle . . . "

"Easy, Newt. I'm not Reggie's agent. I don't imagine he's had a single thought about money since he started broadcasting. In fact, I would bet you that Reggie pays *Billy Earl* every time they go up. Flying lessons, you know."

"Well, it's just that Billy Earl already wants to renegotiate. Damn it, I'm not made of money. I've got a rock-hard written agreement with him . . . but, still, he's a slippery son of a bitch."

I could almost hear Billy Earl saying, "Newt, I always go to the Lord in prayer and ask Him what I should do. And last night, the Lord said to me, 'Billy Earl, you're not getting enough money. Renegotiate.'"

What follows is the partial text of a typical "Eye in the Sky" broadcast:

BILLY EARL. *According to my shiny new Swiss quartz wristwatch with its ebony dial and fourteen karat gold case—I may not mention the brand on the air unless the manufacturer or the retailer wishes to advertize on KARC—the time is seven-fifty on this lovely Arcadian Monday morning. My congregation at the Runway to*

Heaven Ministry—may the Lord richly bless them—surprised me with this beautiful wristwatch as a love offering at yesterday's morning service. Perhaps they're encouraging me to take a little more notice of the time. What do you think, Reggie?

REGGIE. *I have heard that you tend to go on a bit, Billy Earl.*

BILLY EARL. *The sheep who have strayed are sometimes willful, Reggie. The good shepherd labors on until they are all safely in the fold.*

REGGIE. *Well, you know more about that sort of thing than I.*

BILLY EARL. *Dear listeners, I wish that each and every one of you could be with Reggie and me this morning, here in the Flaming Cross, as we soar close to God. Though that's not possible, I invite you all to let your spirits soar as you worship with us at the Runway to Heaven. We meet at the Tabernacle, formerly the Royal Theater, on Main Street. Sabbath services are at eleven a.m. and six p.m., prayer meeting at seven on Wednesday evenings. Plenty of on-street parking.*

REGGIE. *I say, Billy Earl. We've soared so close to God, I've lost sight of Pine Street.*

BILLY EARL. *Right you are, Reggie. Let's go down and have a look . . . Hear that little miss? Listen. Remind me to take a look at this engine when we get back to the airport . . . There's Pine Street, Reggie. And what's this? We have a little backup in the eastbound lane, don't we?*

REGGIE. *There appears to be a stalled lorry.*

BILLY EARL. *That's a truck, folks.*

REGGIE. *I believe he's suffered a puncture.*

BILLY EARL. *He's had a flat, folks. Right between the optometrist clinic and the beauty school. The driver doesn't have enough shoulder to clear his lane.*

REGGIE. *Poor chap. One never wishes to be the center of attention under such circumstances.*

Patrick Adcock

BILLY EARL. *We're pretty well stalled all the way back to the Exxon station, folks. If you haven't passed Caddo Street yet, you need to take a right there. Caddo's clear, and you can scoot right on downtown quick as a whistle.*

REGGIE. *I believe the local constabulary have arrived upon the scene.*

BILLY EARL. *Right again, Reggie. Arcady's finest will soon be directing traffic and moving you good folks right along to your destinations. So let's buzz on down to Tenth Street and see how things are coming along there . . . Well, what do you know—we have some congestion on Tenth Street too. Looks like we've had a little fender-bender in that southbound lane. Right in front of the washateria on the corner of Tenth and Jefferson.*

REGGIE. *Billy Earl, I believe that one of the damaged automobiles is a constabulary motor car.*

BILLY EARL. *Your eyes are sharp this morning, Reggie. The vehicle with that big dent on the driver's side is a police patrol car all right. My guess is that he was hurrying to answer the call on Pine Street and got into this little scrape.*

REGGIE. *If so, it would seem unappreciative to censure him.*

BILLY EARL. *Yes. Well, travelers, if you're trying to get up Tenth Street to State College or beyond, just calm down and be patient. Traffic's moving around that little wreck—it's just moving very slowly . . . We've had a pretty doggone busy Monday morning, haven't we, old copilot?*

REGGIE. *One hopes one has been of some use.*

BILLY EARL. *Friends, our time is gone, and it's back to the old airport for us. Join us again at five when we'll help you get home with your car and your nerves intact. Until then, for Reggie Dipswizzle and myself, this is Billy Earl Hangar saying God bless you and keep you. Now, back to the studio for a word from Miss Dottie and all the girls down at Hair Heaven.*

238

"Reggie and Billy Earl are big hits on the radio," I said.

"Indeed?" Muggsbottom responded. "What can conceivably account for that phenomenon?"

"Oh, part of it is that they flatter us, I suspect. It pleases us to imagine we're urban enough to have traffic problems."

"You Arkansawyers are a curious people. However, one must admit that one eventually grows attached to you . . . Do you suppose that Billy Earl ever allows Reggie to drive the aeroplane?"

"Well, he's charging Reggie for lessons, so I suppose he must from time to time."

"Still, it seems most unwise to me to place Reggie at the controls of an aeroplane. We have never permitted Reggie to take the controls of anything whatever, and I cannot tell that he has suffered from the denial."

On the morning of the accident, I was in my office, reading freshman essays and thinking: If I teach another ten years, I won't be able to spell any word with more than two consonants in it. At about ten-thirty, the Britishers' next-door neighbor, my colleague who has made several previous appearances in this narrative, stuck his head through the door and said, "Have you heard?"

"What?"

"Billy Earl Hangar's plane went down on the other side of the river-—crashed in a little thicket about fifteen minutes ago."

"Crashed?"

"Uh-huh. Billy Earl was killed . . . and another man who was with him. At least, that's what they're saying on the police band. He wasn't on the radio or anything. Just flying around."

"Has the other man been identified?"

I knew instantly, of course, who the other man was.

"I haven't heard a name. They're referring to him as a 'student pilot.' I only know of one person who could be called Billy Earl's 'student pilot.' Your friend Dipswizzle."

When I arrived at the house on the old, tree-shaded street, I parked behind Homer Joe Tennyson's pickup truck. Homer Joe had parked on the street because a car with a light on top and DEAN COUNTY SHERIFF'S DEPARTMENT on the door was occupying the driveway. Sir Monty and Smythe-Gardner had been at home all morning, but Muggsbottom had been at Granny's, swapping lies with Homer Joe and his cronies, when news of the tragedy came to him.

I entered the living room to confront a *tableau vivant.* Muggsbottom and Homer Joe were sitting on the couch, with the old deer skinner's arm around the Englishman's shoulder. On either side of the couch sat Sir Monty and Smythe-Gardner, motionless in their usual chairs. Sheriff Red Birdsong and Deputy Slim Appleseed stood facing them, respectfully holding their wide-brimmed hats in front of them.

Muggsbottom looked up at me and said, "Apparently Reggie was at the controls when the crash occurred."

"I figured even Billy Earl wouldn't have the nerve to take Reggie's money without letting him touch the stick a time or two."

I just blurted this remark right out, and several minutes had passed before I realized it was not the sort of grave euphemism expected of one at such a moment. It could, in fact, even be construed as speaking ill of the dead.

I saw something in Homer Joe's face that I could not then interpret. In retrospect, I understand that Homer Joe had realized immediately what I had not—the ultimate consequences of Reggie Dipswizzle's demise.

19. Dénouement

Billy Earl Hangar, that wandering boy, was buried in Arcady. Despite the briefness of his residence, it was as close to a home as any town in which he had touched down during his years of peregrination. The lease was paid on the old Royal Theater through the end of the month, so Billy Earl's funeral was scheduled to be the last official service of the Runway to Heaven Ministry. More on this point later. The funeral was a jim-dandy.

The preacher from the First Baptist Church officiated, thus giving the service a certain eerie quality from the outset. His resemblance to Billy Earl in physical appearance and manner I have previously noted.

The Ministerial Alliance of Arcady were turned out in full force to honor their fallen comrade, now that he was no longer a threat to proselytize their members. In fact, these preachers had prevailed upon Maynard, who was responsible for his cousin's interment, to make the service an interdenominational affair in which each would participate. Only Father Hal of Our Lady of Wise Counsel had begged off. He claimed to be leading a retreat on that day, a duty from which he could not be excused. I was unconvinced, however, suspecting that Father Hal feared the Runway to Heaven would be too great a shock to his Catholic system.

The Baptist preacher had naturally staked out the sermon

241

Patrick Adcock

for himself on the basis of his and the late Billy Earl's con-
fluent theological and ecclesiastical positions. After an
hour or more of spirited negotiations, the leftovers had
been divided up in this manner: The Unitarian minister
would offer the invocation. The Presbyterian minister
would read the Psalm, the Methodist minister the Epistle,
and the Episcopal priest from the Gospels. Abednego
Aftermath of the Fifteenth Street Communion of the Holy
Ghost would speak the benediction, thereby making Billy
Earl's funeral satisfyingly interracial as well as interdenominational.

The Englishmen and I were in attendance, but Smythe-
Gardner had only been persuaded to come at the very last
minute. Muggsbottom and Sir Monty had argued the
demands of noblesse oblige. After all, the deceased had
been Maynard's cousin, and Maynard was their faithful
retainer—well, anyway, their retainer. Smythe-Gardner had
countered by assessing blame. "That sanctimonious little
snot got Reggie killed, poor sod. Tell me, what honor do
we owe him?" In the end, we were all there, seated together toward the rear of the Royal Theater, but Biffy remained
resentful and sullen. We were fortunate to have found
seats. The sanctuary was filled downstairs, and above us I
could hear the scuffs and scrapes of people filing into the
balcony. During his brief tenure, Billy Earl had acquired a
flock of impressive size.

The Ministerial Alliance of Arcady was arrayed across
the stage, seated on folding chairs. Behind them was the
dingy, tattered screen upon which, not so very long ago,
had flickered scenes of rampant secular humanism. In front
of the clergymen, upon a high catafalque, rested Billy
Earl's coffin.

Some creative element among the Runway to Heaven
regulars had designed a casket with wings. It bore on top
the same flaming cross that had so long adorned the under-
side of the demolished biplane. I believe that the men from

242

the funeral home had voiced some objection until it was demonstrated that the wings readily folded into a vertical position, allowing the grave to be dug to the standard dimensions.

The pianist (the Royal Theater could not accommodate an organ) concluded a mournful number, the title of which I could not identify but which was familiar from many funerals past. The Unitarian rose, looked up to the balcony, and paused for late comers to slip into their seats. When all were finally still, he stepped forward to the apron of the stage and began.

"Will you join with me in a moment of meditation, or please use whatever means you may customarily employ for contemplation of the cosmos and of your place in the cosmos?"

Roughly a quarter of the congregation recognized this sentence as an invitation to bow their heads. The majority then took their cue from these sophisticates.

"Oh, Great Ordering Principle of the Universe . . . Oh, Ultimate Source of Reason and Rationality . . . Oh, Presence Ineffable, that is not white or black, that is not yellow or red or brown . . . that is neither male nor female . . . "

"Dear God," muttered Sir Monty.

"I believe those are the very words for which he is groping," responded Muggsbottom.

"We are here today to commend to You our fellow sojourner Billy Earl Hangar. Billy Earl has undergone that great metamorphosis which awaits us all. Only days ago, Billy Earl was composed of one form of matter. Today, he is composed of another. What is this new form of matter? We cannot say. We do not know whence Billy Earl came, nor whither he has gone . . . just as we do not know whence we came, nor whither we go. We only know that the Universe endures. And, even as we encounter the extra-ordinary revelations of modern theoretical physics, we can say along with the poet, 'Whatever is, is right.'"

"Blasphemy," growled Muggsbottom. "That agnostic booby is quoting *Pope*."

"So today, we remember Billy Earl Hangar—clergyman, aviator, and radio personality. We celebrate his life, especially his contributions to brotherhood and sisterhood among all persons in our community."

I could think of several persons over at State College who might quibble with that assessment.

"In closing, we ask—Oh, Spirit of the Universe—that You draw Billy Earl to Your bosom, which is neither male nor female, and nurture him . . . just as You would have us nurture the exploited and the dispossessed of this, our sick capitalistic, militaristic society.

"We have come to the end of this moment of contemplation."

Although I thought Muggsbottom's characterization of the Unitarian was a bit extreme, I couldn't think that his prayer—or whatever it was—had done much for Billy Earl's fundamentalist flock.

The mainstream clergymen, the Presbyterian and the Methodist, were typically restrained in their rendition of the First and Second Readings. As the Episcopal priest read the familiar John 3:16 and the two verses following— a text which I was pretty damned sure he had not chosen— he glanced apologetically over at his Unitarian soul mate.

Sir Monty roused himself enough to say, "Can't abide that fellow."

What a snoozer Billy Earl's funeral has been so far, I thought, and savored the delicious irony of that fact. The fully immersed majority within the theater were growing noticeably restless, but their time had finally come. The fire-eaters were next up on the program.

The demonstrative and participatory nature of Billy Earl's flock freed the Baptist preacher from certain inhibitions he had developed in dealing with his own, more sophisticated, congregation. When he took the pulpit, things livened up immediately. He preached a stem-winder. No doubt he was especially inspired by Billy Earl's coffin.

I will beg the reader to be satisfied with this extremely brief summary of the sermon. Writing is, after all, largely a matter of proportion, and I feel bound to hurry on to the benediction delivered by Abednego Aftermath. For this benediction was easily the second most arresting moment of the funeral service. The *most* arresting I must withhold for just a little longer.

After we had sung every verse of an exceedingly melancholy hymn, Brother Aftermath advanced resplendently to the coffin. Like his colleagues, he wore a suit of a deep funereal blue, but his wide violet tie glowed against his magenta shirt. And he wore a large gold cross around his neck that had been burnished to a dazzling sheen. He placed one hand upon Billy Earl's fuselage and raised the other in the familiar posture of beatitude.

"Lord, we ask You to bless us as we go forth from this tabernacle today. We are reminded that in the very midst of life we can reach right out and touch Old Man Death on the nose. We are reminded that You could call any of us tomorrow as You have now called Brother Hangar to Yourself. Let me hear 'amen' to that."

The congregation, much energized by the hellfire and brimstone sermon they had just heard, roared, "Amen."

"Brother Hangar's business was saving souls for You, Lord, and we, his fellow pastors, would betray his high calling if we wasted this opportunity to say to these assembled—If you and the Lord ain't right, better get that fixed tonight. Are you saved? Well, if you ain't sho', you ain't ready to go. If you love the Lord, better climb on board . . . I want to hear the Church say 'amen' to that."

"*Amen.*"

"Lord, we know that You mark the sparrow's fall. So we know that You have Your eye out right now for our departed brother, Billy Earl Hangar. 'Cause he's flying up to You, Lord, in the *Flaming Cross*. It's a restored *Flaming Cross* old Billy Earl is flying. Its nose is pointed smack at Heaven. And it don't need no gasoline. And the wind is always at its tail. And its wings are snowy white like angels' wings."

Some of the sniffling in the congregation had turned into audible sobs.

"Keep a lookout for him, Lord. And when You see him, send Your angels out to mark his landing strip. Or if You think You might enjoy watching the old *Flaming Cross* buzz around Heaven, if You should choose to leave Billy Earl in that cockpit he loves, I'm sure that he couldn't think of a better way to spend eternity."

Now cries of "Oh, Brother Hangar" and "Oh, Billy Earl" issued from the faithful.

"Yes, Billy Earl is winging his way to his reward, Lord. And we want to someday follow him. Lord, stir the hearts of those lost in sin. May they confess their sins, repent, and prepare themselves for their own flight to Heaven. Lord, You're everywhere, and we know You care. If we come to You, You'll see us through. We . . . "

The lamentation level was going up like the *Flaming Cross* of Brother Aftermath's metaphor, and there is no telling how much higher he could have driven it had he not been interrupted. But interrupted he was, by an over-wrought sinner who scrambled up onto the stage and threw himself across one wing of Billy Earl's coffin.

"I'm lost," he cried. "A lost sinner. Help me, Jesus."

This sort of thing must have occurred often at the Runway to Heaven Ministry (minus the winged casket, naturally). But I suppose we found it so extraordinary because the sinner was Maynard.

"What, what?" inquired Sir Monty, awakened by the hubbub.

"I believe Maynard has just been saved," Muggsbottom

explained.

After the service, we found ourselves beside the Reverend Aftermath. Muggsbottom complimented him on his performance, a performance powerful enough to effect Maynard's conversion.

"You were like the character actor with the tiny part who steals the film from the stars," he said.

Aftermath winked and said, "Cain't no white man preach up to the black man's standard, Mr. Mulberry."

Reggie was shipped home to Hertfordshire. Muggsbottom exchanged wires with Mama and Papa Dipswizzle, or whichever Dipswizzle was currently minding the family finances. Poor Reggie. He had been the gentlest, the most innocent, the most pacific of men. But he had been also the most star-crossed of men, a fellow to whom unpleasant things happened with such alarming regularity that others finally just wanted him to be somewhere else—witness his many years as a remittance man.

The Phlegm Club convened, discussed the possibility of a memorial service in Arcady, and concluded by voting unanimously in the affirmative. Reggie had been the most outgoing of the Englishmen, the most "approachable," as Newt Parker had put it. Reggie's kindly, sympathetic nature, his unfailing courtesy—these had won him friends among the townspeople. I had personally overheard more than one of the locals make remarks such as, "I don't know about the others, but old Dipswizzle is *all right.*" Also, in his last days, Reggie had acquired a certain celebrity as Eye in the Sky copilot. All in all, the Phlegm Club decided, Reggie was due a service here in Arcady.

Upon Muggsbottom's return from making the arrangements at St. Augustine's of the Wood, he waxed indignant.

"That bloody upstart of a rector asked me if Reggie had been an habitual communicant. Can you imagine? What a question from a Marxist in a cassock! Actually, I never once saw Reggie take the sacrament in all the time I knew him, but I wasn't about to countenance that sort of impertinence from a little pipsqueak left-wing priest. 'The Dipswizzles of Hertfordshire,' I said, 'have been C. of E. since Henry the Eighth.' That may even be true. He replied, 'So Mr. Dipswizzle was at least nominally a Christian then?" To which my answer was, 'If I valued my parish, I shouldn't attempt to sort the nominal Christians out from the rest.' I concluded by instructing him to read the traditional service word for word—none of his barbaric modernisms—and *we* should be entirely responsible for the eulogy."

Reggie's memorial service did not attract the sort of throng that had gathered at the Royal Theater but, in its own way, it was a great success. The small sanctuary of St. Augustine's of the Wood was three-quarters filled. Newt Parker and the tiny staff from KARC were there. Homer Joe Tennyson and the regulars from Granny's had turned out as a favor to Muggsbottom. Homer Joe had composed an elegiac piece of verse entitled "The Day the *Flaming Cross* Went Down," but Muggsbottom had somehow dissuaded him from reciting it. There were a number of people I did not know—I supposed they were Reggie's fans from the radio or, perhaps, stray Episcopalians. I sat with the Englishmen, as did Maynard. The new Maynard was eager to testify before this assemblage, but Muggsbottom had threatened him with bodily harm if he attempted to do so.

Without question, the most striking mourner was Cecilia Luce. Her grief had certainly not impaired her theatrical instincts. She was performing the role of widow in a costume of unrelieved black—hat, dress, hose, shoes. She was even wearing a thin black veil (which did not hide her features) and was, I believe, the first woman I had seen in a veil since my 1940's boyhood. She was the final mourner to arrive and took a great deal of time in finding her seat.

No one could have failed to notice her.

"It's that dreadful woman, is it not?" said Sir Monty so loudly that the question might have been addressed to anyone in the sanctuary.

"Yes," said Muggsbottom.

"I biffed hell out of that boyfriend of hers," said Smythe-Gardner and leaned back in the pew with an expression of deep pleasure on his florid countenance.

With Muggsbottom's baleful glare fixed upon him from beginning to end of the Service for the Dead, the nervous parson adhered to the Book of Common Prayer verbatim. Then, with an audible sigh of relief, he said, "I now call upon the friends of our departed brother in Christ to speak the eulogy."

Sir Monty went first in deference to his seniority. He shambled up to the lectern as though he were not long for this world either, then delivered himself of the following remarks.

"Why Reggie Dipswizzle, such an exemplar in the payment of respect to his elders, should be cut off in the bloom of his youth, no man can say. We can only say that he shall be missed and he shall be remembered. It is not for Reggie Dipswizzle's judgment, but for his nature that I shall remember him. Even we who loved him best could not deny that his judgment was unsound. His much lamented demise, the result of going aloft on one too many occasions with Billy Earl Hangar, attests to this lack of soundness. I could, though I will not, cite other specific examples." Here, Sir Monty stared hard at the woman in black. "Some men are loved for their minds, others for their talent, still others for their charm. Not so with Reggie. We loved Reggie for his nature which, though not sunny, was sweet and generous. Yes, 'sweet' and 'generous' are clearly the adjectives that capsulize our Reggie's personality. And I shall . . . shall, uh . . . deeply miss this . . . this . . . sweetness and generosity."

This brief encomium had expended all of Sir Monty's minuscule store of energy. As he shambled back to his seat, I could not help thinking that he would surely not be one's first choice as eulogist for one's own funeral.

Smythe-Gardner was the next to speak. For this solemn occasion, he had chosen to wear his naval uniform. And due to the earliness of the hour, he was only moderately inebriated.

"My friend Reggie Dipswizzle and I could scarcely have been more different. I come from two long lines of warriors. The Gardners fought for Charles the First at Marston Moor, and Smythes captained ships that smote and scattered the Armada in 1588. For many years, I sailed the seven seas, guarding Her Majesty's—and Her father's—before Her—far-flung interests and biffing Her enemies when the occasion arose. This was my happy lot until . . . until my retirement. Reggie, on the other hand, was the gentlest man I have ever known. What an impossible soldier or sailor he would have made! For he would not, and could not, raise his hand against any man. No degree of provocation could disturb Reggie's inner tranquility." Now Smythe-Gardner stared hard at the woman in black. "I do not pretend to understand this quality, not an atom of which is to be found in my own nature, but it stirred my old warrior's heart.

"I, who have sailed to the four corners of the world and have observed human nature in every race and nationality, can assure you that it is ugly and appalling everywhere and at all times. Reggie, however, loved everyone and trusted everyone. He was the only true and complete innocent I have ever known. Because he could not consciously have done anyone an injury, he could not conceive that anyone would consciously do him an injury. This innocence, of course, meant that poor Reggie could easily be taken advantage of."

Smythe-Gardner gave Cecilia another pointed look. It

was filled with ill will.

"Finally, Reggie was an actor. As a class, I don't like actors. They're a swell-headed lot, and generally pansies to boot. They boast constantly of their exploits when all they've ever done is pretend to be somebody else. But Reggie was not, God knows, egotistical. Far from it. He was self-denigrating to a fault. Not by way of fishing for compliments, as some people use self-criticism. No, Reggie was genuinely modest. The most modest man I have ever known.

"It's hard cheese, the way old Reggie went. But I learnt as a callow midshipman that when the typhoon strikes, we can only batten down the hatches and let the sea have her way until the weather clears . . . Still, when I think how Reggie's life was thrown away by the carelessness and incompetence of Billy Earl Hangar who, while raking in obscene amounts of money from his spurious religiosity, refused to spend the pittance required to keep his aircraft in good repair . . . "

Smythe-Gardner's face assumed a deeper shade of red, and the veins in his neck stood out in knots. Maynard stirred in the pew beside me. I reached over and put a hand lightly on his arm.

"I am overcome and must retire," Smythe-Gardner concluded.

He resumed his seat, all the while exchanging angry stares with the indignant Maynard.

The last word fell to Muggsbottom, as was always the case.

"Ladies and gentlemen, friends of Reggie Dipswizzle . . . we, Reggie's countrymen, thank you for honoring his memory by your attendance at this service. The occasion provides Sir Monty, Captain Smythe-Gardner, and me the opportunity to bid a formal farewell both to our dear old friend and to Arcady."

I was stunned. I should not have been. Homer Joe had

seen on the very morning of Reggie's death that the Englishmen would soon be gone, that without the Dipswizzle annuity they would have to go home to seek out whatever had sustained them before Reggie came into their lives.

"We British are a paradoxical race, for we are simultaneously insular and peripatetic. I believe one reason we have been so happy in Arcady is that we immediately recognized American Southerners as a paradoxical race also. I have often commented upon this particular aspect of Arcadian behavior, sometimes in the public press. We are very different from one another in most superficial ways. Yet, at the core of our beings, I believe we share a number of negative, but no less unifying, beliefs. Not all problems can be solved, not all misunderstandings can be ironed out, not all loose ends can be tied up. Call this fatalism, if you will. I will accept the appellation.

"We must try to be fatalistic about the passing of our dear friend. You know, as I have considered Reggie's life and death, they have come to be to my mind almost the perfect metaphor for the British experience since the days of Sir Walter Raleigh and his comrades. The paradoxes to which I earlier alluded were apparent in Reggie Dipswizzle. He was a man of faultless character and unfailing good will, yet his family could not abide having him within a hundred miles of them. He was an actor, an artist, who had not one iota of imagination. He was a romantic in whom I never saw a spark of passion . . . although others may be more qualified to speak to this point than I."

Now it was Muggsbottom's turn to take a long look at the woman in black. She responded by sniffling daintily and slipping a tissue up beneath her veil.

"Reggie was a traveler, an explorer, an adventurer who totally lacked the spirit of adventure. And like so many of his countrymen since the time of the first Elizabeth, he fell—quite literally—in a foreign land, in a hot country, far from his cool and misty island. And what is the term we British have used for generations to pay tribute to the Reggie Dipswizzles amongst us? I should say it is . . . 'good chap, Reggie. Jolly good chap.'

So the time has come to say goodbye to Reggie and to Arcady, both of which partings are exceedingly painful, I assure you. Again, thank you all for coming."

At the close of the service, Cecilia approached Muggsbottom and whispered from behind her veil, "You know, Muggsbottom, we both loved him, in our ways."

"Yes, madam . . . in our ways."

Outside the church, I found myself standing beside Maynard while the Englishmen were accepting condolences a little ways apart.

"Well, Maynard. The Phlegm Club soon will be no more. I can hardly believe it. Those damned Englishmen have changed my life. I'm going to miss them."

"Jesus has changed my life. But I'm gonna miss 'em too. Even Captain Smythe-Gardner."

"What will you do now?"

"God has told me to carry on the Runway to Heaven Ministry."

"Oh, He has?"

"Yes, sir. I went to Him in prayer, and that's what He told me."

"Have you ever preached a sermon, Maynard?" I asked, trying not to smile at the thought of Maynard in the pulpit.

"No, sir, I ain't. But God will give me the words."

"Well, I suppose operating the Runway to Heaven will have to be a better job than porter at the Caddo Hotel . . . if you can keep the ministry going. Do you think you can keep the contributions coming in? Can you keep up the lease on the Royal?"

"Our Lord said to us, 'Take no thought, saying, What shall we eat? or, What shall we drink? or, Wherewithal shall we be clothed? . . . for your heavenly Father knoweth that ye have need of all these things. But seek ye first the kingdom of God, and his righteousness; and all these things shall be added unto you.' Matthew, Chapter Six, Verses Thirty-one through Thirty-three."

"Maynard, I believe you truly are your cousin's cousin."

"Why, thank you, sir."

While Homer Joe stood clasping Muggsbottom's hand and, close to his ear, was speaking in earnest tones (perhaps even reciting his elegy), most of his deer hunting buddies had crowded around Cecilia Luce. They comforted her all the way out to her automobile. I thought to myself, Cecilia will be all right, for a few more years anyway.

"But why must you go back? You could probably find work of some sort here. The Ol' Perfesser's job still hasn't been filled. You could write that column easily enough. You certainly matched him and Homer Joe tit for tat in Arcady's Battle of the Pens."

"Despite what I may have said at our first meeting, my dear fellow, we did not come to America seeking our fortune. We came seeking a refuge, a sanctuary. Alas, without poor Reggie's brass, it is impossible for us to maintain this delightful retreat where we have been so comfortable and happy. And I'm an old dog, you see. It's far too late in the game for me to seek out some new vocation."

I thought: Muggsbottom, you rascal, what was your *old* vocation? But I said nothing.

"No," he continued, "we must return whence we came and, like Mr. Micawber, hope that something will eventually turn up."

As what I supposed was a reward for handling the numerous arrangements required to get Reggie back across the water, the Dipswizzles had cabled Muggsbottom and his countrymen a sum sufficient to get them back to England. These events seemed to transpire almost with the rapidity with which I have described them here. As suddenly and as unexpectedly as the Englishmen had arrived in our little town, they were leaving it.

I had offered to drive them to the airport in Little Rock, but Muggsbottom had said, "No, thank you. We shall depart as we came, by omnibus."

We had met for one last drink at the Phlegm Club. The new Maynard, wearing an apron of spotless white, had served our drinks "for old times' sake," while declining one himself. "That life is behind me, gentlemen." The poor fellow had almost broken into tears as the Phlegmatics walked out the door for the last time. Even preaching at the Runway to Heaven would have to go some to match the fun of his tenure with the Englishmen. I thought he would miss them far more than he would miss his cousin.

Muggsbottom was the last to step into Eddie Nunn's cab for the ride to the bus station.

"Write," I said, "and tell me how you're getting on."

"I shall try, my boy. I must confess, however, to being a most indifferent correspondent." Then he gave me one of his exaggerated winks. "Unless, of course, I am filled with indignation. Perhaps the sorry state in which I expect, alas, to find my island home will so inspire me."

He shook my hand, ducked into the cab, and was gone.

20. Epilogue

"Where is Chaucer's tomb?" inquired Nadine Twiddle.

"Right back there," I said. "We just passed it."

"No kidding? Where? I didn't even notice."

"Lean out over here. See back there?"

I pointed, as Nadine and I craned our necks around the queue of people shuffling along behind us.

"Oh, I saw *that*," said Nadine. "It doesn't look like all that much, does it?"

"Maybe next year you can visit Napoleon's tomb, Nadine. You'll really like *it*."

At just the moment we were looking back, Stanley Springstead, while apparently paying rapt attention to something on the far wall, the thumb and index finger of his right hand reflectively massaging the skin beneath his pursed lips, reached surreptitiously behind him and brushed the fingers of his left hand lightly across the top of the tomb.

Nadine began to giggle. Taking her by the shoulders, I drew her firmly back into line and pushed her gently forward.

"Stanley Springstead is such a nerd," she said.

I made no effort to rebuke Nadine, for I quite agreed with her characterization of Stanley Springstead. Not, however, because Stanley wished to experience a little brush with greatness. In the past two weeks, the young man had established his nerdhood in far more distressing ways.

"Is his name on it?" Nadine inquired.

"Pardon?"

"Is Chaucer's name on the tomb?"

"The inscription is in Latin, Nadine. Perhaps that's why you didn't notice."

"A-a-h-h-h." The girl's pretty blue eyes resumed their natural, uninquisitive expression. Triumphantly, she made a check mark in her ever present little notebook and began to look at what the people in front of her were looking at. She had shown me this notebook within minutes of the gathering of our group at the Memphis airport, and had told me that Professor Hornbeck was giving "extra points" next term in British Lit for each sight (site?) that Nadine might "experience" on her tour and list therein.

"Where do you suppose they have John Gay?" Having once more consulted her notebook, Nadine was ready to "experience" John Gay.

I had almost shepherded my twelve charges through Poets' Corner when the fruity Oxbridge voice came once again over the public address system.

"Will you pause and offer up with us a Prayer for Peace?"

This was the third Prayer for Peace to punctuate our long, slow tour through the Abbey. I had determined that there must be a clerical equivalent of the royal plural for, although in each instance inviting the visitors to pray with "us," the voice always belonged to the same man. In addition to a general invocation of peace on earth, good will toward men, the mellow baritone implored God to turn His attention expeditiously to a number of specific items— indeed, so detailed was the enumeration of these items that one could not possibly miss the implications of divine inattention. The Lord was asked to aid His servants in the bringing about of majority rule in South Africa, economic growth in the Caribbean and Latin America, racial equality in the American South, increased Israeli sensitivity toward the Palestinians, and salvation of the beleaguered whales, seals, and dolphins.

"But please save our souls," I added silently, "if we just *should* happen to fail in any of these endeavors." I thought of what Muggsbottom—crusty old right-wing C. of E. man—would say if he were with me, and I smiled a wry smile.

Egress was in view, when I realized that Larry Shaw, Gary Frost, and Julia Wallace must have lingered behind. I turned back, to discover the three young people grouped around a rather imposing old lady with a prominent moustache. The campstool on which she was seated conformed to her decidedly martial air. Smythe-Gardner, I felt, would have taken an instant liking to her. The old girl held Larry and Julia each by the wrist, while freezing Gary to the spot with her eyes.

"Another bomb landed," she said in a lecturer's voice, "immediately above the spot where you are now standing. It caused no serious structural damage, but in a building like this, of course, the aesthetic damage is every bit as crucial. How the Dames of Britain effected the renovation of this part of the Abbey is a story, I have found, that Americans particularly enjoy hearing. In 1946, under the spirited leadership of Lady Prunella Stinchcombe, we . . . "

The Americans turned imploring eyes toward their leader, but I could not help them. I knew that in my present weakened state I was no match for a Dame of Britain. To Gary I whispered, "Come as soon as you can," and headed for the street.

There I found the rest of my group, laughing, smoking, and talking of food and drink.

"I hope this doesn't annoy you, sir," said Harold Harkrider, "but I've about o.d.'d on churches."

The date was June 15, the thirteenth, and next to last, day

of the State College tour of Britain for 1989. I was receiving my regular teaching salary for leading the tour group, composed of twelve seniors to be, and was also getting a free trip for myself. In retrospect, the inducements seemed inadequate in the extreme. I had learned much in this, my first and last, stint as tour guide. I had learned that in finding tables at restaurants and seats on city buses, a group of thirteen was not much different from a group of fifty— there was as little chance of seating everyone for the same meal even at a sandwich shop as of getting everyone on the Number 9 bus. I was genuinely proud of the fact that I had lost no one permanently.

During the first week, Julia Wallace had wept nightly for her home beside the rice field—during the second, she had daily proclaimed, in manic high spirits, that she "could easily spend six months in London." Harold Harkrider, who claimed to get lost every time he went to Memphis, had located a gambling club on our first night in London, had somehow gained admittance, and had found his way back to the hotel at four o'clock in the morning, despite being dead broke and (as the British put it) thoroughly pissed. Sylvia Beauchamp had sniffled for days before inconveniently yielding to full-fledged bronchitis on a Sunday afternoon, thus necessitating my circumvention of the National Health Service's treatment policy. Larry Shaw, spiritually never far from the Bible Belt, had been invited to leave services at St. Paul's Cathedral for overly loud and prolonged criticism of (I had silently agreed) a decidedly tepid guest sermon being preached by the Queen's Chaplain. And, in addition to these documented offenses, I was quite sure that after lights out some of my young barbarians were bed hopping for illicit purposes. Although the proposition had never been put to me forthrightly, I was sure that preventing just such behavior was one of my principal duties—if only I had known *how*.

Patrick Adcock

I walked the three blocks from the tube station under leaden skies.

I had finally enticed the last of my wards across the threshold of Hollyhill House. This cramped little bed-and-breakfast hotel was curiously named, for it was a most unbucolic establishment. The proprietress of Hollyhill House was a querulous old lady named Felicity (also curious, come to think of it), who was so fearful of intruders that she locked her doors extremely early in the evening, thereby frequently inconveniencing us. I had announced, "Everyone is on his own tonight. Be up by six in the morning." Then I had struck out on a much delayed pilgrimage of my own.

I was most decidedly not enjoying England, a disturbing state of affairs for an Anglophile. The State College Literary Tour of Britain was an annual offering. For the two week trip, students received course credit. Two members of the English faculty jointly conducted the tour. Too often I found the best of students insufferable under even the best of conditions. I had, therefore, never put myself forward as a candidate for tour guide. But in May, only weeks before the group's departure date, my chairman had called me in for a conference.

The chairman was in all his public utterances a libertarian. In every other aspect of his behavior, he was a Nazi.

He had begun our conversation thus:

"I'm sending you to England next month with the kids." His usual deft touch.

Rather than manfully refusing or cravenly submitting, I had sought an intermediate position. "Why me?" I had inquired.

"Someone has to do it. Besides, with enrollment down as it is, I don't have anything else for you this summer."

"Yes, you bastard," I had thought, "and this has absolutely nothing to do with the Murk-Muggsbottom flap for which, after all these years, you still blame *me*."

260

So here I was. Some people, I thought, would even consider me lucky. I was receiving my regular salary, as if I were teaching a class, and all my expenses came out of the students' fees. Indeed, the tour might have proved considerably less debilitating for me if my colleague Professor Hornbeck had done her duty. But, almost at the last minute (too late to be replaced), she had suddenly taken refuge in a hysterectomy and left all twelve of the highly stimulated undergraduates on my hands.

But thanks to the chairman's spitefulness, I was at least in old London town. And this afternoon, I had finally found a few hours to myself, so that I might go in search of the Flotsam and Jetsam Hotel at Number Two, Bloomsbury Place.

On the other hand, I had half hoped that my commitments in London would be too great to permit this excursion. Over a period of six or seven years, much could have happened to the members of the Phlegm Club. Although it was probable that I would find out nothing at the Flotsam and Jetsam, it was also possible that I would learn something I would rather not know.

The neighborhood was slightly seedy, a faint suggestion of better days still clinging to its facade. I smiled. Just the ambiance for my old friends, I thought. I could have been more cautious and skirted little Bloomsbury Square, but I felt adventurous. What the hell, I *was* having a little adventure. My charges and I had quickly learned the truth of what Muggsbottom had once told me about perambulations through the great city—that when one cut through any patch of greenery in London, one ran the risk of being accosted by winos in soiled and lumpy jackets. These dropouts from the welfare state would beg (presumably) for money in some impenetrable working class dialect.

Bloomsbury Place was a little but not a cozy street, for it was bounded on one side by a busy thoroughfare. The entire block consisted of three attached buildings of moderate size, facing the square across a narrow pavement. The middle building, Number Two, had three storeys and a simple whitewashed facade. It bore no sign, and its shallow porch scarcely gave it the outward appearance of a hostelry. Not until I had climbed the three marble steps did I see the words "THE FLOTSAM & JETSAM," in flaking, fading black paint, on the frosted glass above the unmarked door.

The Flotsam and Jetsam had no reception desk. I could hear the sound of slow and irregular typing coming from somewhere. The tapping noises led me to the manager's office-quarters, tucked remotely away beneath the staircase. In a vaulted cubicle, a florid little fellow was laboring with his forefingers over a tall, old-fashioned typewriter. Through an open door beyond him, I could see into a second tiny room, where the foot of a bed and a table and chair were visible. He abandoned his task—with apparent joy—the moment he saw me.

"May I help you, sir? I am Cyril."

I introduced myself and, of course, the first word out of my mouth identified me as an American Southerner. I soon found that, for two reasons, Cyril was favorably disposed toward me. First, whatever he was typing had proved such an onerous task that he welcomed the distraction. And second, he was one of those Englishmen who saw Americans as childlike creatures, perpetually in need of instruction and guidance. It was the clear duty of his ancient race to meet that need.

I named my three friends and mentioned one or two salient characteristics of each. Did he remember them from their residence of a decade earlier, and had they returned to the Flotsam and Jetsam in more recent times? Cyril was beginning only his third year as hotel manager and, had they occupied rooms during his tenure, he felt he would certainly remember such a trio as I had described.

"These friends," he inquired, "have they not written you

since they left the States?"

"They're not the sort who correspond, really," I said. Then I added as an afterthought, "Except for controversies in the letters column."

Cyril gave me a moment to elaborate upon this cryptic response but, when I did not, he said, "Come on, we'll talk to Basil, the barman. He's been here since Victoria was at school."

I followed Cyril into the intimate little bar of which I had heard Muggsbottom and the others so often speak. It was early yet, and only two patrons graced the bar. They were middle-aged and were having a rather furtive conversation at a corner table. They had more a down-at-the-heels than a martial look about them, I thought. Perhaps the Flotsam and Jetsam had undergone a sea change since Smythe-Gardner's day. More likely I was simply generalizing from insufficient evidence.

I turned my attention to Basil, the barman. He was a small, spare, ageless man with the face of a world-weary, tolerant parish priest. One saw instantly that one might confess anything to him. Cyril introduced me and, after the briefest of salutations, I put my questions to him.

Basil's reply was so immediate and direct that I was unprepared for it. Now, *he* had a martial air about him.

"Of course, I remember them. The last time they was here was a short while before you come, Cyril. They stayed six or eight months, I reckon. The younger one who was with them here before, the actor—they said he died in America. That was a pity, for I really liked him the best. I've always had a soft spot for actors. Don't know why—it's the very devil getting them to settle their bar bill.

"I told you Basil was your man, sir," said Cyril. "If you'll excuse me then, I'll get back to that infernal machine and the bill of fare."

"Anyway," Basil resumed our colloquy, "the old gentleman died here. Did you not know that? One day, a steward comes hotfooting it in here from the reading room, and he says to Mr. Muggsbottom—he's the fellow smokes that awful tobacco—'Mr. Muggsbottom,' he says, 'I believe the old gentleman has expired in his chair.' 'Oh, no,' says Mr. Muggsbottom, 'Sir Monty often gives that impression, but he's only sleeping.' Well, he was that surprised to discover that the old fellow *was* dead, stone dead."

For some reason, I was as surprised by Sir Monty's death as Muggsbottom must have been.

"Do you know where Muggsbottom and Smythe-Gardner are now?" I asked.

"Well, sir, they didn't stay on long after the old gentleman bought it. They was always a bit short of the brass, if I may be so bold as to say it. And the Admiral—that was my term for the naval gentleman—wasn't never very happy here that second time. Said the place wasn't like in the old days. Said we had taken to letting in poofs. He wasn't half wrong neither." Basil cut his eyes censoriously toward the two men at the table. Then, as if my last question had just penetrated his reminiscence, he added, "Spain. I believe they said they was going to Spain."

"Spain?" I said.

"Yes, I'm sure that was it. A gentleman can live very economical in Spain, they said. And besides, men still run that country."

At that moment, a tall, slender man of about sixty entered the bar and, with a long, purposeful stride, headed right toward us. I experienced a shock of recognition. Here came Alec Guinness as the old colonel in *The Bridge on the River Kwai*, dressed for the moment in civilian clothes. Then something, some slight difference in the eyes or around the mouth, told me that this was not that character but rather an uncanny double. I was not in the least surprised when I heard Basil say, "Good afternoon, Colonel Bellamy. What will it be, sir?"

"A bitter, Sergeant Major. You know the drill. No whisky

before the sun goes down." The colonel turned to me and said, "No man will ever become a slave to drink who can wait till nightfall for his first whisky."

"Colonel Bellamy," said Basil, "this gentleman is an American, Mr . . . I'm not sure I caught your name, sir."

I introduced myself.

"Delighted, sir," said the colonel, offering his hand. "I like Americans myself. I don't think they're half as bad as most people make them out. Couldn't very well be, could they?"

Basil said, "Colonel, the American gentleman is inquiring about Mr. Muggsbottom and the Admiral. They was friends in the States." Then the barman flushed slightly, as if suddenly aware that he was intruding himself far too much into the gentlemen's conversation. He hurried away to fill the colonel's order.

"Ah, Muggsbottom. Miss him around here. Prince of a fellow. Can't say I ever warmed up to that mate of his, though. Never warmed up to Navy men as a class, truth to tell."

Basil brought the colonel's bitter.

"There was quite a commotion around here after the old fellow popped off . . . Sir Monty, you know? Did Basil tell you about it?" The colonel gave the barman a piercing "other ranks" look, and the old sergeant major bowed his head, suitably chastened. "No? Let's have a seat over there then, and I'll give you the whole story. Drink?"

"I guess not, thanks. I'm chaperoning twelve American college students, so I should probably either get dead drunk or stay cold sober."

"My choice, I believe, would be the former . . . but as you wish."

Colonel Bellamy picked up his ale and led me over to a table. En route, he cocked his head toward the two men in the corner, making no effort to disguise the gesture, and said, "Pansies. Place isn't what it used to be. Of course, no place is. Chaps used to at least *pretend*."

When we were settled at our table, Colonel Bellamy began to tell me the story of Muggsbottom's final days at the Flotsam & Jetsam. The old soldier gave his account with such relish that I guessed he did not often find a willing auditor.

"Well, as I mentioned before, Sir Monty passed on . . . one day in our reading room. I wouldn't have been surprised to learn that the old boy had bought it long before they moved in here and that Muggsbottom and Smythe-Gardner had just been propping him up in various chairs about the place . . . but I'll say no more on that score. I'm not one to speak ill of the dead. At any rate, Muggsbottom was shaken. Rather startled me, you know. Muggsbottom's usually the stoutest of stout fellows. 'There goes the England of our fathers,' he said—surprisingly lachrymose for old C.P. That little rat terrier Smythe-Gardner reacted totally in character, of course. Flew into a rage and began to threaten the hotel with suits for negligence. As if the management were supposed to have some plan to prevent old relics like Sir Monty from snuffing it.

"Naturally, no one paid any attention whatever to Smythe-Gardner's rantings. But we all sat up and took notice at lunchtime the next day when Muggsbottom returned from making the funeral arrangements in a very high dudgeon indeed. It seems that the papers were unwilling to accept Sir Monty's obituary in the manner in which Muggsbottom had prepared it. They struck all references to the baronetcy. I take it they couldn't find the old boy in *Debrett's*.

"'Who publishes *Debrett's* now?' Muggsbottom demanded. 'A gaggle of scruffy long-haired Labourites, no doubt. Thank God this is the final indignity Sir Monty must suffer at the hands of the Common Man.' It was some time later that Muggsbottom first mentioned leaving the country again, but I think he may have decided to do so that very day. He sent a jeremiad of a letter to the *Times*, I can tell you."

"That's my Muggsbottom," I said.

"It turned out that when the old boy died he hadn't a bean. I canvassed the hotel and collected nearly fifty pounds toward the funeral—I'd be lucky to pry a quarter of that out of this current crowd—but Muggsbottom and Smythe-Gardner turned me down flat. 'There'll be no air of the pauper's burial about Sir Monty's last rites,' Muggsbottom told me.

"He and Smythe-Gardner gave the old boy a bang-up funeral . . . somewhere down in Dorset, I believe. But the expense left them completely strapped. Soon thereafter, Muggsbottom began talking about hot countries. 'Colonel,' he said to me more than once, 'some of my happiest days were spent in hot countries.' 'Mine as well,' I replied. 'Mine as well.' Then one morning, there they were, Muggsbottom and Smythe-Gardner, with their bags standing beside them on the kerb. A cab pulled up, and they got in. Muggsbottom stuck his head out the window and called to me. 'We're off to Spain, Colonel,' says he. 'We'll be back when the counterrevolution succeeds.'"

I said, "That's the way Muggsbottom goes all right . . . and the way, perhaps, he'll come back some day."

"You're fortunate that our paths have crossed, my boy. I'm about the last of the old crowd, you know. The last who knew your friends . . . I say, might I stand you a drink for purposes of toasting old Muggsbottom and his little gamecock pal, wherever they are?"

"I'll accept that drink with pleasure, Colonel."

In my mind's eye, I saw Muggsbottom in the window of that taxicab. As the driver turned out of Bloomsbury Place and into the swirl of London traffic, my old friend was flashing some brave Churchillian sign, the thumbs up or the V for Victory. Charles Pierpont Muggsbottom—off to subdue another hot country.

I checked the telephone table, for it was there that the guests of Hollyhill House found their mail. Among the several letters that Nadine Twiddle received each day from her family and numerous swains I found none for myself.

I affected a tranquil ascent to my room on the third floor, which Europeans, for some curious reason, called the second floor. Once I was alone, however, I immediately gave way to reflection upon the probable life being led by my old, eccentric Anglo-Saxon friends in a Latin land. But a wild pounding on the door soon interrupted my musings. After I had opened it, an ashen faced Julia Wallace continued for an instant to beat at the air.

"What is it, Julia?"

I asked the question not because I wanted an answer (Julia's stricken look foretold some awful inconvenience awaiting me) but because she gave no sign of speaking otherwise.

"We were just going down to Sylvia's room . . . "

"Yes? And . . . ?"

"I think Nadine's broken her ankle."

Oh, Muggsbottom, where art thou at this hour? Living free and easy in sunny Spain, that's where. You irrepressible old dog.